Lying Together

Lying Together

Gaynor Arnold

Tindal
Street
Press

First published in UK February 2011
by Tindal Street Press Ltd
217 The Custard Factory, Gibb Street,
Birmingham, B9 4AA
www.tindalstreet.co.uk

2 4 6 8 10 9 7 5 3 1

**MORAY COUNCIL
LIBRARIES &
INFO.SERVICES**

20 31 80 88	
Askews & Holts	
F	

The following stories were previously published: 'Mouth' was first
published in the anthology *Mouth* (TSFG, 1996); 'Heart Trouble' in
Raw Edge Magazine 1997, also in *Going the Distance* anthology (Tindal
Street Press, 2003). A shorter version of 'In the Street of the Rose-gatherers'
was published in *Salvo* (Cannon Hill, 2006) as 'Guns and Roses'. 'Taking
People In' appeared as 'Hospitality' in *Her Majesty* (Tindal Street Press,
2002). 'Lying Together' was first published in *New Writer* February 1997
and in *The Warwick Review* Vol. IV No.2 June 2010.

A CIP catalogue reference for this book is available
from the British Library

ISBN: 978 1 906994 11 2

Typeset by Alma Books Ltd
Printed and bound in Great Britain by
CPI Mackays, Chatham ME5 8TD

◆Birmingham City Council

For Marjorie Thomas

CONTENTS

Lying Together

TELLING RADNOR

Evie's been going round all her friends. Asking for advice, rejecting it, crying a good deal, losing weight. We all feel helpless. Unsettled, too; we've got problems of our own. But at least we don't have to deal with Radnor.

'How well do you know him?' says Marsha. After a particularly hard three-hour session with Evie, she rings me up at work to discuss it all. She's only known Evie for two years. They were both working for the same company and did a marketing campaign together holed up in Marsha's flat in Moseley every day for the best part of three weeks. To start with, Radnor was simply a name, someone Evie couldn't keep out of her conversation. Then, Marsha remembers him on a couple of occasions suddenly turning up, sliding his black Volkswagen into Marsha's parking space, sounding his horn in three sharp blasts to summon Evie, who was out of the door in seconds: *Honestly, it was like a rat out of a drain. Like she was terrified of keeping him waiting.* Marsha'd only had an impression – pale face, a shock of pale hair – as he opened the car door the second Evie appeared and revved up the engine the moment she was inside.

'Not that well.' I click through some invoices. I don't want to talk about Radnor, particularly at the end of the month when I have to balance the books. Does Clive *never* send out reminders? I tap quietly at the computer keys, hoping Marsha won't hear.

'She said you were both students together.'

'Mmmmm. Sort of.'

'How *sort of*, Anne? Don't be evasive, darling. I'm relying on you for input. I'm trying to counsel in a vacuum here.'

'Marsha – we shared the same territory at roughly the same time. He was a couple of years ahead, in fact.'

'So that makes it – ten years you've known him?'

'I suppose.' Barretts haven't paid for the last three months, and Clive is still giving them credit. I send them a quick email, in my best frightener manner.

'Before he met Evie, then?'

'Yes. A year or two.'

'And ever since?'

'On and off.' I drain the last drop of cold coffee, get back to the keyboard. Bellingham's overdue too. I'll really need to speak to Clive about all this.

'So is he as sexy as she makes out?' Marsha's voice takes on a voyeuristic tone, so God knows what Evie's been saying.

'How sexy is that, then, Marsha?'

'Oh go on. You know how she talks. And what a state she's in. I mean, what man is worth all this grief?'

'The man you love, I suppose. Just a pity it's Radnor, but then Evie always had bad taste.' Whoops, bitchy.

Marsha gives her smoker's chuckle. 'Who'd have thought it? In the year 2000? It's pathetic.'

'Yes. Like that old joke – you know – fish and bicycles.' We both laugh.

I think about it, though. On the way back across the city centre, driving on autopilot till I wake up outside our house and see from the darkness that Steve is on a late job yet again and I've got to start the supper. And then, when I'm slicing onions for the pasta sauce, my eyes start weeping so much I have to go outside and lean against the wall of the kitchen, blinking at the blurry masses of the stars. And then after supper, when Steve slumps in front of the telly and starts coming up with some tired old crap about not having the time to fix a piece of carpet on the landing that we've both been tripping over for days, I find myself getting angry. I find myself shouting, 'Oh God, you men are *really* all alike!' And I stomp off to the bathroom, bang the door, shoot the bolt, and grab my toothbrush. Its bristles are splayed and soft. It needs replacing. Like the carpet. I brush aggressively, tears flowing down my cheeks, swathes of foam dangling from my lips. Marsha's right. What man is worth all this grief? I spit blood into the basin. Evie's my best friend, and yet I can't help her. *You don't understand how I feel*, she keeps saying. *You don't know what he's like.* I can't bring myself to say anything. She doesn't listen anyway. That's how it was before. I tell myself this new crisis is nothing to do with me. And I'm not going to get involved.

As I rinse out my mouth I can hear faint tappings on the landing outside. I whip open the bathroom door. Steve's squatting with a mouthful of tacks, fixing the carpet. He looks up, gives a metallic grin. Even with the tacks between his teeth he still manages to look good. I want to smile with the pure pleasure of seeing him, but I carp at him instead. 'So I have to lose my temper, do I? Before the great British workman pulls his finger out?'

He spits the tacks out into his palm. 'You're still upset, then?'

'Yes. I'm still upset.' I'm angry too, because we're supposed to be avoiding stress just now; relaxing as much as possible. But Steve's idea of relaxing seems to be closing his eyes at the earliest opportunity. Duffing out. Leaving me to get worked up about things like the carpet.

He sighs. 'It looks as if I'll have to end it all, then.' He starts to swallow the tacks, knocking them back, swallowing and wincing with pain. His sleight of hand is convincing for a moment. But only a moment; Steve can never keep a straight face and starts to laugh. And I do too. If it had been Radnor swallowing tacks, I'd have been expecting to ring the ambulance and stay up all night in Casualty feeling guilty as hell. But it isn't and I'm not, and it's suddenly great to be laughing and have Steve drop the hammer and put his arms around me. And go to bed and have nice uncomplicated sex involving only two positions and no angst at all.

'Penny for them.' Steve is watching me, propped up on his elbow, smoking.

'I wish you'd give up. It makes the bedroom stink.' I take the fag from his fingers, grind it out into the huge onyx ashtray Tom and Deirdre bought us for Christmas. The butt end smells worse dead than alive. I push it as far away from me as I can get it. This involves me lying right across Steve's body. He's warm, smelling faintly of sweat, faintly of me. I hear his voice tickling in my ear, his fingers tickling under my outstretched arm: 'That's not what you were thinking about.'

'One of the things.' I roll back, keep my eyes away from him.

'And the other?'

'Oh, just Evie.'

'You mean Radnor.'

'God, Steve, you're obsessed with Radnor.' Just because Radnor has a Ph.D., and Steve is a plumber with six O-levels, he's always imagining I'm comparing the two of them; can't wait to slip something into the conversation to catch me out.

'*I'm* obsessed?' Steve snorts.

'I don't care a twopenny fuck about Radnor. He can cook his own goose. But Evie's my best friend.'

'So you say. But I've never understood what you have in common.'

'What don't you understand?' But I know what's coming. She's outgoing, glamorous, a bit ditzy. Not like me at all.

Steve puts his hands behind his neck. He furrows his brow, his fiercest expression (genial, bland, furrowed: that's Steve's repertoire). 'I don't know. It just doesn't fit. Mind you, she doesn't fit with Radnor either.' This is loquacious for Steve. I wonder what's got into him. I know he's always loathed Radnor, but I really can't make out what he thinks of Evie. He's always nice to her in a way I know she takes for granted from men. *Steve's such a doll*, she's always saying, implying that I'm lucky to have him with his nice brown eyes and his nice big muscles – but with the added implication that, of course, she's luckier to have Radnor. Until now, that is. Until these last weeks of crying and moaning. But I've always had a feeling that Steve's uneasy with her, keeps his distance, as if her sex appeal might be poisonous to the touch. Whenever she comes round, he goes off to watch telly.

'So?' I set my alarm. It's a fiddly little thing with lots of buttons.

'So she's the last person I'd have thought you'd have taken to.'

'Shows how little you know.'

'Aha. Well, I'm only a man.'

'Yup.' I put down the alarm clock, slide down the bed, stroke his belly appreciatively – but only just enough to distract him from further thoughts of Evie. He gives me a squeeze in response, and we curve into each other, ready for sleep. I put the light out, and soon Steve is snoring quietly. He never has trouble sleeping. I'm the insomniac. I start thinking about Evie. And, of course, Radnor.

I don't want to think about him, but he enters my mind unbidden, with his beautiful, bone-white face and crown of flaxen hair. I see him sitting in the sparsely-attended lecture hall, tall, straight-backed, taking careful notes. I see him look across at me. I see him come towards me, holding out his hand, asking if I would like a coffee. He's saying, 'I'm Radnor, by the way – that's spelt R-A-D-N-O-R. People are always getting it wrong.' And my heart starts to beat wildly as I touch his delicate long fingers, and I blurt out, 'I'm Anne' – adding foolishly: 'That's spelt with an e.'
  And he's looking at me so intensely and taking me by the arm so tightly I almost gasp. 'Then come along, Anne-with-an-e. Let's get you a cream bun and the finest coffee money can buy. I need to know everything about you.' And sitting at a rickety table in the student union, I tell him everything. I tell him my whole life: my divorced parents, my mother in Strasbourg, my father in Hong Kong. And how miserable and lonely I'm feeling, in a city so alien and so far from home.
  'It takes time,' he says. 'You'll get used to it, find a soul mate. Believe me, Anne, you'll be all right.' He smiles then, for the first time. And it almost takes my breath away.

I get into work early. I have a go at Clive as soon as he arrives, before the phones start to ring. I tell him about the mess the invoices are in. He says he's no good at paperwork and that's why he employs me.
  'But then you do things behind my back and agree to terms that we *never* give – even to our oldest customers. For example, all that Italian mirror-work for Bellingham's on a sale-or-return basis! What on earth possessed you?'
  'Goodwill, duckie. You know how important that is. You want to listen to your marketing friend, Evie. Talking of which – a little bird

has told me that she's having a few problems with that awful man of hers, the one with that ridiculous name who looks as though he's been in the bleach too long.'

'Radnor.'

'That's the fella. What did a lovely girl like that ever see in him? Dry old stick, or am I wrong?'

'Who told you, anyway?'

'Richie and I were in the White Swan last night when Tom and Deirdre came in, long time no see. They were full of it. Richie said why doesn't she just leave him? And Deirdre says it's much more complicated than that, and Tom raises his eyebrows like he's had enough of that topic for one night, so I never got to know the details . . .'

'Yes, well, it has got pretty boring these last few weeks. I think we've all rehearsed the issues five times over.'

'Now, now. Don't be cynical. Let me make you a lovely cuppa and you can tell old Clive all about it.'

'No thanks. I've just spent half the night thinking about it. I've come to work for a rest. I don't mind the cuppa, though, as you've offered.'

'Oh, yes. Use me, I'm only the boss.' He bustles off but I know he'll come back to it. And I'll put a bit of pressure on in return. This job's only meant to be temporary, just to tide me over after giving in my notice at the school. But I'm feeling the grass grow. I've done all the work he begged me to take on (not just the accounts but a whole new ordering system), and I feel frustrated. I'm a mathematician, not a bookkeeper, but it's all numbers to Clive. He likes the selling side, swans off around the country at every opportunity. *Once they see what I've got to offer, it's no contest. Quality merchandise, you see.* He's doing well; he's got an eye for what's wanted. Meanwhile I'm stuck in the office like a lemon, getting sourer all the time. I keep telling myself it can't be for much longer.

'Okay, I'll tell you about Evie if you take me out on the road with you once in a while. I might even be an asset.' After all, I know every bit of the business; every item that passes through stock. Name, number and code. Material and colour. Manufacturer and delivery times. Cost to us and cost to the customer. And my party trick – doing the VAT in my head.

Clive pokes his head out from the little cubbyhole where we keep the tea things: 'Go on, then.'

'But will you? Seriously this time?' He's reneged before. He's a bit of a one-man-band, likes the matey first-name stuff, doing people favours. He thinks I'll be too stern, won't engage in banter or haggle just to make people feel they've got a bargain. He's a market trader at heart.

'Okay. Don't nag. As long as we don't have to leave Eileen on her own to answer the phone. I'll have a word with Luke, see which days he can cover. Now, come on, what's with the lovely Evie?'

I take the tea from him, give him the edited version. I tell him that Radnor wants a baby. And that Evie can't have one. And she hasn't told him yet.

'Is that all?' Clive stirs his tea with disappointment, sucks the spoon.

'It's clear you don't know Radnor. He's likely to chuck her when he knows. She's completely hysterical.'

'She does tend to exaggerate, doesn't she? Anyway, can't she have treatment? Or adopt or something?'

I wish I hadn't said anything. Clive doesn't understand the issue. He and Richie don't plan their lives around it. I'm angry with him sitting there so plump and complacent. 'You think it's that *easy*, do you?'

He raises his eyebrows. 'I've no idea. I'm just –'

'Exactly. You have *no idea* what you're talking about.' I take a deep breath. I have to remember, it's Evie's problem, not mine. 'Anyway,' I say, 'Radnor wouldn't want anybody else's child.' Oh no. Definitely not.

'Really?' Clive blows on his tea. 'I wouldn't have thought he was the type to care either way.'

'And that's where you're wrong as well. He's obsessed with passing on his genius genes. He's been on about a baby ever since she moved in. And now it hasn't happened, he wants her to go for tests.' I sip my tea: Clive's usual gnat's pee. The steam makes my eyes water. 'I told her not to get involved with him right from the start.'

'He's sure it's not *his* fault, then? Firing blanks?'

'Apparently not.' I gulp the tea, burn my throat a bit.

Clive waits, finds an opened packet of biscuits and rustles around in the Cellophane tube. I know something's coming. 'Didn't *you* have a thing with him once?'

'Good grief, Charlie Brown, whoever told you that?' I laugh.

'Your esteemed other half, no less. That party when he got so drunk, remember? And the fella in question actually turned up with Evie in tow and stood in the corner glowering at us all? To be honest, I couldn't see what all the fuss was about. I said so to Richie at the time – mind you, Richie was goggling a bit himself, saying there *was* something about him, a *je ne sais quoi*, if in a slightly Stalinist vein – but I simply couldn't see it myself. So you and Evie both!' Clive crushes the empty biscuit wrapper between his hands and aims it at the bin, missing by a mile. 'He must be good in the sack, then.'

'Nothing about Radnor is good. Steve's just imagining things.' I'm surprised Steve's even mentioned Radnor. Blood rushes to my head, and to hide it I bend to put my empty mug on the floor. I can see Clive's shoes – shiny old suede, showing the shape of his toes. And his once-natty trousering frayed along the hem.

'Well, it's all very bizarre.' He gets up, cascading crumbs onto the floor. 'I can't see why Evie doesn't take a leaf out of *your* book, Anne. Find some nice ordinary guy who'll appreciate her for what she is. Ability to breed isn't everything, is it?'

'No, it isn't. So shut up about it.' I can hear the sharpness in my voice as I swing back to my screen, bring up the order numbers and scroll down.

Clive, bless him, looks perplexed, addresses the silent multitude: '*Now* what have I said?'

I tell him it's nothing. I tell him I'm just fed up with being stuck in the office all day. 'And I don't feel too good this morning, either.'

Clive backs off. He's anxious to placate me, suggests I have some time off. 'You take as much as you need, duckie. Whatever will help.' He'll take it all back as soon as the phone's going and he can't access the spreadsheets.

'I'll see,' I say.

I decide I'll have to speak to her. I've avoided her the last few days, but it has to be faced. I send her a quick email, and she rings me back almost straightaway. I don't know how she keeps her job in that marketing firm; she's always got plenty of time to socialize. We settle on lunch in Harborne. Two-course menu £9.99. Waiters reasonably speedy and pasta reasonably reliable. I tell her, 'Maximum one hour. I've got work to do, even if you haven't.'

She's already waiting when I get there. You can tell these days that she's a bottle blonde, and her skin's a bit pimply. But her skirt's short and tight and her tits are on display, and the waiters mill around her, as usual. She gets up, dropping her napkin and knocking her shoulder bag off the arm of her chair, and gives me a big hug. 'Annie baby! I've missed you so much!'

'God, Evie, it was only last week. Don't be so melodramatic.' But I can't help smiling. I kiss her back. She smells of wine and crumbs. 'How's things?'

She grimaces. 'Let's order – I'm starved. I've got a bottle already.' She waves the Valpolicella at me. I notice she's drunk nearly half of it already. She slops some in my glass: 'Cheers.'

'Cheers.'

'And bugger all men.'

'For "men" read Radnor, I presume?'

'They're all the same. With the exception of your Steve, of course; he's a doll. And Tom, too. Why couldn't I have chosen someone like that? Or be happy on my own like Marsha? I'm a fool, aren't I?'

I could tell her that she is. I could tell her that she would be well rid of Radnor, that he is trouble incarnate. But I know that wouldn't help – for all her generalized moaning, she won't hear real criticism of him. She says Radnor's the only man who's ever taken her seriously. From the time they started to go out, Radnor was effectively God. I remember her phoning me after their first date, saying he'd given her *the most wonderful evening ever* and why hadn't I told her before that he was so *romantic*? 'Because he's not,' I'd said. 'Don't be fooled by the way he looks at you. He's disastrous around women. Take it from me.' But she wasn't listening – or if she was she thought I was joking. After a few intense weeks, the die was cast. 'I can't believe it,' she'd said, curled up on my sofa, her baby-blue eyes sparkling. 'He thinks I'm perfect. It's a bit frightening, to be honest, Annie. So you must never, ever, *say anything*.'

Now she's starting to cry and I offer her my hanky. The waiters busy themselves with laying knives and forks on adjoining tables, waiting for a suitable opening.

'I wasn't going to do this.' She balls my hanky into a greyish mass. 'I feel I'll run dry, soon. And I get really bad headaches. What I want is to just to *see* you. Have a laugh. Feel normal.'

'Whatever normal is.'

'Yes. Well, more like you. Come on, Annie, drink up.' She beckons a waiter, consults the giant menu. 'I'm going to have the carbonara.'

'I'll have the con funghi. And a salad.' I'm feeling less nauseous, now. There's nothing like making decisions.

'That's two salads, then.' Evie smiles up at the waiter, an intimate, flirting smile. She can't help it.

'Yes, Signora, Signora.' He bows to us both, goes off humming.

She has that instant appeal, Evie. Even when I first saw her and she was looking a good deal worse than she does now. She was dressed in one of those strange hospital gowns, socks and slippers. She was sitting on the next bed to me.

'Hi,' she'd said, leaning towards me. 'Thought you'd wake up soon. Feeling okay?'

'Not sure.' I tried to move, and felt the thick pad between my legs. A flicker of regret came and went.

'They'll have you up in a minute if they see you're awake. I'd close my eyes if I were you.'

I did as she said. It was easier not to think. I dropped off to the murmur of distant voices, the clatter of crockery in the corridor outside. When I came to again, she was still sitting on her bed, but dressed this time. In white. With her baby blond hair freshly brushed, she looked like an angel.

'You look like an angel.'

'Oh my God, she's hallucinating!' She had a deep, throaty giggle.

I laughed, but whispered, 'You *do*, though.'

'Fallen angel, more like. I'm Evie, by the way.'

'And I'm Anne. With an e.' I don't know why I said that. But we both laughed.

'Really? And how are you feeling, Anne with-an-e?'

'I don't know. Yes I do. Awful.' I moved a little, felt the blood oozing out of me. I winced.

'You'll get over it. In a couple of weeks you'll have forgotten all about it. Take it from me – veteran of three campaigns.' She smiled.

I stared at her. In her white dress, with her flaxen hair and peachy skin she seemed immaculate.

A nurse came, took my temperature and went. 'She disapproves of me,' said Evie as she left the room.

'Why d'you think that?'

She laughed. Then launched into all the reasons why women tended to hate her. Her good looks, her easy attitude – and above all her success with men. Not that it was all success; more a series of flash affairs with dubious endings. Dubious men, too – older, invariably married, and always on the make. But she made it sound hilarious.

'I know it's not very *feminist* of me, Annie, but if every stupid man in the world wants to queue up and spend his stupid money on me, who am I to stop them? I mean, would you turn down a flight to New York on Concorde – or a fortnight in the Maldives?' She picked idly at some grapes. 'I take it because it's on offer. Because I like to have a good time. And up till now that's been okay. I've had a lot of fun. But honestly, it's getting now that *everyone* I fancy seems to be married or "in a relationship" already. And if they're not, they're lying about it, like bloody sorry-but-I'll-be-in-London Roger. It's a bummer, isn't it?'

I nodded, as if I'd had the same trouble. But men had never queued up to spend money on me, let alone take me to New York or the Maldives. I'd had a few boyfriends at the Lycée in Strasbourg, the regulation squeezes and fumbles in the back of a battered old Citroën. But no secret liaisons, no illicit weekends, no jumbo-sized bouquets in gilt baskets, no gifts of designer clothes. Nothing serious at all. Until Radnor, that is. But he was the one thing I wasn't going to mention – not that I was saying much, anyhow. But I nodded, enthusiastically: 'Yes, it's a bummer.'

'Still, after next week I'll have one less thing to worry about.'

I looked at her. 'What d'you mean?'

'It's up to me, but Mr Lambourne says I don't really have a choice.'

'Mr Lambourne?'

'You know, our *consultant*? The one who's so gorgeous he just *must* be married? Don't tell me you haven't noticed his big brown eyes? Oh Annie, you're in another world! Well, anyway, he came along yesterday in that beautiful tweed suit of his and sat on this very bed, and said he was so sorry but "the uterus was just not holding up". Made it sound like knicker elastic. I wanted to laugh, except he would have thought me a hard-faced bitch. He was more upset than *I* was, I think. Apparently it's a total disaster area in there. Fibroids and adhesions and God knows what. Trust me not to do things by halves. They've offered me counselling, but I can't see the point.' She fingered the bedspread, quiet for a moment. 'Do you think it serves me right for sleeping around?'

'Of course not.' I didn't believe in that kind of retribution. But I felt a bit panicky for myself all the same.

'But you think, don't you? Like it's Fate. I mean, I've never really wanted kids, but now, well . . .' She blew her nose, then smiled briskly. 'Look, I have to go in a minute. Roger was supposed to collect me an hour ago but he says he's got a meeting, and to get a taxi and he'll pay for it. Honestly, as if *transport*'s the only thing I'm worrying about! Three days I've been in here bleeding like a stuck pig, and he can't get away for a frigging half-hour. The bastard!'

'Yes, the bastard.' I hadn't had any visitors either. Admittedly, I was only in for the day and no one knew where I was, but it gave me satisfaction to say the words.

'Yes. They're all bastards!' She passed an elaborate fruit basket done up in a ridiculous amount of artificial yellow ribbon. 'Have a plum! Roger's guilt offering.' She pushed one into my mouth. 'Go on! Sink your teeth into it! Hard.' We laughed again.

When she finally went off to her taxi, I felt bereft. I realized suddenly that my head was aching, and I had cramps in my belly. I hadn't noticed the pain when Evie was there. I looked at her empty mattress with its plastic cover, and watched my tears trickle down over Roger's best quality purple plums.

A few hours later I was home. Back to the house I shared with two glum geography students who were away on a field trip. There was no food in the kitchen except half a box of cereal and two sprouting carrots, but I wasn't hungry anyway. I locked the door, unplugged the phone and went to bed. I just wanted the day to be over as soon as possible; I wanted to erase it from my consciousness. But I couldn't sleep, and when I did, I dreamed of babies – lines of them lying dead and blue in their cots because I'd forgotten to feed them. A woman in an apron and starched cap kept saying, *You're a fine mother, aren't you? You don't deserve such lovely children.* I woke up feeling sick, convinced I'd done the wrong thing. I wanted someone to reassure me. And there was only one person I could speak to.

As soon as I decently could, I rang her. I was a bit afraid it might have been one of those hospital friendships – like holiday friendships – that don't make it into real life. But she sounded genuinely pleased to hear from me. 'I'll come round to your place if that's all right. I'm sick of sitting around taking it easy. I've read every magazine in the place and if I have any more lifestyle guidance, I'll go nuts. I'll get a taxi – put it on Roger's account. And I'll tell you *all* about the bastard. You won't believe it!' So next thing we were sitting in front of my gas fire on Tiverton Road, eating our way through a box of éclairs she'd picked up at Druckers on the way. The white cardboard box was open between us, and we were cramming like schoolgirls. She was telling me about how Roger had finally rung up the night before. 'From his carphone! Somewhere in Edgbaston! Couldn't even be bothered to come and *see* me. Is that cherishing or what?' She'd told him it was all over between them and he'd not believed her, could *just not see why* she was so upset, kept telling her he'd sorted 'this whole thing' out for her and what more did she want? 'And I told him that if having half your insides removed was sorting anything he could just piss off. And he said "Now you're just being unfair." So I said, "*Unfair*! Well, pardon me! I'm sure you'll be better off with someone who appreciates you more. So sod off and don't ring me again – or I might tell your *wife*!" And I could tell down the phone that he went pale.' She made a comical face and we both fell about laughing.

I knew Radnor's knock immediately. Short and imperative. And then his pale face at the window, pressed icily against the glass. My heart was pounding, but I had to let him in. I'd got my story ready, but wasn't sure how good I'd be at lying to him. He hardly acknowledged Evie, just edged me into the kitchen, holding me by the top of my arms, demanding to know where I'd been: 'I've looked everywhere for you, Anne. I've been at my wit's end.'

I didn't trust myself to look him in the eye. 'Something came up. I'll tell you later. I can't talk now.' I indicated Evie, who was sitting on the sofa in a red bustier and five-inch heels.

He threw a short, disapproving look in her direction. 'Tonight, then. Seven fifteen. I'll collect you.' He turned and left. He'd been in the house about thirty seconds.

'Wow, who's that?' Evie stared after him, like men usually stare after women. I should have known then, I suppose, that things might take an unexpected turn. But I thought Radnor was hardly her type.

'That's Radnor,' I said, carefully fitting the lid back on the cake box.

'He's the bastard in question, then?' She raised her eyes to me, half an éclair poised in her hand.

'Good grief, no. No. Just a friend. Someone I see at lectures.'

'Really?' She made big eyes. 'Maybe he likes you more than you think. He was standing very close.' She laughed. '*Kissing* close, in fact.'

'Don't be daft.' I put the cake box back on the table.

'Daft? I beg your pardon, Annie, but if there's one area that Evie Richards is expert in, it's the body language of men. And that man's is perfectly *smouldering*.' She shivered appreciatively.

The shiver ran through me too, but for different reasons. 'Not my cup of tea,' I said airily. 'He's altogether too intense.'

She perked up. 'You mean brainy?'

'That too. He'll be a professor before he's forty. He's got it all planned.'

She licked her lips dreamily, savouring the last hint of cream from the cakes. 'I'd like to date a really clever man for once. Someone to look up to.'

'You're supposed to be off sex, remember?'

'I can still look. That won't hurt. After all, he's not *married*, is he? Maybe my luck will change.'

'You'll have to tell him,' I say when we're on to the zabaglione. (Or rather, when I am; Evie's not eating pudding, and she's only toyed with the pasta.)

'I can't. I'm just too scared.'

'But Evie, what's the alternative? He's going to smell a rat if you won't have those tests . . .'

She gives me a beatific smile. 'There is a way out. It's perfect. You can tell him, Annie dear.'

'Me?' She has no idea how horrifying that is. I feel the sweat along my back. 'What good would that do, for God's sake? It won't matter who tells him, it's –'

'He'll listen to you. You're a serious person. You'll be able to put it in the right way.' Her faith in me is pathetic. And misplaced. Eight years on, she still thinks Radnor and I are some sort of intellectual chums. She doesn't notice we never talk to each other.

'There *is* no right way, Evie. And you'll do it just as well as me. Just don't go into detail. Fib if you have to. After all, he can't exactly look at your medical notes to check.'

'He'll get it out of me. You don't know what he's like with his questions. I'll just break down and tell him everything. Then he'll leave me. Please, Annie. *Please.*'

I know why men fall for her; that sumptuous beauty, that wide soft mouth; she's irresistible. But I can't help her; I mustn't.

I say it's out of the question.

The traffic's bad on the Bristol Road, and Clive's out by the time I get back. Eileen's on reception downstairs, Luke's off taking the second lot of replacement glass shades round to Waterside Court, and I've got the upstairs office to myself. I try to get on with the VAT, but I can't concentrate. I look at the phone. I pick it up. I put it down again. I try translating the technical specifications of the latest stuff from Milan. Clive's left the diagrams on my desk with a note – *You're a scientist, work this out.* I'm not and I can't. I look at the phone again. Suddenly my fingers are tapping out the numbers like old friends. I'm not breathing as I count the rings. He won't be there, I'm sure. He'll have changed his extension, moved up in the world. It rings a long time. I imagine it ringing away in some dusty office, some unoccupied Portakabin. I'm just going to put the receiver down when he answers: 'Dr Messiter.'

I force my voice, brightly. 'Hello, Radnor. It's Anne.'

Long silence. If I didn't know him I'd think the line had gone dead, but I know he's there. I try upbeat, assured: 'Look, I really need to see you.'

Another long silence. 'I can't imagine why.'

'It's about Evie.' I rush it out.

Another pause. '*Evie?* Why?'

'Well, it's something she wants you to know.'

'Why can't she tell me herself?'

'That's the problem.'

'It sounds highly dubious.' He's off-hand, irritable. 'I'm not sure –'

'Are you busy now?'

'Well, I've got –'

'Like this minute?' I know I have to pressure him. I have to do it today before my courage drains away.

'I see. *That* important. I'm almost curious. Well, Anne, you'll have to come to *me*. I'm very busy.'

'Give me half an hour.'

'Very well.' I tell Eileen to hold the fort, get back in the car. It's hot and I'm almost out of petrol, but I'll have to risk it. Radnor hates people to be late. I look in the mirror, comb my hair and take a deep breath. I drive off, feeling a bit like Thelma or Louise, taking a flying leap over the precipice.

Afterwards, I ring Marsha. I have to dampen her need to meddle, stop her saying something silly to Evie at this stage. 'I've had a word with Radnor,' I tell her. 'Over the baby business.'

'My God, Anne! Talk about biting the bullet! What did he say?'

'He was pretty furious –'

'Oh God.'

'Furious with *me,* actually.'

'With *you?*' Marsha is shrieking down the phone. 'That's so totally unfair!'

'A case of shoot the messenger, I suppose.'

Marsha's excited voice goes up an octave. 'This guy gets crazier by the day! But are you saying Evie's really off the hook?'

'Well, he seems to accept that it's not her fault.'

'Clever girl! You've managed to deflect his anger onto you. I am *so* impressed.' I can feel Marsha's deep forensic interest vibrating the phone line. 'How exactly did you do it?'

'Just one of my hidden skills.'

'Anne, I need detail! It sounds like you've worked a miracle.'

'I just happen to know a few of Radnor's weaknesses.' I twiddle with a free ballpoint Clive's picked up from somewhere – a horrible green and orange with a white button and 'Daley's Garage' written in black. I thought Clive was supposed to have taste. I throw it in the bin.

'Ah, I thought so. You and Radnor did more than share the same bit of space, then?' Marsha never forgets a conversation, sod her. 'Which exact "weakness" did you exploit?'

'No comment.'

'Anne, you're so secretive! I could kill you.'

'Thanks. I appreciate the negative energy.' Marsha believes in all that stuff, her flat's been Feng Shui'd out of existence.

'Oh, I didn't mean that literally! It's just that for Evie's sake . . . you know how she relies on me. I need to have accurate information –'

'Well, let's just say I called on some shared experience.'

'Well, thank God you did. I guess Evie's over the moon.'

'I haven't got hold of her yet. For once she seems to be out earning some money. Unless she's gone home with a hangover, which wouldn't surprise me the state she was in at lunchtime. I've left her a message. Basically he wants her to carry on as usual. Not talk about it. Not mention it.'

'What?' Marsha's roar nearly deafens me. 'That Radnor is really *weird*.'

'You're in a funny mood tonight.' Steve watches me over the dining table. He's come home early, done his famous Chicken Surprise, using up all the pans and leaving his toolbox on the worktop. He feels he's owed some sort of thanks and I haven't managed it. I feel a little queasy. Reaction, probably. I go on eating, avoid his eyes, wonder whether I should say anything. Eventually, and in a casual way between bites of bread, I mention that I'm pleased because I think I've sorted things out for Evie.

'What? This thing that's been going on for weeks? Her and Radnor?' Steve picks up a chicken bone, savages it with his teeth. Then a thought strikes him and he looks up. 'You've been to see him, haven't you?'

I should have known he'd guess; he's got antennae a mile long where Radnor is concerned. 'Well?' He sits there, holding the chicken bone, brow furrowed.

'Well what?'

'Well, *did* you?'

'Ten out of ten. This chicken's terrific, by the way. Good thing I like garlic.'

'Bugger the garlic. Are you completely mad?'

'What d'you mean?'

'You know what I mean.'

'Not really. And anyway, I don't want a big scene about this. I was only getting him to see sense.'

'And?'

'And I did.'

'And?'

'And that's it.'

'That's it? I thought women liked to *share* things. Details. So we men are always being told.'

'Well, I'm just bucking the trend. Especially when you're so paranoid about everything to do with Radnor.'

'I'm not paranoid. It's just that every time you talk about him – or even think about him – you get upset.'

'Rubbish.' I concentrate on the chicken breast, cut it up very small.

'Why do you always deny it?'

'Because you always exaggerate. He's in the past.'

'Oh yes?'

'Okay, then. Tell me. Am I upset now?' I look him full in the face. Surely even Steve can't tell how fast my heart is beating.

'Don't pretend with me. I can practically *see* his face behind your eyes. Just like last night. And the night before. In fact, I'm fucking sick of being in bed with him.'

'Now you're being stupid.'

'Stupid. Thanks, Anne. Yes, that's my level. I'm not Doctor Professor bloody Radnor, M.A. Ph.D., honorary this, prize-winning that. I just don't match up, do I?'

'What's so great about a couple of degrees? When he's such a psycho underneath? You're miles better than him in every way. Why don't you believe it?'

'Why don't you?' He looks at me fiercely.

I try evasive action. 'Why does it matter so much anyway? What d'you think he did – seduce me on top of his desk?'

'I wouldn't put it past him.'

'Or me, apparently.' I get up, remove the plates, move out of his sight line.

'Okay, I didn't mean that. Sorry.' Steve grabs for my hand as I pass. 'It's just the way he goes around looking so stiff-necked and pleased with himself. I just want to punch him in the face.'

'You don't need to prove anything to me, Steve.'

'So you keep saying. But then you go and do something that makes me feel I have to –'

'I know, I know. I'm sorry. But Evie was so desperate.'

'You care more about her than about me, then.'

'Please don't put it like that, Steve. It wasn't a choice.'

I didn't do it just for Evie. No one's *that* altruistic. But I didn't mean to upset Steve, either. I don't really know what I had in mind when I made that phone call. Up till then, I'd managed to avoid a face-to-face with Radnor. It hadn't been difficult; he's never been a social animal – and the rest of us had got used to Evie arriving everywhere without him, breezing in with a 'Hi, gang!' and a raft of excuses for why he was occupied elsewhere. Over the years, he and I had found ourselves in the same room a number of times, but I'd given him a wide berth; hadn't met his eye; hadn't addressed him at all. I'd keep repeating to myself all the time, like a mantra, 'Don't forget, this man is a bastard.' Yet when I stepped into his office that day he looked exactly the same as when I first saw him: pale face, blond hair, freakishly beautiful. And yet with a look that was almost kind. Maybe I had misjudged him. Maybe he wasn't so bad. Maybe we could be grown-up about things.

He put down his pen, scrutinized me carefully. 'You look tired, Anne. Husband of yours not looking after you?'

'I'm not here to talk about Steve, thank you, Radnor.' Defensive already.

'Ah. No of course, it's about Evie. Well?'

'She's in a state.'

He raised his eyebrows. '*In a state.* What exactly does that mean?'

'Haven't you noticed how much weight she's lost?'

He hesitated. Clearly he hadn't. But he wasn't going to admit it. 'Women are always losing weight. And gaining it. That can't be what's brought you here at such short notice. I told you how busy I am.' He indicated the piles of exam papers, folders, sheets of paper, all stacked neatly: annotated, labelled, assessed, valued.

'She's desperately unhappy, Radnor. And she feels she can't talk to you.'

'Nonsense. Evie is not secretive like you, Anne. She's a high-spirited, open person.'

'Yes, I know all her good points. She's my best friend, remember?'

'So she is. And therefore you're aware that there isn't a devious bone in her body. That's what's so lovely about her.' He'd apparently forgotten how he'd once called her 'that tarty-looking girl who takes up all your time'; how for a year he'd tried to break up our friendship because she was 'trivial-minded'. He had a different view of her now she belonged to him.

'Look, she may be lovely, Radnor, but she's afraid of you, all the same.'

'Afraid?' He seemed genuinely taken aback. 'What *is* all this nonsense about, Anne? Please come to the point.'

'Okay.' I was in for it now. I took a deep breath and the words came out in a rush. 'Evie can't have children. She had a hysterectomy ages ago. I don't know the details. Evie finds it too upsetting to discuss, even with me. And she couldn't face telling *you* at all. So I'm here instead – the fall guy.' I gave a stupid little smile.

He stared at me. He didn't look shocked, or even surprised, although he raked his hair a little with his fingers. 'Yes, I suspected something like this.'

'You *knew*?'

'Well, Anne, it's not rocket science. We've been lovers for four years. There must have been something wrong. I'm not totally obtuse.'

'Oh, Radnor, why didn't you say? She's been going half-mad about these tests. Afraid you'll dump her, even.'

He frowned at the distasteful word. '*Dump* her?'

'Leave her. Throw her out. You know what I mean.'

'How badly you think of me, Anne.'

'You've been known to do it, though, haven't you?'

His eyes deepened with anger, but he said nothing. He was in super-control. 'The difference in this case, Anne, is that Evie is the innocent victim. So I can hardly let her down – even when things are, well, disappointing.' He adjusted a pile of papers a quarter of an inch to the right, and I saw the tightness in his throat.

'Disappointing? Is that all you can say? I thought – she thought – you wanted a child more than anything.'

'You know I did. You of all people know how *much* I did. But some-times things don't work out just as we want. Fate takes a hand. Or people help Fate along a little, don't they, Anne?' He gave me a hard look. 'But Evie mustn't worry. You can pass that on, as you seem to be the appointed messenger. Tell her I just don't want to hear any more about it. End of story.'

I was totally perplexed. It was all too easy. But I nodded, grateful. He'd dismissed me; the interview was over; I had actually done it.

I turned to go. But even as I turned, he spoke again. 'But tell me, Anne. Why have you of all people taken it upon yourself to be the bearer of bad news?'

'I told you. Evie asked me.'

'And do you do everything she asks?'

'Obviously not. But she'd got herself into such a state that I thought –'

'That you'd come in person and see how I took it.'

'No, that's not it at all. I'm sorry about it. I really am, Radnor.'

'*Sorry*? I find that hard to believe. Coming from you, after what you did.'

'Please don't rake that all up.'

'Why ever not? Why should I spare you? You have a nerve, I must say. Coming here and gloating.'

'*Gloating*? You think I'm gloating?'

'It seems awfully like it, Anne.'

I sighed. 'I knew you'd take it out on me.'

'Are you surprised?'

'Not really. It's what I expected. You've always had to beat me into the ground.'

'You speak as if I'm some sort of sadist.'

'Yes,' I said. 'That's how you appear.'

'Well, appearances can be deceptive, as you full well know. I thought – mistakenly as it seemed – that you loved me once.'

'I did.' The words jumped out unbidden.

'So why did you see fit to break my heart?'

'I don't know.' I really didn't know any more. His presence confused my thought processes. I was back swimming in a vast emotional sea, feeling the heavy tug of his body as he enclosed me in a drowning embrace. All I could say was: 'It was just too much for me. You were too much for me. You never let me breathe.'

He stared at me, unbelieving. 'I see. But that doesn't exactly explain why you killed our baby.'

I could feel the tears collecting behind my eyebrows, my nose, my forehead, making everything ache. 'You can't imagine that I *wanted* to do it.'

'Then, for God's sake, Anne, why did you?'

'I don't know.' I felt unable to account for it, even to myself. 'I suppose a baby made everything too complicated. Closed down my options in life.'

'So you weighed the life of my child against your "options"? Did you never think you were being the slightest bit selfish?'

He was glaring at me from the moral high ground, but I wasn't going to be intimidated. 'Of course I was being selfish – I was nineteen, for heaven's sake; I wanted to have a life. And don't imagine I haven't blamed myself ever since – wondering what it would have been like to hold a child in my arms! Don't imagine I don't think of it every day now.' I choked and stopped, ambushed by my tears. 'But I knew you'd never let me go once I had your child.'

'And would that have been so bad? Us together for ever?' His voice had softened and he looked at me in his old intense way.

'I don't know, Radnor. I really don't know. But it's all in the past. I made my decision and you made yours.' I felt exhausted; I wanted to go.

But he got up. Came round the desk, eyes fixed on me. Stood over me. 'Is it really all in the past?' He grasped my arms, his fingertips finding the old places as if the bruises had never healed.

'Please don't.' I tried to break away.

'Oh? Would your husband not like it? I daresay you run rings around that poor sap of a plumber.'

'Don't call him that.'

Radnor smiled. 'I'm so sorry. I beg his pardon. No doubt he has his good points. Although he hasn't given you that longed-for child, I notice.'

'And he hasn't turned his back on me, either. He's stuck by me. He's a nice man.'

Radnor went on gripping my arms, and I felt the utter helplessness he always induced when he touched me. I knew I had to resist him, to forget the feel of him, the smell of him, the look of him. I had to turn my mind to Steve – Steve who let me be myself, who made me feel relaxed. Steve who pottered around the house, whistling through his teeth, taking a fag break at the back door, smoke curling away from his face. Steve who turned to me in bed, with his lazy, confiding wink: *Okay, babe?*

Radnor's voice was insistent. 'Nice. Yes, no doubt, *nice*. If that's what you want, Anne. If you want something ordinary. I don't suppose your poor plumber makes many *demands*.'

'Let me go.' My voice was very faint.

He went on holding me. I went on letting him. My head might be remembering Steve, but my body remembered Radnor. I could hear his voice insistently in my head. 'The plumber may have his good points, but I don't suppose he takes your breath away, does he? *Does he, Anne?*' His voice sharp now, probing.

I didn't answer.

He relaxed then, smiled down at me. Such a sweet smile; luminous. And his eyes – like stars in the frost. 'Anne,' he said, pulling me close.

I thought the word 'stop' in my head. I tried to speak it. But I had no breath. My lungs were full of grief, and love, and regret, and I sank beneath the water line, into the darkness.

Steve and I sit over the remains of the meal. He's on his second fag, but he's still grumpy. I try again.

'Okay, you're right about me getting upset about Radnor. There've always been a lot of unresolved issues.'

'Like why he dumped you and took up with Evie?' Steve's feeling brutal.

'It didn't happen quite like that.'

'Oh? I never knew the full story.'

'They got together much later – just after I met *you*, in fact. She ran into him in a cake shop.'

'A cake shop? *Radnor*?' Steve looks astounded.

'Well, even Radnor eats cake.' Although I'd wondered about it, myself, questioned how much he'd planned it all. 'I admit it was a bit of a surprise. She's hardly his type. Although I suppose any bloke would give his eye teeth to have someone like Evie hanging on his arm.'

Steve grunts. 'Except that Radnor is not *any bloke*, is he? Isn't that what all this fuss has been about?'

'Who can say what people see in each other? He thinks she's perfect.'

'Perfect?' Steve laughs. 'Is he completely off his head?'

'Evie's not very complicated. It looks like innocence. It appeals to him.'

Steve is unconvinced. 'That's not the message I've been getting these past weeks. I thought it was the relationship from hell. But maybe I wasn't listening properly. Or I don't have the A-levels to work it out.'

'Oh-oh. Your chip is showing again.' I can't help laughing.

Steve laughs too. The atmosphere lightens. I feel able to put my arms round him and not risk being pushed away. 'Look, why are we wasting all this time on Evie and Radnor, when *you* are so extraordinarily sexy and nice?' I kiss his ear.

'Oh, *nice*! I'm a bit sick of that.'

'It's a good quality. It'll make you a great dad.' I stroke his dark curls. They're so tight they spring back under my fingers. I love his hair, his dark, smooth skin, his male smell. Even the fags. 'I know you're annoyed about it. But seeing Radnor today *did* help. Sorted things out. You know – closure.'

Steve snorts. 'Closure! God help us, you sound like Marsha.' He broods a bit, takes time to finish his cigarette, then suddenly blows the last of the smoke into the air. 'Okay, Annie-pannie. Let's see if it's worked.' He plants a big sploshy kiss on me. It has a sharp tail of desire in it and I think this might be the night.

Clive is organizing a farewell party. I'm not supposed to know, but there's much rustling of wrapping paper and clinking of bottles in the cubbyhole. 'Just a few friends,' says Evie, who has crept in to tell me the wonderful news that Radnor's taking time off to come along too. She goes on again about how Radnor has forgiven her, and how he is in such a good mood these days she can't imagine why she was so worried about telling him.

The last few months I've closed my mind to Radnor, just refused to think about him. I concentrate on Steve. I concentrate on the baby. Positive vibes. Good karma. Willing things to be the way I want.

I was worried about how Evie would take the news, but she's been up for sharing every bit of the experience – making sure I'm taking all the right advice, buying all the right things. She says that being godmother will be much more fun. 'All the gain without the pain, Annie darling! Now doesn't that sound like me?' And she thinks Radnor agrees. 'He's too wrapped up in his work for fatherhood. At least that's what he says. And to be honest I can't imagine him putting up with a load of noise in the house. But he's really pleased about *your* baby, Annie. He's always asking how you are getting on. There's a whole new side to him you just don't know.'

I don't want to know the new side. I feel it will be awfully like the old side. I can't cope with it. And now he's coming to the party, and I know it's significant. He wouldn't come just to stand around talking to people he despises. While Evie chats on, unwrapping lemon Babygros and tiny vests – *Oh, aren't they sweet!* – I feel a cold sensation creep up through my body.

When the time comes, we all cram into the upstairs office – Steve and me, Clive, Richie, Eileen, Luke, Tom, Deirdre, Marsha, Evie

– and Radnor. Radnor stands at the back and smiles a lot. Marsha's gobsmacked, whispers aggressively in my ear: 'Hey, the guy's totally charming. A real pussycat. I think you and Evie have been holding out on me.'

Radnor doesn't say much, doesn't speak to me directly, but I can feel his scary smile all the time. I think of crocodiles and little fishes. I feel exposed. I want Steve to take me away somewhere quiet and safe, but I'm the centre of attention and have to stay and laugh at Clive's jokes. When he's finished saying how much he'll miss me bossing him about at the office, he pops the corks and fills the tall flutes that Eileen's holding out on a wobbly tin tray. He's fussing as usual, getting champagne foam all over his trousers, and before he can organize himself to speak, Radnor raises his glass.

'To Anne's baby!' he says, standing tall and proud in the middle of the room.

Everyone looks at me. Except for Steve.

Steve looks at Radnor.

LOOKING FOR LESLIE HOWARD

Seeing him sitting at that awkward corner table made me jump a bit. I normally didn't put customers there unless we were really full. He must have sat himself down when I had my back turned, even though there were lots of empty tables much more convenient. His head was turned away from me, so I couldn't see his face, but his hair was very dark and thick. He still had his overcoat on, and his trilby was placed neatly on the empty chair beside him. He was reading, and the little table lamp threw a small circle of light onto his hands as he held the book.

And that's when I saw his skin. I always notice people's skin. In fact, it's the first thing I notice. His was a lovely golden colour. And I knew it would be soft, too – meltingly soft – just like the kid gloves rich women wear. And his nails were neat and pink as he turned a page with his finger and thumb: a quick, neat movement that made me shiver.

I left off cutting up the Victoria sponge, and squeezed my way through the empty tables until I was standing in front of him – or as far in front of him as I could manage in that corner – with my pad and pencil at the ready, white cuffs well pulled down, collar well pulled up. He didn't move, as if he had no idea anybody was there. I waited, wondering what kind of book he was reading. It looked like a library book, with a dark red cover and very small print. I couldn't read the title. After a few moments standing there like an idiot, I coughed and jiggled the empty chair a bit. And then he looked up. Brown eyes, of course, to go with the golden skin. Soft eyes too, fine and bright, with thick, dark lashes that made his eyes look made-up, as if he had drawn a black line all round them, like a film star. He was so good-looking I could hardly take my eyes off him. But I managed to look nonchalant: 'Can I take your order, sir?'

He stared for a moment as though he didn't understand the words, and I thought perhaps he was a foreigner. But when he spoke, it was in perfect English. 'I beg your pardon – miles away. Just tea, please.'

'Nothing to eat?'

He seemed surprised, and then, 'Why not?' His eyes flicked to the teatime menu in its little silver stand. 'Why don't I have some . . . hot buttered toast?' It was the first item on the list. And the cheapest.

'Certainly, sir. Strawberry or raspberry?'

He looked perplexed.

'Jam's included,' I said.

'Is it? Then I'll have strawberry.' He smiled. He had a beautiful smile – pleasant, interested, but not too familiar. A gentleman's smile, in fact. You could tell he was a gentleman, even though there was this mysterious, foreign look to him. When I came back with the tea and toast, he was deep in the book again. Hardly lifted his eyes when I put down the tray and took off the heavy teapot and hot water jug – just murmured a little sound that might have been 'thank you' when I put the plate of toast in front of him. I slid the milk jug next to the teapot and placed the cup and saucer to the right of the toast, turning the cup the right way up, and moving the menu stand to a position near the wall. I placed the jam next to the milk, moved everything round again. I made as much noise as I decently could, hoping he'd look up. All the time I couldn't take my eyes off the beauty of his skin, his narrow face with its long, nice-shaped nose, and his eyelids drawn down slantingly over his eyes. 'Is that all right, sir? Anything else?'

He looked up, surprised. As if he'd never seen me before, let alone given me an order; as if I might have been a Martian come to stand in front of him. Then he looked down at the table as if the tea and toast had come from another planet as well; as if he hadn't heard me clash about for five minutes right under his nose. 'Yes. Thank you,' he said, smiling up at me. 'Everything looks very nice.' And he opened his napkin, laid it carefully across his lap and stretched out his beautiful brown hand for the teapot. His skin looked so much like velvet. I couldn't help staring, wishing my own was half as lovely. I wanted to stroke it. And, yes, kiss it, too. Let my lips feel the soft smoothness, let the feel of it go straight to my brain.

I was completely daft about nice-looking men. But it was all in my head, all romance and daydreams; I wasn't a good-time girl who'd flirt with anybody. The man had to be dead right – well-dressed, and well-mannered – or he meant nothing to me. I was always looking out for the perfect gentleman. A man like Leslie Howard, in fact. Leslie was my ideal. I loved all his films. I'd go to the Odeon on my afternoon off and sit through the programme two or three times, until the anthem came up and the lights came on, and I'd walk out in a kind of dream. I kept wishing the men I met in my life were more like Leslie. Most of our customers were genteel, of course, and I'd married myself off to doctors and solicitors on no end of occasions since I'd started work at the hotel. But behind the scenes, there wasn't much choice. I'd given up on the porter's boy by the end of the first week. He liked to tell stupid jokes, and whistled loudly if your petticoat was showing even a little bit. And Mr Reeves and Mr Mullan were far too old for me. I'd once had a fancy for Keith Beddoes, the delivery boy from Smollett's, who winked at me with his arms around a cardboard box full of veg and asked, '*Anything doing, kiddo?*' But in the end, I gave him the cold shoulder. He was good-looking, but a bit full of himself, and I could tell he was just waiting for a chance to pinch my bottom or put his hand up my skirt. I couldn't bear the thought of that. One day, I knew, I was bound to find a man like Leslie. He'd come to the restaurant and our eyes would meet.

Miss Jennings always laughed at my ideas. 'These people – they're ships that pass in the night,' she'd say, as she collected up all the forgotten scarves and umbrellas left behind in the cloakroom. 'Don't you get any romantic ideas, Elsie, or you're bound to be disappointed.' And although I loved the idea of two great lit-up liners passing each other, bright white against midnight blue, with me leaping across the gap into the arms of a handsome stranger, I realized that she was right. Most of my customers behaved as if I didn't exist. They came in a rush, taking off coats and gloves, and talked amongst themselves without so much as a glance at me. Just one or two were chatty and used to tell me what they got up to when they weren't tucking into cream teas or crêpes suzette. Mr Reynolds, for example. He came nearly every lunchtime and had a lamb chop or a piece of steak, always with season's vegetables and rice pudding afterwards. He was quite old, with mottled skin like a toad, but always had some story to tell me and didn't seem to notice my neck and hands. 'You always brighten my day, Elsie,' he used to say with a wink. 'You're a lovely girl.'

Did he really think I was lovely? Sometimes I'd try to get a glimpse of my reflection in the floor-length mirror in the lobby and persuade myself I looked normal enough in my tailored black dress and white starched pinny.

Now I hovered over the handsome young man, loath to leave him. It was nice, just to be so close to him, to be breathing the same air. 'Let me know if you want anything else, sir. I'll be just here.' I indicated the sideboard where the silver cutlery lay in baskets, where the clean napkins were folded and stacked, where rows of cruets waited to be filled, and where Winnie sat at the cash register totting up the lunchtime takings. It was three o'clock; a quiet time. Lunch had finished and tea had not yet begun. In half an hour Mavis would come on duty, the rush would start and I'd be up to my eyes in orders for Welsh rarebit and 'a choice of pastries if you don't mind, Miss'. But in the meantime I could get away with standing at the counter and feasting my eyes on the young man's beauty as he sat there in his heavy coat, idly stirring his tea, his hot buttered toast left untouched in front of him as he devoured the contents of his book instead. I pretended to give an extra shine to the knives and forks as I watched him from the corner of my eye. He went on reading for ages, drinking his tea absent-mindedly, so in the end I went across to him, squeezing again through the empty tables and chairs, my tray like a shield in front of me.

'Finished, sir?'

'By all means.' He pushed his teacup away, still reading.

'You haven't touched your toast,' I said, as I removed his plate.

He looked up. Then looked at the toast. Again, that look of surprise, as if he hardly recognized it. 'Oh dear. I'm afraid I forgot.'

'Well, it's gone cold now.'

'Yes, indeed.' He looked at it unhappily; almost guiltily. I felt slightly guilty too, as it had been me that had pushed him into having the toast, and now he had wasted his money. I didn't know if this mattered to him. I couldn't tell if he was well-off or not. His coat looked as if it had been expensive once, and his hat had a nice curl to the brim and, all in all, he had a well-kept kind of look. But I had an idea that money didn't come easily to him, and that he spent it carefully.

'You were too busy reading,' I said, adding boldly, 'It must be a good book.'

'Very good. Food for the mind. I'll have to make do with that.' He smiled again and my heart fluttered again. But if I'd hoped he would share the contents with me I was disappointed. He closed the book and slid it into his pocket. 'How much do I owe you?'

'Two and threepence,' I said, tearing his order off my pad. 'Pay at the desk, sir,' I added as he started to rummage for change in his trousers.

'Of course. But I was looking for . . .' He put a shilling on the tablecloth.

'Oh, that's too much!' I cried.

He looked even more surprised than he'd done before. Nobody turns down a tip, especially a generous one.

'I mean, it was my fault you had the toast,' I added lamely.

'Not at all. And it certainly wasn't your fault that I didn't eat it. I'm always letting food go cold. My mother despairs of me.' He was getting up, picking up his trilby, trying to slide his chair back and getting stuck in that awkward corner, chair and table legs tangling in their usual stupid way.

'Here, let me move it.' I reached to pull the table out and as I did so, my sleeves slid up my arms an inch or two. I saw his glance fall on the backs of my hands, my wrists, and I hastily pulled my cuffs back down. 'Sorry,' I said, feeling the blood pulse in my neck and cheeks.

'Nothing to apologize for,' he said, and I didn't know whether he meant he had seen or not seen. Or whether he had seen and forgotten it, as a gentleman should. Then he said, 'Good afternoon,' made his way to Winnie's desk and paid quickly before walking out into the lobby. He checked his watch before putting on his hat, descending the hotel steps and turning right. Another ship passed by, I thought.

But after supper, when I was lying on my bed, still in uniform, trying to ignore the sound of Winnie's wireless from next door, I thought about him again. I reckoned he must be five or six years older than me – around twenty or twenty-one. It was difficult to judge his age as he was quite boyish-looking, but when he spoke, it was in a grown-up way that was completely different from Keith and the other lads. He was clearly very clever, because no one read a book – especially such a dull-looking book – in that concentrated kind of way unless they were. And he lived with his mother. I imagined she'd be dark-haired and dark-eyed like him – a foreigner perhaps, come to England for the love of an Englishman but left a widow with an only child and a small private income. I decided his mother would have just enough money to stop her son from having to work, but not enough to allow them to live in style. Their clothes would be good quality but not new, and she would, I thought, do her own cooking, while the young man would sit at the table in their artistic dining room with his nose in a book, letting the food go cold while he read about – what? Not romance, I felt sure. Not Mary Webb, Ethel M. Dell, or American detective stories. Something serious and quiet. Philosophy, perhaps. That was the most serious thing I could think of, although I had no idea what it really was. However, I imagined the young man taking me back to his house in the leafy suburbs and introducing me to a dark-eyed lady with black hair plaited over the top of her head and coloured shawls over her shoulders, and who would keep a gramophone continually on the wind with gypsy music while she presented dish after dish of exotic fare. Hungarian goulash, possibly, like we had in the restaurant sometimes. 'My son is very absent-minded,' she would say. 'I despair of him. He needs a good woman to look after him. Someone just like you, Elsie.'

'Elsie, can you do me a favour?' It was Miss Jennings, rattling my doorknob. She was always bothering me about something or other at bedtime. I got off the bed and opened the door. She had on her satin dressing gown, as usual, and her hair was wound in pin curls and covered with a heavy-duty net. Her skin was shiny with cold cream

34

and gave off a smell I always thought was too sweet – almost sickly, in fact. 'Oh, Elsie,' she said, taking my hand in her clammy one. 'I've just put my hair in curls and now I need something from the late chemist. Can you be a love and go for me?'

'It's quarter to ten,' I said grumpily, not wanting to get my swollen feet back into my shoes.

'I know, dear, but it's, you know' – she lowered her voice – '*time of the month*. Come on, Elsie, I'll do the same for you. Hurry up, or they'll be shut.'

So I put on my hat and coat and shoved my feet into shoes that seemed to have shrunk two sizes since I took them off, took the slightly greasy two shilling piece, and scuttled down the back stairs with a bad grace. I liked the chance to be friendly with Miss Jennings, to have cocoa with her and chat about how she did her nails, but sometimes I felt she seemed to be taking advantage of the fact that I was the youngest girl on the staff – and although she always promised she'd make things up to me, somehow she never really did.

The late chemist was on a corner down a side street, three blocks from the hotel, just where Stephenson Street ended. I'd never been inside. It had two big glass flasks of coloured water in the window, blue and red, lit up from inside and casting queer stripes of colour everywhere. The rest of the shop was dark. I was afraid it was shut, but the door opened when I pushed it, the bell jangling loudly. A man in a white coat stood silently behind the long counter, as if he had been there for ever, waiting for me to arrive. His freckled skin seemed to glow in an eerie manner in the red and blue light. His spectacles were the magnifying kind, and made his eyes look three times as big as normal. I stopped for a moment, not sure what to say. I never liked asking men for sanitary stuff, and would usually wait ages to get a lady assistant – but there was no one else in the shop so I rushed the name out as quickly as I could. 'A box of Dr White's, please.'

He sighed, casting a glance up at the clock. 'You leave things until the last minute, don't you, young lady? I close at ten. You've only just caught me. What would you have done if I'd been closed, eh? Eh?' He put his white speckled face close to mine, then drew back and gave a kind of laugh that wasn't really a laugh at all.

I said it wasn't for me, but for 'somebody at the hotel'. I tried to imply that it was a guest, somebody important – and it seemed to work, because he stopped laughing and produced a box from under the counter. 'One and three.'

'Can you wrap it, please?' I wasn't going all the way back advertising Dr White's, even in the dark.

The chemist slowly pulled out a brown paper bag, slipped the box inside it in rather a pointed way and slid it across the counter. I put the two shillings down and he took it, opened the till and, after a few minutes chinking about in the coin box, came up with the change, which he put on the counter with a smack. I stretched to pick it up, not thinking about my skin because the shop was so dark and the man so old – but the next minute he was gripping my wrist. His hand felt horrible and sweaty. My mother had always warned me to be careful of men like this, and there had been one or two at the hotel who had tried to grab me from behind. But now I was on my own in a dark and deserted shop. I couldn't help thinking about the crazy scientist I'd read about in *Her Present Danger* who kidnapped young girls so they could extract the essence of their youth. This man was a chemist; he might know how to do it. 'Let me go!' I cried, my voice not bold at all, but high and wobbly.

'Don't be such a silly little blighter! I'm not going to hurt you. I just wanted to take a look at your skin.' He pushed up my cuff and ran his thumb roughly across the raised ridges of my arm, sending white scaly flakes drifting onto the counter.

'Please,' I said, trying desperately to slip my wrist out of his grasp. But he ignored me, pulled my arm closer, and looked at it over the top of his glasses.

'You've been scratching, haven't you, naughty girl? I can see – scratch, scratch, scratch.' He looked at me crossly. 'Don't you ever put any-thing on it?'

'Nothing's any good.' I said, more sure of myself now – after all, I'd spent years putting calamine on it, getting myself stiff and powdery to no avail. 'Ma says it's incurable.'

'I know *that*,' he said tetchily. 'I'm a medical man, for heaven's sake. But there are treatments that can tone it down a bit. You're a young girl; you don't want to have to hide away under layers of clothes for the rest of your life. Let me have a proper look. Take your coat off.'

I knew there was nothing that would persuade me to take off as much as a hair-ribbon in front of him, but he still had hold of my wrist. 'No, thank you,' I said, making another attempt at sounding self-possessed. 'I'm in a hurry. People are waiting for me at the hotel.'

'Oh, hoity-toity! Well, it's not my funeral,' he said, suddenly losing interest. 'Here you are, silly child. If you want to suffer, suffer.' And he released my wrist with a flick of annoyance, as if my scaly arm was something useless he was throwing to the dogs.

I pulled down my cuff, grabbed the Dr White's and the change, and turned tail, almost throwing myself at the shop door. The doorbell jangled madly as I wrenched the handle up and down in a panic, all sorts of wild imaginings surging through my brain. I nearly fainted as I heard the chemist come up behind me. I thought he was about to drug me with chloroform and make me a prisoner in his cellar and no one would ever know. But the door suddenly opened, smooth as silk, and I fell out into the street.

I began to run. I could see some people coming out of a building up ahead. Men and women laughing and talking, but not like people when they come out of a pub. Excited, I thought, but more serious. There was quite a group of them and they spilled over the pavement and into the road. In my panic I headed straight through the middle of them. Someone jostled my arm and the box slipped out of its paper bag onto the pavement. A man bent to pick it up. 'Sorry about that! We're a fearful lot when we get excited. Here you are.' The speaker rose and looked at me. It was the young man with the lovely skin. His face was even handsomer in the lamplight, his eyes even blacker around the rims. 'Why,' he said, with a look of such pleasure that my heart battered against my ribs. 'It's my little waitress! My little waitress who thought a shilling was too much for a tip.' I didn't know what to say as he stood there smiling with the box in his hands. He must have seen what it was, although he gave no sign. I was tremendously excited to see him, of course, and felt relieved to be in the middle of a group of normal people after my fright with the chemist, but I was embarrassed about him standing there with that box on display.

'I've just been running an errand for a friend,' I explained. 'Well, not really a friend – someone from the hotel.'

'Well, don't let us keep you. It must be urgent. You're quite out of breath.' He handed back the box. I realized I was panting hard with fright, and that my hands were shaking so much I couldn't put it back into its bag. The cheap brown paper began to tear as I tried to shove it in.

'Let me do it.' Another pair of hands came forward. A woman's. Work-worn and sensible, with a silvery wedding ring. A kind face, pale dried skin, as if she had powdered with talc. 'Jack told us about you, you know. We thought you were rather marvellous, refusing a tip. Jack always overdoes the compensation.'

I was astonished that the young man had discussed such a thing with his friends, and with this woman who I thought for a moment might be his wife, but who looked too old. 'Oh, it just didn't seem fair,' I replied. 'I thought maybe he needed it more than me.'

There was a burst of very hearty laughter from the small group around us. I felt very silly and very young. 'I have to go now,' I said hastily. 'Miss Jennings is relying on me.'

Jack smiled. 'Off you go, then,' he said. 'Sweet dreams,' he added, raising his hat.

I couldn't think of anything else that night – and for every night afterwards – except for the mysterious Jack raising his hat and smiling at me. Each teatime I waited for the sight of him, hoping to see his narrow head bent over that old red book. On my first afternoon off, I even gave up the chance to see Leslie in *It's Love I'm After* so I could walk to the building where I'd seen him. There was a brass plate on the door. It said 'The Carlton Rooms and Exhibition Hall'. The door was shut and there was no way of telling what went on inside. Mr Reynolds, when I asked him later, said all sorts of things happened there. People hired out rooms, he said. He had himself been to a meeting of the Antiquarian Society there only last week. 'What's your interest, Elsie?' he said. 'You should be going out dancing or to the flicks, not bothering about a musty old place like that.' I said I had run into someone I knew there, but didn't know where that person lived to look him up. 'Ah,' said Mr Reynolds. 'He'll be doing the looking up himself, if he's got any sense.'

But I knew Jack was never going to look me up. He didn't know who I was, and even if he remembered me kindly, it was simply as a 'little waitress'. I was too young and too common to interest him in any other way. And of course there was my skin. It was flaring up badly then, spots creeping up my neck and behind my ears. But all the same, on my next day off I was back at the Carlton Rooms, like a moth to a candle. This time the door was open and there was an elderly gent on duty in the lobby. 'What can I do for you, young lady?' he said in a friendly sort of way when he saw me hovering around. Then he made a lot of fuss getting out a big ledger from behind the desk, and after much turning of pages, checking and re-checking of dates and tracing about with his finger, he finally came to it: 'Wednesday 19th – Photography Club in the Charles Ramsden Room, Peace Pledge Union in the Main Hall, and Philosophy Society in the library.' I was delighted with myself. Jack was a philosopher just like I'd imagined. I thought that if I waited outside the hall when the Philosophy Club ended the next Wednesday I was sure to see Jack coming out. I worked out a number of excuses as to why I should be there at that particular time, and what I would say to Jack when he saw me; and I imagined how he would offer me his arm and take me back to the hotel and raise his hat and ask when he might see me again. But even though I waited for several Wednesdays, watching all the different people coming out and drifting down the street in twos and threes, Jack never appeared.

I realized that I'd been kidding myself, anyway. No real gentleman who came and ate in the hotel was going to fall in love with a mere waitress. I told myself that I needed to give up my stupid imaginings and concentrate on bettering myself. That's what my mother had hoped for when she sent me off with my cardboard suitcase and one change of clothes to 'learn how to lay a table and talk ladylike'. She thought I might even get to be a housekeeper at a big house if I was lucky and took my chance when it came. Every letter she wrote ended with the hope that I would 'get on', and every time I went home for a weekend she'd make sure I hadn't forgotten. 'Don't be like me, Elsie,' she'd say, rolling out soggy pastry on the kitchen table, all the kids running round, and my sister Peggy trying to keep them in order. 'Make something of yourself. Don't let a husband and kids drag you down.'

By then I was pretty good at silver service, and I started to learn all the French words on the menu and say them in the proper way. As well as that, I used to hang around in the kitchen in the mornings while Mr Mullan prepared the food. Then, when the customers asked about Hollandaise sauce or Cutlets Reform, I was able to explain what they were straight away. Mr Reeves the manager said I was the best trainee he had come across, and after Mrs Walsh left to look after her sick auntie in Teignmouth, he made me head waitress, even though I was two years younger than Mavis. 'It's not years that count,' he said. 'It's what you've got up here.' And he put his finger to his forehead and tapped it knowingly.

Then, six months later, when Winnie left to marry the encyclopedia salesman who'd always come in for a grilled plaice on Fridays, I was put in charge of the cash desk – 'A position of great trust', said Mr Reeves as he counted out the float in front of me that first day.

Lots of things started to change, then. Of course I'd seen the newsreels with Hitler spouting off in front of all those thousands of Nazis, but I'd always thought he was somebody comical, with his silly moustache and staring eyes. Keith Beddoes used to mimic him in the store-room with a finger under his nose and his arm stuck up in the air as he marched about: *Sieg Heil!* He made Mavis and me laugh. But now people were talking about things getting serious, and other countries getting invaded. Sometimes we had guests with foreign accents in the hotel. 'Refugees,' explained Mr Reynolds. 'People who can see the writing on the wall.' And then all of a sudden, with just a week's notice, Miss Jennings left to join the Wrens with her very best friend Miss Carter. 'War is on the cards, Elsie,' she said, as she gave me a big, and rather sticky, kiss of farewell. 'Look after yourself, my love, and don't get taken advantage of.' Six months later, Mr Chamberlain was on the radio telling us the terrible news.

Well, half the men at the hotel joined up straight away, and we were so short-staffed that Mr Reeves had to do a lot more work than he was used to. He was always rushing about looking exasperated and never wanted to be asked anything at all, even if you needed something important like keys to the pantry or the linen cupboard. At the same time, everybody in the world seemed to want to come to the hotel for afternoon tea, so we started doing tea dances twice a week in the ballroom – which was a lot of extra work for me and Mavis. All the enlisted men came in to show off their new uniforms, and parents and sweethearts came to say farewell over iced buns and petits fours. Mavis and I would do a bit of a foxtrot with the trays as we swirled in and out. Life was so hectic that I only had time to get up, do my work, and go to bed. I had no time for dreams. Even about Jack.

In fact, the only spare time I had in those days was between breakfast and lunch, when Mrs Willacott was doing the morning coffees. If the weather was fine, I'd go up with Mavis to the little bit of flat roof over the ballroom and sunbathe behind the wall. No one could see us, and I used to take down my thick stockings and let my skin feel the sun. Mavis would look at my scabs with pity as she stretched out her white legs next to my mottled ones.

'Do they hurt?' she said once, eyeing the shiny red patches on my knees that looked like continents rising from the sea, with a whole lot of separate islands dotted about up and down from my ankles to the top of my legs.

'Flaming agony,' I said, although this was a lie. It was just that the scabs itched a lot and sometimes I couldn't help scratching. Then the blood would seep through my stockings, even though I wore two thick pairs. I always had to be on the lookout for the stains.

'You're lucky they're not on your face,' she said.

'Yes,' I said. 'Although I'd be a blinking sight luckier if I didn't have them at all.' Then she asked me if I thought it would make any difference to my getting married, and I could see her thinking of my poor husband and the shock he would have on our wedding night. 'I don't think I'll get married,' I said.

'Don't you want kids? I want to have three kids,' she said, as if that were the only point in getting married.

'Maybe you won't stop at three. Maybe you'll have seven. One every eighteen months like my ma,' I said callously. 'I'd rather keep out of all that. Anyway, I want to get on in life.'

And get on I did, although I never forgot Jack. He kept himself in some hidden part of me even when I thought I'd grown out of my romantic stage. I still went to the flicks, of course, and I still held a candle for Leslie Howard, but I knew a bit more about the way of the world. I almost blushed thinking how I must have appeared to Jack that day – a flat-chested kid with bad skin and cow's eyes, holding a box of sanitary towels. My only comfort was that Jack wouldn't have remembered me at all; and that we were never going to meet again.

So it was a shock to me when I saw him a few years later. It was about the middle of the war and I was dead tired with all the endless work and making do – not to mention the sleepless nights in the cellars because of the bombing. It was Mr Reeves' half-day off (he had a lot of half-days then), and I was on my way to the kitchens to check the rations with Mr Mullan. As I passed the dining room I glanced in casually to check on the new girl, not expecting anything out of the ordinary. But there he was, silhouetted against the window, handsome as ever. I caught my breath, thinking I must be imagining things. Maybe it was just someone else who looked like him; someone else slim and dark. Then he glanced towards the door where I was standing, and I was in no doubt.

Just like the first time, the dining room was pretty empty. The tea dance was in full swing in the ballroom and the sound of a saxophone was echoing down the hall. I could see the new waitress sauntering towards Jack's table in a half-soaked sort of way, and I headed her off quickly. 'I'll see to this gentleman, Jean,' I said, pulling down my cuffs and pulling up my collar.

He wasn't reading this time; he was alert, on edge, eyes flicking from window to door. I knew the signs, of course: he was waiting for someone. It was bound to be a woman. Why wouldn't it be – he was young and handsome, and if I'd fallen for him on sight, surely some other woman would have? I wanted him to myself, though, to talk about tea and jam and hot buttered toast. I didn't know if I could bear to see another woman sitting across from him, taking his lovely soft hands into hers.

'May I take your order, sir?' I smiled, hoping he'd recognize me. But he gave no sign. His face, as he turned to look at me, was thinner and paler than I remembered and the dark lashes around his eyes looked even more intense.

'Not yet, thank you. I'm waiting for someone.' He added, 'My mother and sisters. They're always late. Ah, here they –'

He rose with a smile, colour coming to his cheeks, and I turned and saw in the doorway a plump, middle-aged woman in a mushroom-coloured two-piece, followed by two very smartly dressed young ladies. They all rushed forward and clung to him, laughing and crying at the same time. Jack had trouble keeping upright underneath their assault, and it struck me again that he seemed rather frailer than before. I knew what all the excitement meant, of course: Jack was off to battle, and his family had come to say goodbye. We'd had plenty of scenes like this in the last two or three years. The only thing that was strange was that he wasn't in uniform – just a plain dark suit which didn't fit him very well. He still looked lovely, though, and I wanted to eat him with my eyes.

I was a bit disappointed that his mother had no exotic scarves and no plaits of foreign-looking hair. In fact, she looked just like any of the women who regularly came to lunch at the hotel – little hat with a feather perched on her head, a fox fur around her shoulders. Only the colour of her skin marked her out. It had that old rose colour and velvety texture that I so admired in Jack, and she had the same striking eyelashes. The sisters were equally dark, with lots of black curls. Their velvet tams, worn on one side, were especially fashionable. All three took a long time to get seated, deciding who should sit next to Jack and who should sit opposite. 'Oh, Jack!' they kept saying, jumping up and down, and kissing him over and over, and, 'Oh, Jack,' again when they finished. And even when they were seated, it seemed the mother could not take her eyes off her son. She patted his hand and even leant across the table and stroked his head. He didn't seem at all embarrassed and looked at them all and gave a smile which was much wider than I'd seen from him before. He seemed full of love for them, and not at all absent-minded.

'Would you care to look at the menu?' I asked, once they were slightly more settled. 'We have a selection of cakes and pastries as well as muffins and hot buttered toast.' I handed the menu to Jack. 'Jam's included, needless to say.' I wanted to see if he'd remembered. He looked up at me for a moment, as if an old memory was stirring but he couldn't quite place what it was. But seconds later his sisters had distracted him, saying, my goodness, didn't they know there was a war on down here in Devon and gosh, he must have a custard slice, or was he hungry and did he want sardines on toast or an omelette? 'Oh, Jack,' they kept saying. 'We can't believe you're back with us.' They touched him again and again as if to make sure he wasn't a ghost. And he laughed and raised his hand to pat the younger sister affectionately on the back.

And that's when I saw his fingers. The skin was black and blistered and scarred right up to the knuckles, and his nails were uneven and torn. I wanted to cry out with shock. It was like a pain going through me to see his lovely hands in such a state and I couldn't imagine what had happened to them. But I kept my pencil steady and wrote down the entire order, crossing it out as they changed their minds and changed them back again. 'Oh, we're so sorry, Miss,' said the older sister. 'Please excuse us. We're just so excited.'

When I came back with the tray, they were all so wrapped up in each other that they didn't notice how I was trembling, how I nearly spilled the tea and the hot water, how I seemed to get egg custard on the fruit cake and trailed a line of sardine scales along the milk jug, how the spoon fell out of the strawberry jam, and the tongs over-balanced from the sugar basin. 'How lovely,' murmured the mother, as she surveyed it all, tea and children. 'How long has it been since we all ate a meal together?'

'Now, Mother! Don't be morbid,' the younger and livelier of the sisters piped up. 'The worst is over. We have to think of the future, now.'

How could the worst be over? And as for the future – was I about to lose Jack as soon as Fate had brought him back to me? I watched them from the till as they talked and laughed. It was such a different Jack, so lively and happy. I wanted to be part of his family, to be able to touch him and joke with him as they did in their easy way.

When I was clearing the dishes, the mother opened her handbag and discreetly passed a five pound note across to him, but he shook his head and wouldn't take it. 'You have to have some money, Jack. However you feel about it, you can't live on air,' she said. I couldn't help wondering what had happened to the private income and why his mother was giving him money like he was a child. She then tried a pound, and finally a ten shilling note, which he took as if he really didn't want to and only because his sister pushed it into his pocket, saying, 'Even a saint like you needs to eat and drink.' It struck me as a funny thing to say about your brother. None of my brothers were anything like saints, especially Douglas, who was always in some sort of trouble, pinching things and being places he shouldn't be. Dad had had to take the strap to him more than once. I was surprised, though, when they all got up and said goodbye in quite a happy way. Much too happy, I thought, considering that next week he could be sunk in a convoy or shot down from a burning plane.

Jack's mother paid the bill and said they had to hurry or they would miss the train to London. Jack ushered them out, and I followed, loitering in the doorway, thinking he might ask for his hat and coat and I could help him on with them, feeling the soft cashmere or the silk lining as I made my own private farewell. It was only when his mother kissed him again and said, 'Goodbye, darling. And don't forget to write!' that I realized they were going without him. And then, when he'd waved them off, he turned back and went past me up the stairs. I could hardly believe it. I slipped behind the counter and checked in the visitors' book. There on the bottom line, *Jack Thompson, Cavendish Square, London*, in dark, neat handwriting. Such an English name. And such a posh-sounding address. And how posh all of them had been, his mother and sisters. I must have seemed really stupid to refuse his shilling three years before.

I wanted to make amends for my stupidity, by serving Jack the very best cuts of meat and one of the secret desserts Mr Mullan kept in the cold larder for favoured customers. I'd show Jack how sophisticated I'd got and perhaps, this time, he would tell me something about his real self. From seven o'clock on I had my eyes trained on the dining room entrance, and nearly ran into Mavis three times. 'What's the matter, Elsie?' she said. 'You're a real clodhopper tonight!' But nine o'clock came, the dining room emptied, and Jack hadn't come.

'How long is Mr Thompson staying?' I asked Mr Reeves casually when we were laying up for the next day's breakfast. Mr Reeves said only the one night, booked from London by telephone he believed, and could I be a dear and take some cocoa up to twenty-one as Mavis was washing up and the new girl had gone home with a sick headache. 'I wouldn't normally ask you to do room service, but I know I can rely on you when the chips are down.'

'Of course,' I said. 'Anything to help the war effort, Mr Reeves.'

In fact, I made two cups of cocoa and after taking the first to twenty-one, I knocked on the adjoining door. Jack opened it. His shirt sleeves were rolled up, his arms all golden and smooth. He must have been reading again, as his book was open on the bed. I could see the dent on the coverlet where he'd been lying. 'Your cocoa, Mr Thompson,' I said.

He frowned. 'You've made a mistake, I think,' he said.

'No, it's for you. I made it specially. Only you mustn't let it go cold like you usually do.'

'I beg your pardon?'

I felt embarrassed now. He clearly didn't remember and I was near to making a fool of myself. But it was worth one more go.

'We've met before. Three years ago. You gave me a shilling tip and I didn't want to take it.'

He laughed. 'Good lord! When I came down for that PPU meeting! I'm so sorry – I didn't recognize you. You were a lot younger, I think. Well, obviously you were, but I mean – not so elegant and grown-up.' I blushed, glad I had put my hair up before dinner and dabbed on a little lipstick. He surveyed me as I stood in the doorway, cup in hand, and I wondered whether he was considering if I was now more worthy of his notice. But he only said, 'I'm afraid I can't give you any kind of tip this time. I've only got a ten shilling note.'

'Take it anyway,' I said, holding out the cocoa. 'Or I'll have to pour it down the sink, and that would be a waste of rations.'

'Well, we can't have that.' He took the cup, then paused. 'Are you allowed to come in while I drink it? I could do with some company. Or is that against the rules?'

My heart thudded in my chest. 'I'm off duty now,' I lied. 'So I can do as I please.'

'*Will* you come in then?'

And so I found myself stepping into Jack's bedroom with Jack there in his shirt sleeves and his book on the bed, and the bedside lamp glowing just as dimly as the one on the corner table three years before. I didn't care if Mr Reeves saw me. I didn't care if I got the sack. I was alone with Jack. It was like the night before battle when men and women do all kinds of foolish things.

'Do sit down.' He removed his jacket from the back of the rickety bedroom chair, moved his book onto the chest of drawers and sat on the edge of the bed. He lifted the cup to his lips. I didn't look at his fingers, just concentrated on the burnished shine of his forearms in the lamplight. I could feel myself trembling. I had no idea what was going to happen.

We sat in silence for a bit while he drank. He didn't seem to mind the silence but I felt so wound up that I had to speak. 'What is it you're reading?' I said, nodding at the book. I almost bit back the words as I said them, because I hated it when people said the same thing to me. Mr Reeves and Mavis were always asking me that question, though they had no interest whatsoever in the answer.

He hesitated, and I could see he didn't want to seem too highbrow. But he just said, 'Bertrand Russell.'

I'd heard the name, but I'd never seen his books in the lending library. 'What sort of thing does he write?'

'Philosophy, mainly.'

'Really?' I couldn't help grinning. I really had been right in that old guess of mine.

'And mathematics too. But I don't understand a lot of that.' He smiled, and I knew he was trying to make me feel better about being uneducated. That was the sort of gentleman he was.

But I put him right. 'Oh, I'm pretty good at figures. I'm responsible for the till and have to do the balance at the end of the day. Mr Reeves hates it if we're a farthing out – not that we are usually, but Mavis forgets things sometimes.'

'Oh,' he said. 'Arithmetic. Rather you than me. I could never do all those calculations – you know, the ones involving thirty pounds of bananas at fivepence halfpenny a pound.' He laughed.

'That would be: five thirties are one hundred and fifty, plus thirty halfpennies is fifteen pence, equals a hundred and sixty-five pence, which is – divided by twelve –' I paused '– thirteen shillings and ninepence.'

He stared at me. 'Good Lord!'

'It's not difficult,' I said, blushing a bit. 'I mean, I have to do it every day, so it's second nature.' Then I felt foolish. What was I doing showing off like a child in front of the teacher, when I wanted to impress him with my grown-up charm?

'Well,' he said. 'I'm impressed. Not that we have any bananas to count, these days. My mother says she hasn't seen one in I don't know how long.'

'We got hold of a few last year. Mr Mullan put them in a trifle to make them go further.'

'Trifle, eh? You do well for yourselves down here, don't you? Eggs, cream, butter, cakes. My sisters were envious. They can't get much of that in London . . .'

'Well, we've got our own chickens out the back. And Mr Mullan deals direct with a couple of farmers for the butter and so on.'

He raised his eyes. 'Ah. Black market, you mean.'

'Well, not really. We all have to do what we can, don't we?'

He smiled. 'All of us have to. In our different ways.' And I felt suddenly tawdry, and I knew Jack would never buy anything on the black market, and would always be straight as a die.

There was another silence. Again, Jack seemed not to mind, but I felt awkward. 'Where are you off to?' I asked, hoping he'd say he was stationed in the local barracks – somewhere I could meet him when he had leave, where we could go to the pictures together and then have tea in a café and be waited on by somebody else.

'Oh, somewhere in the country,' he said, vaguely. 'I'm afraid I've forgotten the name.'

Obviously, he couldn't really have forgotten the name if he was having to get there, so I realized he must be doing something so secret he couldn't even tell me. Careless words cost lives, after all. Perhaps there was a country house somewhere out on Dartmoor where he'd be taught wireless codes and then dropped behind enemy lines. He was so cool and nonchalant, I imagined he would make a good spy, risking his life like Leslie in *Pimpernel Smith*. 'I suppose it's a bit nerve-racking,'

I said. 'Not knowing what's going to happen to you from now on. Where you'll be sent, I mean.'

'Oh, I know what's going to happen.' He said it with a kind of sureness, as if he knew what he was in for. 'It's pretty run of the mill stuff, after all.'

'I think you're awfully brave.' (They said that on the films: *Awf'ly brave.*)

He frowned. 'Do you? People don't normally say that.' He looked down at his mangled fingers. 'Still, it'll be good to get active again. I feel as though my body's atrophied these last eighteen months.'

Atrophied. I loved the long word, and the fact that he didn't mind using it with me, although I could only guess what it meant. 'Which Service are you in?' I asked. 'Or can't you say?'

He stopped, and gave me a long look over the rim of the cup. Then he set it down. Paused. Gave me a rueful smile. 'I'm afraid, young lady, that you may be under a misapprehension.'

Another complicated word. 'What do you mean?' I said. 'What *misapprehension?*'

He paused again, but for such a long time that I thought he wasn't going to answer. Then he said, 'I'm not in the forces, I'm afraid: quite the opposite.'

'And what would the opposite be?' I asked, jokingly. 'Something terribly secret?'

He looked me full in the face. 'Not secret at all. Open for all to see and despise. I thought you must have guessed – my lack of uniform, I mean. I'm a Conscientious Objector.'

The horrible words seemed to float in the air between us. I thought for a moment that he was joking, but one look at his face told me he wasn't. I felt almost sick. A Conshie, a coward, the lowest of the low. Even my useless dad had tried to join up, although his chest was too bad and they'd sent him to an aeroplane factory in Bristol instead.

'There,' he said, lightly. 'I've disappointed you. You thought I was one of Our Brave Boys. Now you think I'm a coward and will want your cocoa back.'

'No,' I said quickly, embarrassed at the way he'd guessed my thoughts – except for the bit about the cocoa, which I wouldn't have begrudged anyone. 'I expect you have your reasons.' Although I couldn't imagine what they could be. I didn't understand why anyone wouldn't want to fight. I'd wanted to fight myself when I heard Mr Churchill's speech, saying we would never surrender.

'Well, I do have my reasons, of course,' he said. 'Although not everyone appreciates them. Not even my mother, sometimes. In fact my mother and my sisters don't share my embarrassing principles at all.'

'So why *are* you a Conshie – entious objector?' I asked, thinking as I said the words that it was not my place to question him, a guest at the hotel. Mr Reeves would have sacked me on the spot. 'If you don't mind my asking,' I added, quickly.

He sighed, as if tired of explaining it. 'I happen to believe that war is fundamentally wrong,' he said. 'That we human beings can settle our differences another way. Haven't we learnt from our mistakes? Take the War to End All Wars? Well, it didn't, did it? We have to forge a different understanding if we are to survive; if we are to change the way we live. I won't have other people's blood on my hands.'

'But don't you love your country?' I asked. I'd imagined myself making a last stand on the promenade, alongside Mr Reeves and Mavis, kitchen knife in hand.

'My country?' he said. 'Well, I'm not sure about that. I mean, I love the individuals in it and I'm not scared of dying for them – at least not more than any other man. But I would never say "My country right or wrong." Because my country is often wrong. Most ordinary people on both sides don't want war and we shouldn't allow ourselves to be bullied into it.' He spoke quickly, quietly, seemed so sure of himself that I could tell he'd said the words before, probably many times. 'Look,' he said, as if passing on a really important thing, 'the fact that a bomb might one day kill my sister in London – and God knows I'd be half-crazy if it did – it doesn't justify me flying off and bombing someone else's grandmother in Berlin. And it's equally wrong that the person whose grandmother was killed should come and bomb, say, your uncle in Taunton. Don't you see how cruel and illogical it is?'

What he said made sense in a sort of way, but I couldn't see Hitler taking any notice of the logic. I was surprised that Jack even thought he might. I didn't know what to say, so I stayed quiet. He was quiet too. He probably thought I was too stupid to understand. 'So what are you doing down here, if you're not joining up?' I asked at last. 'I mean, you live in London, don't you? It said Cavendish Square in the book.'

'What?' That old absent-minded look. 'Oh, yes, I do have a flat there. Or, at least, I did. My mother has it now and I just perch there from time to time. I didn't have much use for it before the war with all the travelling I did.'

'Travelling?' I thought of my midnight ships and tropical islands, and thought of Jack in a white suit, leaning over the rail. 'Abroad?' I said.

He laughed. 'Good Lord, no. Just lots of train journeys to obscure places. Lots of strong tea and stale buns. And lots of high-minded talk. We thought we'd get our way, in those days. I had a very successful Peace Pledge meeting here in this town – that's why I was here, you know, that day I gave you the shilling. I didn't think I'd be coming back as a prisoner eighteen months later.'

He said the word 'prisoner' lightly but I still got a shock. 'You were in prison?' I said. It made sense suddenly – the skin and the nails, and the way his clothes didn't fit. But it didn't seem the right sort of place for him.

He nodded. 'Well, you know what they do to us Conshies. We mustn't contaminate the general population. But why they sent me *here* of all places I don't know. It was difficult for Mother and the girls to visit. Another subtle punishment, I suppose.'

'Was it very bad?' I'd heard the Conshies were half-starved. Mrs Willacott's nephew worked in the prison kitchens and said they were poor little specimens who didn't eat meat and were probably too weedy to fight even if they wanted to. I hadn't taken much notice at the time; I'd thought Conshies deserved all they got.

Jack gave a funny kind of smile. 'I wouldn't exactly recommend prison life. I had nothing to read for six months. I think that was the worst thing of all; I think that might have broken my spirit if anything would. And then of course I got to know the size and shape of mailbags more intimately than I cared for. That black waxed thread was the very devil.' Jack turned his hand, showed me his stained and mangled fingers. I cast down my eyes, unable to look. 'But it gives you time to think, to see if you can stand up for what you believe, in practice.'

'But you're out for good, now?' I said. 'They've let you out?'

'Yes, they let me out. The Government and I have come to an understanding. I shall be working on the land. After all, I have no conscientious objection to people being fed.'

I couldn't help being relieved. I didn't care if Jack had funny ideas. He wouldn't be going to the Far East or Africa. He wouldn't be manning a convoy in the North Atlantic or battling in the skies above our heads. He would be safe on a farm. Even if I never saw him again, I'd know he was alive.

He drained his cup. 'That was very welcome. Even if I got it on false pretences.'

I shrugged. 'I thought you might need it. You didn't come down for dinner.'

'Oh.' That old absent-minded look again. 'I forgot, I'm afraid.'

'Weren't you hungry?' I was famished if I missed a meal, but there was always something to pick at in the kitchen as long as Mr Mullan didn't see.

'I'm used to being hungry. You're hungry all the time in prison. And anyway, I had a good tea. An extremely good tea, as it happens.'

'And you were reading, too.' I nodded towards the book.

'Yes, Bertrand Russell kept me busy. You should try him some time.'

I wasn't sure I could read hard books like that but I said I might try. He held out the finished cup and I stretched out my hand to take it. As I did so, my cuff slid back and a flaky red patch of skin slipped into view. He frowned. 'Oh dear, have you scalded yourself?' He put down the cup, and bent forward, taking my hand in his, examining my wrist in a probing way, like a doctor.

I felt myself go scarlet. All evening I'd kept imagining how it would feel if he touched me, but not in this pitying way because of my wretched scabs. 'No, it's a skin disease,' I said quickly, pushing down my sleeve and pulling my hand away from his. 'Don't worry, it's not catching.'

'I'm not worried. And don't be ashamed. There's nothing to be ashamed of.' His voice was very gentle.

'But it's ugly, horrible. People don't want to see it. It makes them sick.' I couldn't let myself speak any more, I was so afraid I would cry.

'People are fools. I don't mind looking at it.' He delicately lifted the edge of my cuff. 'May I?'

'But it's really awful,' I said. 'And it's all over me. Except my face. I don't get it on my face.'

I was gabbling with nerves, but he seemed not to notice as he edged my sleeve further up my arm, revealing the horrible red mess around my elbow, all the shiny scales and flakes fluttering onto his trousers. 'People pay too much attention to the surface of things,' he said, letting his fingers caress my skin in a dreamlike way. 'It's what's inside that counts.'

'Yes.' I closed my eyes. His fingers were calloused, but they felt like gossamer to me, just as I had always imagined. I couldn't stop trembling. I wanted him to slide his hand further and further, right up to my armpit. I wanted him to unbutton my blouse and touch my breasts. I wanted him to touch me all over, even where my skin was at its worst. He was very close, now, his face near mine, his hair brushing my cheek. I could hear his breathing; I was sure he could hear mine. I closed my eyes, ready for him to ravish me.

But instead I felt him pull my sleeve back down, and I slowly opened my eyes. He was watching me, a strange look on his face. Then he patted my hand. 'I'm sorry,' he said gently. 'I shouldn't have done that. I've overstepped the mark.'

'I don't mind,' I said. 'It felt nice. You've got nice hands.'

He raised his eyebrows. 'Hardly. But it's getting late. I don't want to get you into trouble.' And he got up and handed me the empty cup. And I got up and took it. And he opened the door. And we both said goodnight in a fumbled sort of way. And I went downstairs with my heart pounding and the stupid cup in my hand.

He didn't come down to breakfast so I asked Mr Reeves if I should take a tray up. He said there would be no need for that as Mr Thompson had already gone on the early train to Taunton. I nearly dropped the coffee jug, and had to put it down quickly. 'Gone?'

'Yes, *gone*, Elsie. People come and go, you know. In a hotel.'

'Didn't he leave a message?'

'Message? Why should he leave a message?' he said sharply.

I thought quickly. 'I mean, Mr Thompson owed for a cup of cocoa. Last night.'

'Well, that's gone west then,' he said crossly. 'There was nothing on the spike.'

'Sorry, Mr Reeves,' I said. 'I must have forgot.'

'We can't afford "forgetting" – now there's a war on. I'm surprised at you, Elsie.'

'It won't happen again, Mr Reeves.' I was so heart-stricken, I thought I might break down and cry in front of him, but I managed to turn away and take a big breath. Miss Jennings was right. I could never mean anything to a man like Jack. He'd been kind, but nothing had happened between us in spite of the low light and the soft, inviting bed. He'd drunk his cocoa and answered my questions and showed a kind interest in my skin condition. That's how he'd been brought up. But he'd probably forgotten me the minute he went back to his book, as soon as the taste of cocoa had faded from his tongue.

Then as I turned to go past the till, I saw something propped up there. It was a small parcel, wrapped in yesterday's newspaper. Written on the front was 'For the Waitress with the Cocoa'. I couldn't think who else it could be from, but I hardly dared to hope. I unwrapped it carefully. It was a man's spotted scarf. Fine silk, the sort Miss Jennings used to say could be pulled through a wedding ring. There was something else, too – a note on a piece of hotel paper. Neat, dark writing: *I owe you for a charming evening and I always like to pay my debts. This scarf is a bit grand for life down on the farm. Have it please, with my regards, Jack Thompson. P.S. I'm sorry, but I don't know your name.*

MOUTH

S he's always mouthing off at me. I call her The Mouth. In my mind, that is. I call her The Mouth in my mind. To her face I say Yes. Thank you. Mother.

When I was little she'd yank my hair back in a rubber band. Give me a ponytail so high it seemed to grow out of the top of my head. So tight it would never come undone. *Go and Play*, she'd say. *And don't get dirty*. I'd go off in my white socks and hand-knitted cardigan to stand by the fence and watch the others.

Who did you play with? she'd say when I came back. *What did you play? Were those Bates boys out there? They didn't give you any of that bubblegum, did they? Let me see your hands.* I'd have the gum in my knickers, just inside the elastic. I'd chew it in bed after I'd said my prayers. 'God bless Mummy . . . God bless Daddy . . .' I'd slip my hand down to the side of the wooden bed and pull it off, hard and cold and shiny, but still sweet.

I don't know why you don't play with Sandra Smith. My mother liked Sandra. My mother liked me to go to tea with Sandra. They had proper tea with serviettes. Mr Smith had an office job and a typewriter in the bay window where he did Invoices. Sometimes Sandra and I played at Invoices. Otherwise Sandra's house was boring.

When it rained I'd stay in and read. Enid Blyton, The Famous Five. Sometimes I'd go through the bookcase in the front room. Dreary titles: *Silas Marner*; *Bleak House*; *Kenilworth*. I tried *A Christmas Carol*. It started: 'Marley was dead.' I didn't read any more. My mother would look over my shoulder to make sure I wasn't reading comics. *I want you reading proper books. What about* Black Beauty?

I didn't like horses.

I used to hear her talking. *Geraldine has a lot of Potential.* I hated the name Geraldine. The Bates boys called me Gerry. My dad never called me anything, except 'chicken'. When he spoke. Which wasn't that often.

Geraldine is a natural dancer, she'd say. She took me for private lessons with Miss Standish in a big house three bus stops away. *Now, mind you hold your head up! Don't look at your feet! I want to be proud of you.*

Elocution, too. Mr Moon with a moustache and an old mother, making me recite 'The Charge of the Light Brigade'. He'd put his sweaty hand on my shoulder and breathe into my ear. Warm breath, smelling of sherry. My mother paid him two pounds for half an hour. *Geraldine has a lovely speaking voice.*

She wanted me to be a model, a TV announcer, an air hostess. My hair was long and shiny and she waved it with tongs. When I was twelve, I cut it all off with Brenda Morris's kitchen scissors and I thought she'd have a heart attack. When I inked a tattoo into my knuckles (D. A. V. E.), she slapped me across the mouth so hard my lips started to bleed. Called me a little trollop. How could I be an air hostess with hands like that? *You realize you're disfigured for life?* She took me to the doctor. Asked about plastic surgery. Slammed out in a temper, dragging me by the arm.

The next day I dyed my hair orange.

Do something about your daughter! She held up my spikes of hair by the roots. Dad cleared his throat. He usually went into the garden when The Mouth was at full blast, but she was barring the way. So he just shook his head and went upstairs, leaving his imprint in the armchair cushion. He wouldn't look at me.

It's that school. You used to be a lovely girl in the Juniors. Nice friends. Now it's people like Brenda Morris and this Dave, whoever he is. It's not good enough. She brushed my stubbled hair until my scalp turned red. She pulled up my socks and straightened my cardigan. *Now I don't want you messing about after school. Come straight home. I'll be waiting.*

At break time I took off the cardigan and hid it behind the rubbish bins. I never wore a cardigan again. I borrowed a baggy sweater from Brenda. She said I could keep it. She always had plenty of clothes. I never let my mother see it; stuffed it in my schoolbag on the way home. She went on a lot the first day. *Where's your cardigan? How can you have lost it? Do you know how much these things cost?* Then she noticed my nails. She didn't like purple. *Do they let you go to school with nails like that?*

'Can't stop us,' I said. 'Everyone does it.'

The Mouth exploded. On and on. A load of crap about me and my friends. On and on.

'Mum, you're doing me head in!'

What kind of expression is that? That's not a nice expression!

'I don't want to be nice!' Not her nice; not what she thought was nice. I fought her, mouthing back. But her voice cut through my brain. I felt she was inside me, bursting through my skull. '*You're doing my head in!*' I looked round at Dad. 'Tell her, will you?'

He just cleared his throat.

I worked out what to do, what would keep her quiet. Lies. It was easy. I'd say: 'I'm going round Sandra's' or 'I'm staying behind at school to help with the netball' or 'I'm going shopping for Mr Moon's mother.' Then I'd go out with Dave and Griff and smoke in the bus shelter by the Rec. We'd have a laugh. Griff used to pick at his wrists with a razor blade. He said it didn't hurt. I did it too. It hurt, but I didn't say. I pulled my sleeves down to hide the cuts.

Have you been smoking? She'd smell the fags on me when I came home and she'd come across the room to pull the hair out of my eyes.

'It's the bus. I had to go upstairs.'

How's Sandra?

'Fine. Her mother asked after you.'

I wish you'd wear something nice when you go round there. Where did you get that terrible old jumper?

'Sandra said I could have it.'

Does she think you can't buy your own? That we're poor? I'll get you a nice new one.

She did. But it wasn't what I wanted. It was from Marks & Spencer's, all neat and fitted into the waist. And the wrong colour.

Why do you want black all the time? Black, black, black. Like a funeral! And it doesn't suit you. Makes you look washed-out. This bottle green's much more cheerful. Isn't it, Dad?

'Much more.'

'Yes, Mum. It's lovely. Thank you.'

I should think so. I spoil you. You don't deserve it. Not the way you carry on.

She never liked the way I looked. Even when I tried to tone it down. Even when I wore a skirt to please her. *Look at the length of that! You look just like a tart! A little trollop! You'll get yourself into trouble one of these days.*

Whenever I went out, I could hear her voice still in my head. It made me tense. Brian said I was tense. Frigid, he said, when he tried to make it with me behind the toilets at the Rec: 'What's the matter with you? Afraid what Mummy might say?'

So I let him do it.

After that we used an empty flat he said belonged to his brother. Cold and gloomy with a black vinyl suite and a broken gas fire. Brian would open me a couple of lagers and I'd sit astride him in the armchair, give him the works; anything he wanted. I'd grind away into his body, keeping at it, wanting it to hurt. We didn't even stop if Dave or Griff came in. Then I'd have another lager, sitting on the chair arm with the wet running down my legs. Then I'd do it with them too.

In the bathroom, I'd pick my wrists a little bit deeper. Make the blood flow. Feel the pain. Brian said I was a nutcase.

What's the matter with your wrists? Show me your wrists! She pulled me out of bed, gripping my arms by the elbows, shaking them till my fingers nearly flew off. *What stupid idea is this? What's the matter with you? I've had just about enough! You're going to have to see someone!*

She dragged me down to the doctor's again. He said the cuts weren't deep. He said something about girls of my age and gave me a prescription. The Mouth was going all the way to the chemist's. Why, she wanted to know, why? Hadn't she given me everything? Didn't I know what I was doing to her? And to Dad?

'Sorry, Mum. I won't do it again.'

The thing was, I didn't know what it was doing to Dad. He sometimes opened his mouth as if he was going to say something to me, then closed it again, like a goldfish, silent. The morning he heard me heaving in the bathroom he just said, 'All right are you, chicken?'

'Just something I've eaten.'

'Right you are, then. If you're sure.' I heard his footsteps creaking off down the landing.

The pills were quite pretty. Cheerful two-tone, red and yellow. I took twenty-five. Then I lay on the bed, closed my eyes, hoping it would be quick. Next thing I was spewing all over the bed, sick streaming up my nose, choking me. I lay my cheek in the mess, not caring, hard clots in my throat, desperate to sleep. Then, suddenly, ambulance men were carting me out on a stretcher round the bend of the stairs saying I was lucky. I could hear her screaming *Lucky!!* somewhere behind my head. I lay in the ambulance, feeling her voice between my ears, going on and on.

She turned up in the morning. Powdered, in her best coat. Without Dad. She pulled up a stool, hissed in my ear, told me what a lot of worry I'd caused. How she'd never be able to trust me again. *You're very selfish. I hope you realize, now, what a worry you are. This is what happens when you go your own way. You just don't listen.*

She didn't listen either. I tried to tell her, but I was too tired. The doctor did it in his little glass office, looking at me when he spoke. I could see her face, the Mouth suspended for a second, blank. Then on the go again, silent to him, then loud right up against my face. *Who was it? Geraldine, answer me! It's that Dave, isn't it? Isn't it? Does he know you're only fifteen? Does he? Does he know what he could get for this in court?*

I said it wasn't Dave. It wasn't anyone important. 'Anyway, it doesn't matter, I'm not having it.'

She pointed her finger at me. *Oh yes you are! I'm not having my grandchild done away with, whatever you think.*

She was always asking, *Who's the father?* And I'd keep saying I didn't know. I didn't. I'd done it with Brian and Griff and Dave, and loads of others. And Brian's brother once, though he was supposed to be engaged; he said it was the least I could do for letting us use his flat. They never came near me now, any of them. I was a problem. A nutcase.

She started knitting jackets. *Have you thought about a name? Nigel's nice. For a boy. Or Jonathon.* She seemed to have calmed down. She got Dad to redecorate the spare room. She chose the wallpaper. Primrose. She let me sit in front of the telly all day. She brought me cups of tea and sandwiches. She was very smarmy to Mrs Davies, the home teacher. Asked her if I could still become an air hostess.

Nigel was six weeks old when I ran away. She'd left him alone with me for once, gone to get mushrooms for tea. I put on my old black skirt and sweater and wrapped him up in a blanket. I thought about the empty flat, the gas fire, the vinyl settee. I reckoned Brian's brother wouldn't make a fuss if I made myself useful. But a woman opened the door. The fiancée. She stood in my way in a cotton dressing gown and too much scent saying I had some bloody cheek, and trying to close the door. In the end, she said she knew someone who might help. Someone with a room to spare for services rendered.

'A housekeeper?'

'Kind of.' She smiled.

Wayne was used to having his own way. He told me I had to smarten myself up. And learn to cook. And relax in bed. Or else I'd be out.

'There are plenty of sluts in this world. I can take my pick. I don't have to have you.'

'Yes, Wayne,' I said.

I used to dream about her breaking in on us, yelling, screaming. One night, it happened, blue lights flashing on the ceiling, walkie-talkies blaring, The Mouth shrieking through it all. Wayne jumped out of bed, got out the bathroom window quicker than greased lightening. The one thing that he didn't want was the cops sticking their noses in his business.

She stood in the doorway pointing me out with her finger, like I was in an identity parade: *That's her!* Then she rushed to the cot to get Nigel, walked round with him against her shoulder, saying *There, there!* though he wasn't crying. She told the cops she wanted them to make me come back home. *That's where she belongs! A decent place, not this hell-hole.*

She started poking round, looking in the ashtrays, counting the empties in the corner. She opened the cupboards, my dressing table, Wayne's wardrobe. *Where are the child's clothes? Sold them for drink I suppose? Or drugs?* She grabbed my bag and pulled out my tranx. *What are these? LSD?*

'Leave my effing stuff alone!'

Don't tell me what to do! You're only a child!

'I'm sixteen. I can do what I like.'

She'd brought a bloke from Social Services. He started to talk about co-operation. The Mouth started yelling. Didn't they realize what sort of life I was living? They'd be sorry if that baby was found starved to death. *Look at him! Just look at this filthy nappy! The girl's not capable!*

In the end, she took Nigel home with her. Better than a Court Order, said the man. And I wasn't really up to caring for him just at the minute, was I? I could see that, couldn't I? He could stay with my mother for the time being. That was a safe place. They'd come round and see me in a day or two. Try and sort out the future.

Wayne came back later, thought it was a good idea, handing Nigel over. 'I've had enough of all this. I'm telling you, it's doing my fucking head in as well. Let her have the fucking kid. It'll get her off your back. You can forget about her, then. Start being a bit fucking normal, you know?' He grabbed my wrist, jabbing at the scars. 'Stop this bloody nonsense, too.'

I could see it might be better without having to wake up all through the night. Wayne didn't like me getting up. He'd say, 'Let the little bugger wait. See to me first.' I had to fill my mouth with his cock while Nigel screamed next door. Then I had to sit in the cold and feed him. Then I had to take something to make me sleep. Sometimes I wouldn't wake up till the afternoon, Nigel screaming again. And me still tired.

'You'll get over it,' said Wayne. 'You can have plenty more little bastards, no problem. Only they can be mine this time.'

She was all sweetness and light when we went to talk things over. Wayne surprised her with his suit and gold cufflinks and the shirt I'd ironed that morning and the way he agreed with everything she said. They got on like a house on fire. They had a lot in common: they both had a problem with me. Wayne smiled and said he was going to sort me out. Stop my bad habits. Make me smarten myself up. Take a pride. Help him in his business. 'There's a lot she could do.'

She got Dad to get out the photo album. Showed Wayne the snaps. Me, shy, neat, squinting up at the sun at Mablethorpe. *She was a lovely little girl. No trouble at all, then.*

I went over to look at Nigel. She'd got him all decked out in white. Perfect. Spotless. Tightly wrapped like a Christmas parcel. She saw me looking, said, *You don't have to worry, Geraldine. I'll look after him. I'll see he has the best of everything. The very best. Just like I gave you.*

ANGEL CHILD

I didn't used to think you could give a child too much attention. I thought if you put the effort in, they'd return the compliment and be a credit to you. Clifford says you don't have children in order to expect anything from them, but I reckon that where Geraldine's concerned, he's as disappointed as I am. Except that he sits down under it all. Sits in that damned armchair and sighs as if I'm not worth listening to. As if it's all mouth-breath to him.

It's not as though he wasn't as keen as me for her to have all those private lessons; as if he didn't pipe his eye when he went to see her do a solo fairy in the ballet concert and play an angel in the Christmas play. He thought she was lovely, took snaps by the dozen, showed them to all our friends. But he never understood that children don't bring themselves up. You have to work at them. But Clifford never worked at anything. 'As long as she's happy,' he'd say, in that stick-in-the-mud way of his. As if happiness was an alternative to success.

I'd get worked up then. 'Can you be happy stuck in a little terraced house with no education and no prospects? When you're clever and talented and could do all sorts if only you had the chance?'

He'd say, 'Calm down, Theresa. Don't shout.' But I'm one of eight and I've had to shout all my life to get noticed. Geraldine has never needed to shout, though. She's an only child and I used to listen to her every word with bated breath. Anything she asked for she could have. Yet by the time she was ten she started to turn on me, saying of all things, 'You don't listen! Why don't you ever listen?'

'I've listened too much, my girl,' I said in the end, the day she wanted to go out shopping in my best high heels. 'Now it's your turn.' She didn't like that; she turned sullen, scowled at me. But you've got to be firm. That's why I know it's not my fault she went off the rails.

It was gradual of course, the onset. When she was little, she was a sunbeam. Lovely blond hair, almost white. Skin you could nearly see through, so delicate. Big clear eyes. She was a wonderful child to dress, never spilled her drinks, never played in the muck, sat nicely on the grass in the back garden and arranged her dolls in rows, or read a book. She was a real prodigy with reading, went through all Clifford's classics by the time she was eleven. 'That girl's got a future ahead of her,' I'd say. 'She's exceptional.'

They tried to bring her down to their level, of course. The rowdy element I mean – the Bates boys, Brenda Morris and the like – common kids. That's the trouble with living in a mixed area like this. Clifford could never see it. 'Live and let live,' he'd say. That would have been all very well, if the rowdy element had let us live how we wanted to. They'd sit on our front wall and suck horrible sherbet-dabs from that cheap shop over the bridge, yelling out names to everyone who passed. I started to find flat grey plasters of chewing gum all over Geraldine's knickers and I knew they'd put them there. No respect for property, those kids. God knows what sort of behaviour they'd get away with, day in and day out. I told Geraldine to keep away, to play with Sandra Smith instead.

Sandra was a really nice child. She lived in The Avenue. That's where we should have been if Clifford had had more go in him. There was a house going cheap there when we were first married. But Clifford was always frightened to take a chance. He said Coldstream Terrace would see us out and why did we need a great semi-detached place like that? It makes me mad to think of that now. It was before the prices went silly and we could have had it easily. Then I wouldn't have had Sylvia Smith patronizing me with her coffee mornings and jumble sales. I'd have been there throwing my own house open to cardboard boxes and piles of National Geographic. After all, what's Malcolm Smith but a jumped-up salesman working out of his front room? *The office* Sylvia calls it, but who has a sideboard, a dining table and eight straight-backed chairs in their office?

But Geraldine was a contrary little madam. She dug in her heels every time Sandra invited her, whining, complaining, not wanting to go. 'I suppose you prefer those awful Bates boys?' I said.

'Yes,' she said. 'I do! I bloody do!' She almost spat at me. I wasn't having that. I had to shake her. Hard.

'That girl's got a temper,' I told Clifford, but he wouldn't have it.

'Leave her alone, Theresa,' he said. 'All your questions – you make things worse.' It was easy for Clifford – it's easy for a man to shrug off responsibility. He used to go in the garden so he wouldn't be there when she came home late from school, so I had to be the one to ask her where she'd been. I could see his back bent over the marigolds, saying, 'I'm on your side, chicken.'

I had plans for St Bridget's when Geraldine was eleven. A good school, strong on discipline, and a nice bottle-green uniform. 'The nuns'll have none of your nonsense,' I told her. 'You won't be able to try your tricks with them.' Clifford went so far as to raise himself out of his armchair on this one. Said I'd done nothing but complain about the nuns all my life and now I was proposing putting Geraldine through the same process. Well, I've lapsed, I admit, but the discipline never did me any harm. The thought of Sister Mary-Margaret still frightens me to death.

It was no go, though. Clifford and Geraldine got together, had a strategy all worked out. Said Sandra Smith and Everybody was going to Marston Road Comp and what brilliant results all the pupils got. 'Oxford and Cambridge,' said Clifford. 'You'd like that. Theresa.'

So she went. But my first instincts were right. I'd seen those kids lolling about in town – the hair, the clothes, the carryings-on. In a couple of years Geraldine was as bad as the rest. One person can't fight against it. And you get no help from the teachers. They just tell you to calm down. Mr Anderson, for example, just pulling his beard and saying he'll investigate matters and he's sure it's not serious, and you know damn well you won't hear another word, as if behaviour and manners and bad influences are nothing to do with them.

Doctors are just the same. They're supposed to help, be up with the latest trends. I said, 'These tattoos can be surgically removed – I've seen it on the television – and I want it done for Geraldine. He said I was over-reacting, to 'keep calm'. I'd like to see how calm he'd have been if it was his daughter with 'DAVE' all over her knuckles. He'd think it was too common for a doctor's daughter. But I suppose he thought Geraldine was just a working-class trollop. He took a bit more notice when I hauled her back with her wrists cut to pieces. I got a prescription out of him then. 'It's only superficial,' he said. 'But bring her back in a fortnight.'

A lot he knew, giving her pills like that. Six days later she was in St Luke's, taken out on a stretcher, red blanket, the lot, and all the rowdy element gawping. Kevin Bates had the nerve to ask if he could go and see her at visiting time. 'You scum can keep away,' I said. 'Haven't you done enough?'

It took something to walk down the street after that. I knew what they were thinking. Gloating, in fact. But I wasn't going to give them the satisfaction of seeing me in pieces. I put on my best green coat, powdered the blotches on my face, walked out in front of them all, and stood at the bus stop daring them to say a word.

Geraldine was propped on pillows, her dyed hair sticking up in spikes. She said, 'Hello, Mum.' No apologies.

I didn't know about the baby then, of course, but the young doctor called me to the nurses' office. I stood watching her through the glass partition while he was telling me. She looked so innocent, with her white skin. So pure. How could she have let anyone mess her about? I remembered those plasters of chewing gum, the stained knickers she thought I didn't know about, stuffed behind the wardrobe. She'd never confided in me. Nobody did. Certainly not Clifford. He never gave me any support. He'd gone to work as usual. 'Give her my love,' he said, his back to me. 'Say I'll pop in and see her tonight.'

They thought the baby was all right. She hadn't taken very many. A cry for help, they said. All I could think of was who had driven her to this. That Dave? Those boys Mr Chislett had seen her with in the park – those leather boys, the ones with the jackets and chains, the ones who smoked all the time – who she pretended she didn't know?

'Who was it?' I shook her. 'Tell me which one!' I'd see he had his come-uppance. There was a law about these things. She was only a child.

The little bitch wouldn't say. 'Anyway, I'm having an abortion.' She'd got it all worked out. But if ever I've done one good thing in my life, it was getting that idea out of her head. I didn't even let up when that staff-nurse came and told me to calm down. Sister Mary-Margaret would have been proud.

And Nigel, when he came, was an angel of a child. Blond hair, skin you could almost see through, big clear eyes. Geraldine never had to lift a finger for him. I did everything. She just sat around, watching TV, eating. 'Why don't you go back to school, or college?' I said. I thought she might take some exams, train for something. Be an air hostess, like she'd wanted as a child. Or a TV announcer. Now that I'd got her out of all those dead black clothes, permed her hair a bit, she looked pretty again. I said why didn't she go for an interview, or go to night school? I said I'd look after Nigel, full time if necessary. She needn't worry about him at all.

I should have realized that she was too quiet, that something was brewing. While I was out one afternoon, getting some mushrooms for tea, she went. Taking Nigel and only one change of clothes. Clifford came back early, said didn't I have any sense and couldn't I see I'd driven her away? And went to dig the garden, of all things. I wouldn't let him get away with that, followed him down to the greenhouse. 'Why is it my fault? Haven't I done everything, absolutely everything, for her?'

'Too bloody much. That's your trouble.' He started making mincemeat of the slugs with the edge of his spade. 'She'd be all right if you'd leave her alone.' The usual Clifford story: Do nothing; let his little chicken have her way. Well, she'd had her way for too long. Now I was going to have mine.

The young copper they sent wasn't up to much. I said I wanted someone a bit more senior on such a serious matter. He said this sort of thing was pretty routine. 'They go off all the time, these young girls.'

'But not if they're suicidal and involved in drugs; not with a six-week-old baby. You'll all be for the high jump if something happens to my grandson.' He took more notice then.

'Who is she likely to have gone to?'

I said if I knew that I wouldn't be involving them, would I? But he kept going on about her having to have school friends, boyfriends, 'that sort of thing'. He asked about the father of the baby. I said that was a closed book. I wasn't having Dave sticking his oar in, claiming custody or whatever. I suggested that Mr Anderson might earn his wages for once by parting with some information from the school. 'And you could try Brenda Morris, somewhere over the bridge.'

It was weeks before we heard. Every day I thought about Nigel, wondered if she was remembering to feed him, change his nappy. Clifford said, 'Aren't you worried about *Geraldine*? How *she's* managing to live?'

'Speak for yourself.' He was the one who'd let her go to the dogs.

In the end, they found her just round the corner, on the Westwood Estate. Living with an older man. Rough sort, they said, as if I needed telling. With a record for GBH.

'Take it easy now, madam,' said the copper when we went down in a police car with a woman PC. 'He could turn nasty.' But by the time we'd arrived he'd skedaddled the back way.

Geraldine was on the sofa, all in black again, great rings around her eyes, wrists covered up. 'Wayne doesn't like the pigs,' she said with a laugh. 'They make him nervous.' I'd have made him nervous, too, if he'd laid a finger on Nigel.

The place was a tip. No housework happening there. That's not what was making her look worn out. And the child was a disgrace. Caked was the word. Encrusted. I could hardly bear to pick him up. There were bottles everywhere, cider. I could smell drink on her breath. And her bag was crammed full of pills. 'What's this?' I said, holding it up.

'Valium,' said Geraldine, grabbing at it. 'Now leave my effing stuff alone!'

She refused to come back with me. Argued the toss as usual, said she was sixteen now and could make her own decisions. I told her she could do as she liked but I wasn't going to have my grandson living in that place, being brought up by a drunkard. She fell over then, started to cry onto the filthy vinyl floor. I made her a cup of tea in the only mug I could find while the social workers were called. They took one look at Geraldine and said she wasn't fit to cope. Asked me if I was in a position to help. 'A temporary measure,' said the one with the beard. 'Until we can assess the situation properly.' I noticed he didn't sit down.

Clifford missed all this, said, 'Where's Geraldine?' when he came home and saw Nigel in his cot. I told him she's shacked up with a violent ex-con, drinking and drugging herself to death, and is he satisfied?

Now, it's not often I'm wrong about someone, but I've had to eat my words about Wayne, in spite of his name. He was very frank with Clifford and me when he came to tea, explaining about his childhood and how he was taken advantage of by his friends. He always seemed to be in the wrong place at the wrong time, he said. That was why he'd gone to prison. He was just in the off-licence buying a beer when these lads had come in. He'd known them of course and he'd tried to take the gun off them, but they had stuck together and Wayne had got the blame. He runs his own business now – buying and selling videos – and I must say he was very presentable; neat collar and tie. More than I can say of her, dragging around in a dirty old top with sick stains down the front, scrabbling in her bag for tranquillizers and cigarettes. Wayne says she needs taking in hand, given a bit of discipline. I'm amazed how quickly he's cottoned on to that, but he says prison opens your eyes to a lot of things. Geraldine says nothing, just gives me one of her dull-eyed looks. But I feel happier in my mind that she's with someone who'll keep her up to the mark.

Wayne and I agree that Nigel is best left with me. Wayne says I'm a marvel with babies, and he can see Nigel's looking better already. He says Geraldine has no patience. Motherhood, I tell him, is a job for the experts.

THE GINGER ROGERS
OF BATH AND WELLS

S he's Licensed for Music and Dancing. It's written above the fanlight of her five-storey Regency house. But Lydia Pendleton's dancing days are done. In fact, her moving days are pretty much done as well. When the weather is warm, she has a little freedom in her hips and knee-joints, but her feet, once so nimble and dainty, are swollen and near useless. She can manage to hobble from her bed-settee to her easy chair, but has to rely on the kindness of others for almost everything else. Her old friend Matty comes every morning and spends a brisk hour setting Lydia's room (the first floor front) to rights, plumping up cushions and pillows, running a vacuum cleaner between the pieces of heavy furniture and flicking a duster at the few uncluttered surfaces. But she's a poor conversationalist and is always off on the dot of eleven o'clock. The rest of the day Lydia has to herself. She might read the local paper, or thumb through some old programmes, or watch a small portable TV with the sound down. Or she might just stare at the sky. But her ears are always pricked for any footfall on the landing outside. Lydia has nine tenants, all theatricals, inhabiting assorted accommodation over five floors, and although they sleep on late in the mornings and come back late at night, she usually manages to waylay one or two. She leaves her door ajar specially, and can hear the lightest of steps. She hears one now.

'Is that you, Miss Henshaw, dear?'

Vicki Henshaw hears the old lady's feeble query, and stops. Damn, she thinks. Caught again. She inclines her head around the massive mahogany door. She is wearing a chic beret and a shiny black mackintosh. 'Did you want something, Mrs Pendleton? I'm just going up to the theatre.' She knows better than to enquire after Lydia's health; it is an inexhaustible subject. She pulls on her gloves with a briskness she hopes will deter Lydia from asking more questions. Her feet are still outside the door.

'Would you do me a favour, Miss Henshaw, dear?'

'It'll have to be quick, I'm afraid. I'm due in rehearsal at three.' The words are firm, but Vicki senses she has lost the advantage. Invalid ladies are difficult to refuse.

'Just bring that little table over here, would you?' Lydia indicates an octagonal carved object, vaguely Indian in style. 'I meant to ask Matty, but she's so impatient. She's always off home before I've finished with her.'

Vicki is wholly in the room now. She is tall, with long legs and long hair. She puts down her shoulder bag and attempts to move the heavy table, rucking up the Kashmiri rug and banging her thin knees against the ornate carving. Lydia squeals out for her to stop: 'Ooh, careful, dear! I daren't injure Mr Rolfe's leading lady!'

'Oh, I'm not his "leading lady"!' Vicki straightens up, smiling. 'We're an ensemble group.'

'*Ensemble*?' Mrs Pendleton frowns. 'You mean like a chorus?'

'Well, not exactly. It just means we do all the parts, big and small. One minute I'm the waitress with two lines, the next I'm the woman who's going to kill herself in a big scene. It's not like it used to be – one big Star and a lot of also-rans. It gives everyone a chance to shine.' She makes a move to the door. 'Anyway I –'

'Perhaps you wouldn't think that way if you *had* been the Star,' Lydia reflects, not altogether unkindly, as she glances with delicate reference to the framed black-and-white photographs massed in ranks on the flock wallpaper. 'Of course, I wouldn't go so far as to say I was a *big* star, but I was pretty well known in the West Country during the War. "The Ginger Rogers of Bath and Wells" they called me. That was an exaggeration of course; I was never as pretty as Ginger.' She cranes round. 'That's me in *Hit the Deck*. One of my best photos, although it makes my hair look on the dark side. Mind you, I never had a leading man anything like Fred Astaire. Wartime, you see, Miss Henshaw. I had to make do with poor old Laurie Burnett.' Lydia sighs, leaning back in the deep easy chair. 'I don't expect a young thing like you re-members Laurie – but he was quite a name in his day – the thirties, I mean. Star billing, always his own dressing room. But you can see how he was in 1943.' She reaches back perilously and unhooks the photo from the wall. 'I mean, how could anyone take him for the Romantic Lead with his hair dyed so black it looked like a wig, and that terrible spluttering when he got out of breath? Quite frankly, Miss Henshaw, he was a shocker. I used to long for a younger partner, someone with a bit of zip.' She sighs, then chuckles a little. 'You know, some nights I'd try and speed things up – ever so slightly, just to get a bit of pace in the big numbers – but all he'd do was start to wheeze.' She shakes her head. 'And now, look at me – I'm even worse than he was. Heart trouble's a terrible thing.' She lies back as if exhausted by the power of reminiscence. But she is not done. 'What I would find useful,' she says pathetically, 'is somewhere to put a tray.' She gestures vaguely in the vicinity of her armchair, as if hoping for a space to materialize.

'A tray?' Vicki thinks that if she does this one simple thing, she can leave Mrs Pendleton with a clear conscience. She is already in danger of missing the bus up the hill, but she feels sorry for the old woman. She glances round for a tray, but there is no sign of one. The room is grand and high-ceilinged, with three full-length sash windows, but it is dark red, ill-lit, and chock-full of elaborate furniture. Every hori-zontal surface is loaded: records in old green paper sleeves, theatre programmes in top-heavy piles, copies of *Spotlight* and *The Stage*. And newspapers, millions of newspapers. It looks as though every *Avon Gazette* ever printed has found its resting place on Lydia's red and blue Axminster carpet.

'If you could just move these, dear' – Lydia indicates the pile near her left elbow – 'then I could make room for my biscuits and my Thermos.'

Vicki fears this business with the tray will go on for a long time. She glances at her watch, and lets Lydia see her do so. The old lady remonstrates. 'Oh, I'm making you late. Selfish me. I must let you go.'

But her dismissal is faint; and Vicki hears herself offering to clear a space after all. She says brightly, 'It won't take long.' She thinks less brightly of the walk up the hill to the Arts Centre, of the way Justin Rolfe hates people to be late, of the sarcasm that will result. She begins to move the mound of papers. 'Where shall I put them? On the floor?' She stacks them against an ebony étagère where the dust-furred remains of half a dozen bouquets are displayed in their faded red ribbons. A dark oak tea-trolley is gradually revealed at Lydia's elbow. Under direction, Vicki finds the flask of tea and the packet of ginger nuts and settles them cosily on a tray beside the transistor radio and the big old-fashioned black telephone with its twisted purplish cord.

Lydia opens the ginger nuts. 'Have one, dear.'

Vicki, in reflex, accepts. It cleaves hot and dry to the roof of her mouth. She says thickly, 'I really *have* to go now.'

Lydia waves a valedictory ginger nut at her. 'Give my love to Mr Rolfe, won't you? Ask him when he's coming to see me again. He used to call me the best landlady in the western hemisphere. Mind you, he said a lot of silly things. He was a terrible flirt. I used to say, "No woman's safe from you, Mr Rolfe." That made him laugh.'

Vicki sucks her cheeks. 'I bet it did.'

'Now don't forget to tell him. Say "The Ginger Rogers of Bath and Wells requests his company." No excuses – or I might remember he still owes me a month's rent. Now off you go, Miss Henshaw, dear.'

'Yes, I really must.' She glances more explicitly at her watch. There is no chance she will catch that bus, now.

'You think I'm an old nuisance, I know.'

The remark catches Vicki as she rounds the door's edge. She looks back hastily. 'Oh, no, I love your old photos – and your stories. I could stay here all day, honestly. It's just that they'll have started working things out without me. We're improvising, you know.'

'Improvising? Well, I *don't* know about that really, dear.' Lydia's remark lassoes Vicki back into the room. 'I'm glad to say there was none of that sort of thing in my day. Someone else wrote the words; we just said them. I must say, it was a lot fairer. Everybody knew where they were. Just like a family.'

'Really? I thought these old musical comedy troupes were full of jealousy and drama . . . or is that just Hollywood myth?' Vicki wonders why she cannot put an end to this conversation.

'I expect it was, dear. Though there was one occasion . . . Plymouth, I think it must have been, because there were so many Navy boys. We were doing Ivor Novello and I'd had this meat pie . . .'

It is dark when Lydia wakes up. Only the horizontal red bar of the electric fire lights the area around her. She reaches over the back of her chair and her plump hand feels for the trailing cord with its egg-shaped switch. She turns on the standard lamp: more reddish light. Brighter this time, but still heavily obscured by the fringed red shade. Lydia likes red: it is both cosy and theatrical. It reminds her of the Gaiety Theatre in King Street where she'd danced as a child. That was shut, now – turned into a Cash 'n' Carry – and they'd opened the new Arts Centre instead, up near the University. She'd been there a few times. Mr Rolfe had given her complimentaries, and she and Matty had put on their best clothes and taken a taxi up the hill. But the place hadn't felt right. Not like a theatre at all: just rough brick and black paint, with plastic seats – and no curtain. No scenery to speak of either; you had no idea where you were supposed to be. As for costumes, she'd said to Matty that it looked as though they'd been out to Oxfam and picked the cheapest cast-offs they could get. 'There was no glamour,' she'd complained. 'No glamour at all.'

Glamour had always been Lydia's watchword. She believed anything in life could be improved by a touch of it, and the meanest of lives could be enhanced by an hour or two in the presence of beautiful clothes, lyrical music and elegant dancing. She loved Hollywood films, of course, with Fred and Ginger twirling impeccably round the floor doing steps few could emulate. But for a real heartbeat thrill there was nothing like tripping the light fantastic yourself. There was nothing like standing in front of an audience and hearing the swell of applause. Lydia had never wanted to give up that feeling.

However, after the war, she had found herself less in demand as a leading lady. And then, imperceptibly, less in demand for any kind of part. She'd still dressed like a diva, but she spent more time 'resting' than she ever had. With each day that passed, she found it harder to keep the notion of glamour alive in her heart. Gradually it occurred to her that a new strategy was needed, one where she was in control, where she did not have to wait to be summoned at the whim of others. The choice was obvious for a person of her talents: she would run a dancing school. And not just any dancing school. It would be a lavish enterprise with a proper ballroom. There would be formal dances, as in a country house. As the Principal, she would be the hostess, the central figure gliding across the boards, drawing all eyes.

But first, she needed a suitable property. And that was where Arthur Pendleton had come in. He'd been one of her more elderly admirers; someone whom, in earlier days, she'd tended to disregard at the stage door in favour of younger men. But he was, she learned from Matty, the possessor of a large Regency house, and a private income sufficient for her plans. So she turned the full blaze of her charm upon him, and within six weeks she was stepping over the threshold as his bride. She entered her new domain with relish, and began to convert the elegant but dowdy house into a palace of dreams. Up went mirrors and chandeliers. On went rose-coloured paint. Red velvet curtains were swagged across every alcove with tasselled ropes. Red carpet adorned every staircase. Potted palms filled the entrance hall. And in the basement Lydia created a ballroom with a ceiling of stars, phalanxes of gilt chairs around the edge, and a smoothly sprung floor in the middle. 'I shall hold classes in the daytime, and formal dances at night,' Lydia exulted. 'I shall be Licensed for Music and Dancing.'

Mr Pendleton had watched with rising agitation as his once tasteful home took on the aspect of a Grand Hotel. He'd wanted his glamorous wife to be happy; to be given the environment she so clearly loved. And he'd wanted to be part of it. But he was an old dog and he couldn't bring himself to learn new tricks. Once the dance lessons started, he found there was too much bustle and noise and music and clattering of feet. And the hallway was always filled with coats and umbrellas and boots and dancing shoes. It was all very well to have that kind of hectic excitement once a week at the theatre; it was another matter to have it every day in his own home. Gradually he retired to the upper reaches, where the music was only faint and the sound of voices didn't penetrate, and took to spending his days on a battered sofa with a glass of brandy and a detective novel. Within six months of the wedding he had quietly passed away. Lydia followed his coffin in the smartest of black dresses and the most elegant of widow's hats. But, as all good troupers do, she pinned orchids onto her bodice that very night, and soldiered on.

For a long time after that, she queened it in the ballroom, partnering the very choicest of her pupils to the strains of the Dorchester Trio. Her silver shoes twinkled; her supple arms embraced disinterestedly the worsted suiting of each ardent young man (any suggestion of more intimate contact was met with a closed-up smile that gave nothing away). If bouquets arrived with declarations, she put the flowers in water and the notes, unread, in the fire. And stepped forth once more under the rotating mirrored globe that sent measles of tinted light over her smooth face and bare shoulders. Head extended, arms poised, she whirled and pranced, dreaming she was Ginger gliding over acres of glassy Hollywood floors, with suitors falling literally at her feet.

However, ten years after Mr Pendleton's decease, the thickening of Lydia's body was matched by a slackening in the popularity of formal dance. She began to have difficulty managing the spiral stairs down to the ballroom, and she found it harder to keep her balance during the unforgiving spins of the Viennese waltz. The classes themselves became painfully small: fewer young women, almost no young men. They were all elsewhere, in cramped cellars and coffee bars, doing hand-jive or the Twist. They didn't want to bother with glides and *chassées* and reverse turns. Even the cha-cha-cha failed to interest them. One day, Lydia shut the baize doors of the ballroom for the last time and retired upstairs – the red room on the first floor, always her favourite. Surrounding herself with memories of the past, she began to dig in.

For years she resisted the idea of taking in lodgers, inhabiting her elaborate museum alone until it occurred to her that she need not demean herself with travelling salesmen and cat-owning spinsters: she could take colourful tenants from the acting profession. And now there were three floors of them, poor Miss Henshaw included. And Lydia was like the jam in a sandwich, spreading thickly and redly along the first floor front.

* * *

The door creaks open. There are two heads peering in. Lydia can't make them out in the gloom. 'Who's that?' she calls out, a little nervously, as she rarely has visitors this late. 'Miss Henshaw, is that you?'

'Yes, it's me.' Lydia recognizes Miss Henshaw's rather breathy voice. The girl needs a good voice coach, she thinks. She'd never have reached the back of the Birmingham Hippodrome with a voice like that. 'And I've brought you a visitor,' she says.

'Not Mr Rolfe!' Lydia brightens. Her hand strays automatically to adjust her faded grey hair. She wishes she'd had time to tidy herself up, to put on a fresh cardigan, get rid of her old slippers and put on the court shoes that were all right as long as she didn't stand up.

'No, not Justin. But I gave him your message. He says as soon as the show's up and running he'll be here to toast you with the best champagne – but until then he's in monkish isolation. And he says he hasn't forgotten the rent.'

Lydia is mortified. 'Oh, I didn't mean it about the rent! He didn't take me seriously, did he? Such a nice young man, always doing me little favours. Permed my hair for me, you know. And did my nails. But never mind that, who *have* you got there?' Lydia squints into the darkness eager to know her visitor. She doesn't have many. The Theatricals, contrary to her expectations, don't have much time for her, always rushing past her door, always in a hurry. Only Miss Henshaw gives her the time of day. She's a sweet girl in spite of that gawky figure and all her strange enthusiasm for "ensemble", but she never takes Lydia's advice on the importance of glamour.

Miss Henshaw comes forward and squats in front of Lydia's chair. She takes her hand, squeezes it excitedly. 'I've got a surprise for you.'

'Surprise?' Lydia doesn't much like surprises at her time of life. They are usually bad ones. But Miss Henshaw looks as if she can hardly contain herself with delight. 'Does the name Alan Treloar mean anything to you?' she says with a *This Is Your Life* kind of smile.

'Alan Treloar? . . .' Lydia stares at the young girl, horribly aware that she cannot reward her with the instant name recognition she clearly expects. She tries to catch at the memory, which whirls and circles like an elusive fly. Lydia knows the name. She knows it very well indeed, but where – and when? She runs through all her leading men, all her directors, all the young men from choruses all over the country, but to her great annoyance she cannot – cannot – place the name. It's all very well for Miss Henshaw to be hovering over her as if she is about to bestow a big birthday present on a child of five, but the poor girl has no idea how many people Lydia has worked with; and how many she has forgotten. Perhaps it's not a theatrical visitor after all, she thinks. Maybe it's a star pupil, or a long-lost relative of Mr Pendleton's.

'Perhaps I can help.' The man emerging from the shadows has a West Country accent; so, probably not an actor, Lydia thinks. As he comes into the dim red light of the standard lamp, she sees that he is short and almost bald, wearing a good quality camel-hair coat with a tartan muffler neatly folded inside. Lydia is disappointed; he is definitely not a Theatrical; more like a shoe salesman. Yet he bends and takes Lydia by the hands in a way that is almost courtly. 'You've never met me, Miss Landon, but I can honestly say I've never forgotten you.'

'Miss Landon!' She's taken by surprise, and giggles. 'Oh you must be from the past! I've been Mrs Pendleton for years.'

'I don't know about that. All I know is you were Lydia Landon the night you came to Plymouth with *An Angel in Calico* – the night I called you the "Ginger Rogers of Bath and Wells".'

'Alan Treloar!' It all comes flooding back. 'Of course, how could I forget! I must have read your name a thousand times! My best ever review! I've still got it.' She twists around in her chair, flustered, excited. 'It's somewhere in that cuttings album. Miss Henshaw, can you pass it to me? You know where it is, don't you? On the what-not. Under the magazines. Be careful with it, mind. It's showing its age – like me!' She turns to the balding man who, she can now see, has very attractive eyes. 'Was it really *you* who wrote all those nice things?'

'All my own work.' Alan Treloar smiles shyly as he finds a corner of a dining chair to sit on. 'My *only* published work, in fact. It was my first chance to write a review – and, would you believe, my last? I was called up the next week. Never went back to the newspaper business. Went into ironmongery, in fact. Got a fair-sized place near Chard – garden supplies, that sort of thing. I don't do badly, but I've always hankered after the theatre, Miss Landon, and I try to see all the old plays, all the musicals. I've looked out for you over the years, seen your name here and there. But things are different now, aren't they? They don't put on things like *Angel* any more. Glamorous stuff, I mean.'

This is a man after Lydia's own heart. 'Oh, youngsters these days don't know what Glamour means,' she says. 'Miss Henshaw here' – she turns to watch as the girl carefully pulls out the old cuttings album – 'She's a lovely girl but she seems quite happy to play three minor parts a night in brown sacking. I couldn't have borne to do that when I was in my prime. But it's the modern way, I suppose. I'm always being told I should march with the times.'

Alan Treloar shakes his head. 'But it's not always an improvement, is it? Your Arts Centre, for example. I normally never go near it, but I had an hour to kill on my way back to Taunton and thought I'd just see what was on – have a cup of coffee in the bar, perhaps. Rub shoulders with the profession, so to speak. And that was when I heard Miss Henshaw –'

'Oh, call me Vicki, please,' she says, approaching with the album clasped to her chest. 'I keep asking Mrs Pendleton to call me that, but she won't.'

'That's because I have old-fashioned values. When I was the star, I always insisted on my full title. You might do better to insist on it yourself, you know. Respect breeds respect.' Lydia would hate to call this young girl 'Vicki'. It would be like referring to Mr Rolfe as 'Justin'. It implied a kind of intimacy, a suggestion that everyone was on the same friendly level when they clearly weren't – even if they spent half their rehearsal time rolling around on the floor together, in the so-called "ensemble work". 'Anyway,' she says, turning to her visitor, 'What was it you were saying, Mr Treloar?'

'Well, I heard *Vicki* here saying to her director – Mr Rolfe, that is – "The Ginger Rogers of Bath and Wells has bidden you to tea." I was flabbergasted. I mean, it couldn't refer to anyone else, could it? It was my phrase – my property, if you like. It was me who'd coined it all those years ago. To hear someone else saying it – some pretty young lady I didn't know at all – well, to be honest, I couldn't believe my ears.'

'And now I don't expect you can believe your eyes – me sat here like a fat plum pudding.' Lydia leans forward, confidentially. 'I'm afraid I can't walk, now, let alone dance. My heart, Mr Treloar.' Lydia's faulty heart is making its presence known, beating a strange rhythm inside her tight pink jumper. She feels he must be able to see it, fluttering away.

'Oh indeed, I know. Bodies can let us down.' Alan Treloar pats his almost bald head with a rueful wince. 'But in you I see the Spirit of Glamour lives on regardless.'

'Oh, you are still a flatterer I see!' But she is inordinately pleased all the same, and smiles as she opens the cuttings album Vicki has placed on her knees. She smoothes the page, squints at the faded type. 'Here it is!' She reads the first paragraph aloud. '*A touch of Hollywood glamour was brought to us tonight at the Theatre Royal when Lydia Landon danced her way into the audience's heart as if she were the Ginger Rogers of Bath and Wells . . .*' She leans back. 'But why Bath and Wells, Mr Treloar? I thought it made me sound a tiny bit like a bishop.'

Alan Treloar laughs. 'I don't know, to be honest. It seemed to trip off the tongue when I was writing it. And you did come from Bath originally, didn't you?'

'Well, that's true. But Laurie Burnett came from Cromer, and you didn't mention that.'

Alan Treloar looks her in the eye. 'I wasn't madly in love with Laurie Burnett,' he says, tightening his grip on her hand. Lydia feels a frisson of the kind she hasn't known for years. They sit for minutes, hands clasped. Then Alan laughs, breaks the spell. 'Laurie was an awful dancer, anyhow. Couldn't keep time – and what a wig!'

Lydia laughs too. She is enjoying herself now. 'It wasn't a wig, you know, although everyone thought so – just a terrible dye-job. He insisted on doing it himself, got black stuff all over the sink in his dressing room. And he thought no one knew.'

'He let you down, Miss Landon. You deserved a wonderful partner like Fred Astaire.'

'Oh Mr Treloar! I was never that good.'

'Yes, you were. You were *better* than Ginger, in fact. There was always something a bit hard about her. You were so warm and lovely. You still are.'

Lydia's eyes moisten. She can hear the music, the applause; see the rows of white upturned faces; smell the bouquets. This is the sort of conversation she has missed all these years, the sort of conversation that can take her back to such exquisite memories. Having Theatricals in the house has been a poor substitute. The actors come, they go, they admire her old photographs, but no one really wants to talk about the past. And none of them know about the glory days, even if, like Miss Henshaw, they humour her for fifteen minutes or so.

She looks up at the young actress, so young, so inexperienced, so very different from herself. She thinks, not for the first time, that the poor girl has absolutely no figure. And with those pale lips and great black eyes, it's no wonder she never gets a leading part. She turns to her graciously. 'Off you go now, dear. Get your beauty sleep. I'm sure you have another heavy day tomorrow.' More rolling around, she thinks. More first names and brown paper sacks and total rejection of Glamour. When Mr Rolfe comes to tea, she'll have a word with him. Even with 'ensemble playing', there must be an opportunity to shine. It's the least she can do after Miss Henshaw has been so kind.

'Will you be all right? Do you need anything?' The girl is wringing her hands a little. She seems, for once, reluctant to go.

'Oh, don't worry. I think I have everything I need. And if not, I'm sure Mr Treloar and myself will be able to *improvise*.' She laughs, and Alan Treloar laughs too.

'I'll go then,' she says.

'Yes, dear, do.' Lydia waves her away. 'Now, pull up that little Indian table, if you don't mind, Mr Treloar. You and I have a lot to catch up on. I've a Thermos, if you'd like a cup of tea. And some ginger nuts if you're hungry.'

Alan Treloar takes off his camel-hair coat and tartan scarf and puts them carefully on the floor beside him, then pulls the table close. He settles himself next to Lydia as if he is thoroughly at home. He's humming a song, now. It's 'Dancing Cheek to Cheek'. And Lydia's feet tap out the rhythm on the red and blue carpet.

HEART TROUBLE

My mother's collar had rain on it. Perfectly circular beads of rain. On the black coat she always hated wearing. 'It reminds me of death,' she'd said when she brought it home on appro. But Dad and I had said it looked nice, with its swagger back, its stylish yoke, so she gave in and hung it up in the wardrobe. But she pulled a face every time she put it on: 'Dull old thing.'

She liked bright colours. She had an appetite for life – singing, dancing, acting the fool. Everyone said she looked young for her age.

But not now. She looked a hundred years old, now. And black *didn't* suit her. She stood at the front door, her eyes small, screwed up, staring inward. 'Sorry to ring the bell, love. I've forgotten my key.'

She'd just come back from the hospital, seeing Dad again. Everything was supposed to be all right. The operation had been a success, and she'd told me I needn't bother to visit any more. But I didn't like what her face was saying to me, now.

'How is he, then?' The calls came from behind me. The family had the kitchen door open. I could hear the sound of frying and Uncle Ron's radio: the *Light Programme*.

She kissed me, wet collar rubbing my cheek: 'Has she had her tea?'

I turned to see Gran wiping her hands on her apron, patting her secret Woodbines in the pocket, her thin old wedding ring loose on her bony finger. 'I gave her a bit of bread and butter, but she wanted to wait for you.'

Mam took off her coat. It looked heavy and dull as she hung it over the banister. 'I think I've got some soup. Something, anyway.' She slumped; her hands still in the folds of the coat.

'Come on! How is he?' Uncle Ron shouted down the passage, sports page in hand.

'I've got to ring them later. They said to come home. There was nothing I could do.'

'I knew there'd be something. It was like this with my Frank.' Auntie May's head was in the kitchen doorway now, curlers under chiffon scarf.

Gran pushed past her: 'My legs. I've got to sit down if it kills me. And your Frank was years ago, May. Things have come on since then.'

'Bloody women!' said Uncle Ron, and disappeared out the back, seeing to his sausages.

'You won't have to go back, will you?' I didn't like it when Mam went out in the evening – although Gran would let me watch what I liked on television. I wanted to go with her, but the hospital was two long bus rides away and I knew I'd feel sick. Sometimes I *was* sick, throwing up the minute I got off the bus. Mam said it wasn't worth it.

'I don't know, love. It depends what they say. Dad's not so good just now.'

I wanted her to stay home. After all, the operation had been a success. The doctors would look after him. Why did she need to go back? I didn't think about Dad. It was Mam I needed to be there with me; Mam who kept a watch on my whole life – plaited my hair, took me shopping, sent me out to play when the weather was nice, worried about me being warm enough without my cardigan, made sure I had my mac when it looked like rain. Without her, there was a hole in my life.

Dad was more distant. He'd spend his evenings sitting in the armchair reading the *South Wales Echo*, or tinkering with the innards of a watch, his black eye-piece monocled fiercely in his right eye, tweezers in hand. He was irritable if disturbed. On Sundays he'd fiddle about in the only bit of our garden that got any sun, tying up zinnias and asters, checking for slugs. On his days off he'd spend the afternoon in the cellar developing and printing our summer snaps – Ilfracombe, the bandstand talent competition, the harbour full of boats – until my mother told him to come up before he froze to death. When he came up his fingers would be white, and my mother would start on him: 'Why do you keep on doing it? That damp old place? You know it does you no good.' And she'd chafe his fingers and make him sit down and hold a cup of tea bowled in his large hands. 'Stubborn as hell, you are.'

And quiet, too. My dad was known for being quiet. Conversation was my mother's domain; she had words enough for two. But he'd hug me and give me a kiss, and sometimes he'd show things to me, explain them: like the piston engines on the Campbell's paddle steamers, and how to build a proper three-tier sandcastle. I loved him, of course – because loving him was unquestionable, best in the world, next to Mam. But his being away made little difference to my days. Except making play-ground talk more interesting: 'My dad's got a bad heart. He's having a New Operation.' I felt pleased to have something new to tell them. We kids loved everything new, everything bright and clean and modern. As we dawdled home along Albany Road, we took excited detours around the new British Home Stores with its pastel flooring, plastic fittings and enormous plate-glass windows – and turned up our noses at Woolworth's dark wooden counters and splintery floors. We watched with joy as our houses grew brighter with jazzy curtains, mix-and-match wallpaper and (if we could afford it) the picture of a Chinese woman all done in green. We adored television and *Quatermass* and the progress of science. We hated anything old-fashioned.

The hospital at Llandough was new. At least it seemed new, compared with the tall, church-like infirmary where I'd gone to have the stitches in my forehead just the year before. The first few visits there had been exciting. I felt important, going all that way, walking along the drive with the grown-ups, my mother hissing quietly at me 'Remember to say you're twelve!' But I hated the journey, juddering along in the smelly Western Welsh diesel, trying to gulp fresh air from the window as the bus twisted and turned up the hill away from Cardiff. And the visit itself started to be less interesting – me sitting night after night by the bedside with the stiff white coverlet at eye-level, and the whispering of hushed voices all around the ward. I'd listen to my mother talking – her raconteur style, imitating voices, the arguments of Uncle Ron and Auntie May, the quirks of the customers at the shop, all the people who sent good wishes. I would smile, not knowing what to say. He'd

make an effort: 'How's school?' and I'd tell him we were doing a pup-
pet play Mr Williams had written about the women of Fishguard. And
that Andrea Jenkins had the main part because she had a loud voice,
and other kids had parts because they had good puppets. But that I'd
helped to paint the scenery. He'd pat my hand: 'Good girl.' Then we'd
pause, no hooks of small talk between us. Sometimes I'd read a book.
(He'd taken a photo of me reading like that, sitting on my own on the
deck of the *Bristol Queen*, absorbed in *Malory Towers* while the sea
washed over the rail.) But really I was hoping to be in time for a bit
of television when we got back. I'd kiss him goodbye as soon as the
bell rang, anxious to get the bus.

And now something was wrong. I couldn't understand it. After the
operation he'd been fine. 'He'll be all right, you'll see,' Gran kept saying to Mam. Saying it over and over again as she laid the cloth and
put out the plates: 'He'll be all right. He'll be all right.'

Tea was quick; devilled ham sandwiches. Mam cut herself on the tin
and cried all over the plaster. When we'd cleared away, she crossed the
road to ring from the phone box on the corner, came back not looking
at me and mouthing over my head: 'They think I'd better go back.' She
asked Uncle Ron to go with her. As a rule she'd never go anywhere
with him. He was a bit touched, she said, and liable to make a scene.
It was all right for him to pick rows at home, but you kept away from
him outside because he'd shout and show you up. But now she was
asking him, and he was saying, 'All right, love,' and looking serious
like a normal person. Mam said she'd already rung for Glamtax, not
to waste time.

We only ever had taxis to get to the Pier Head to catch the boat for
holidays. I had this feeling in my stomach like before a ballet exam,
or going back to school. Horrible, but exciting too. 'Can I come?' I
said, following Mam around as she put things in her bag. Mam kept
hugging me and saying, no, it would be all right, I'd be better staying
with Gran; Dad would understand. She put on her coat. It made her
look suddenly grey.

The taxi arrived – a man in dark red uniform and cap – and I saw
Mrs Marks next door holding back the curtain to see what was going

on. We stood on the front step, waved them off, Auntie May going on about Frank that last time, and Gran whispering, 'Quiet, you. Think about the child.'

I stayed up late, watching a film about a tap dancer with a ribbon in her hair and a tiny cupid-bow mouth. And a blond friend who talked fast and smoked, and wore a fox fur round her shoulders. And then hundreds of smiling dancers marching out of nowhere on a vast shiny stage with a boom of coordinated feet.

'Stay home tomorrow,' said Gran, which was another treat. She let me sleep in her feather bed, which dipped in the middle.

When I woke up, Mam hadn't come home. Gran said no news was good news, and gave me toast and Marmite. Then Uncle Ivor (not my real uncle, just a friend of Auntie May's) came knocking on the door with a message from Mrs Rice across the road who had a phone and was always willing to take a call. 'Sticking her nose in, mind you,' said Uncle Ivor, heading for the kitchen. 'But you can't complain.' They shut the kitchen door, shut me out, but I hung over the banister, trying to catch the words. No words, only the sudden wail. I galloped up the stairs two at a time, heading away from them. I knew they'd have to come and tell me. Sit me down like David Copperfield to give me the news. I waited in my bedroom, in the little armchair Dad had made, drawing doctors and nurses, patients in bed. And coffins and crosses and graves. Plenty of shading, thick 2B pencil. I listened for the rattle of the kitchen door as I built up the shadows.

It was Auntie May who came, knocking on my door like a servant in a play – but not knowing her lines, and crying all the time. She said she'd come to say my daddy was in heaven. She was holding her best white prayer-book with the shiny cover. I'd been asking her for weeks if I could have it, and she'd said no, not until you're grown-up. She handed it to me now.

She tried to say something more, but I told her to leave me alone. That's what people said in plays and films. *Leave me alone!* I threw myself down on the bed as she closed the door, and writhed around on the shiny green eiderdown. The prayer-book slid sideways and fell open onto the rug. The bookmark fell out so I could see the picture of the Infant Jesus, swaddled like a rolled-up parcel, halo curling round his head like a giant turban. I looked at it covertly through my tears. The halo was interesting. I thought of copying it in my new drawing book, shaded to look more shiny round the edge.

At dinner-time, Pat and Jenny came from school, wondering where I'd been. Laughing up the path, expecting influenza or a cold. Standing on the front tiles, ringing the bell.

I told Gran I'd answer the door. I felt important, and wished I had a black dress with a veil like a Victorian orphan, not a tartan skirt with straps and a Fair Isle cardigan with a button off. But, opening the door and seeing their smiles, their questioning faces, I found I couldn't say a word and started to cry. Uncle Ivor, temporary man of the house, took over, said the necessary words in a whisper, and: 'Tell the school, will you, girls? Save us going down.' They ran off, sad and gleeful, hoods up against the rain.

Not much for dinner. Bread, and Gran's sugary butter from the still-laid table. A bit of paste, some jam. I sat and drew whole funerals, paying special attention to shoes (I'd just learned how to draw high heels and feet from the front). I sat in the front window and watched for my mother. But she didn't come. 'She'll have a lot of things to sort out,' said Gran. Other people came, though. Relatives we only saw at Christmas. The neighbours. Friends who'd heard. Someone's daughter who was a nurse. Gran made tea and smoked in the back kitchen with the door open: 'I wish to God they'd all go. Fly their kites.'

Time dragged. I drew clocks. Uncle Ben and Auntie Flora came in see-through macs, she very jolly, discussing the sales and the new black wallpaper they were having in the bathroom: 'Well, you got to keep going'; he telling funny stories, glancing round for an audience, noticing my half-smile: 'Liked that one, did you, love? That's the way.'

The curate came in a wet cloak, had a cup of tea and went again. 'Hoping for something stronger,' said Gran. 'Well, he won't get it from me.' She swept up sugar from the tablecloth, threw it in the fire. It crackled and burned briefly blue. She stood, hand on the high mantelpiece, staring down.

Half-past four. Still no Mam. No food for tea either. Nobody'd been shopping. Uncle Ivor fancied chitterlings and sent me off: 'Something for her to do.'

I stood in line on the sawdust floor at the pork butcher's, an orphaned child out in the Wide, Wide World, blinking back tears. The man behind the counter paused as he swung the bag closed by its corners. He looked in my face, kind for a minute: 'All right are you, love?'

The kindness was the worst thing. The tears rose but I nodded, brave. He gave me the bag. 'Two and six, then.'

I walked home slowly, head down. I splashed through the rainbow puddles on the pavements. I didn't care if I got my shoes wet. I wanted wet shoes. And wet hair. And a wet face. I trudged in a funeral procession, holding the wrapped chitterlings in front of me like an offering. I went down the lane to the back of the house. And in through the back gate – wood swollen and needing a push. And past Dad's roses hanging their heads. And up the high kitchen step and into the house. With the parcel of meat in one hand and sixpence change in the other. Expecting Gran and Auntie May and Uncle Ivor round the kitchen table. But not expecting Mam. In a black coat that didn't suit her. With pale face and red eyes and rain on her collar. And the hot tears bursting from me as I leapt across the room.

REMEMBERING THE FLOWERS

'Anything planned for tonight?' Chris gave a little boogie with his hips and winked.

'Not really,' said Stephen, closing his desk drawer.

'Not even – *nudge-nudge*?' Chris gave it nose and elbow action.

Stephen gave a half-smile and reached for his coat. He always reacted badly to Chris's heavy bonhomie, even though he recognized all too well the symptoms of loneliness that lay behind it: the extended working hours, the intrusive conversations, the pathetic attempts to batten on to the details of other people's lives. Stephen had been there once himself. But that was a long time ago, and now he couldn't find it in himself to humour the bloke.

'But flowers – you're going to give the little woman some flowers on Valentine's Day, tell me that at least.' Chris affected hand-on-heart concern.

'That'd be telling. Anyway, I'm off now. Don't stay too late.' Stephen picked up his briefcase and quickly made his exit, knowing he had absolutely no intention of submitting to the annual flower-buying binge: trashy bouquets, even trashier sentiments. Real love, he thought, was worth more than that.

But then, rushing up from the Tube, he saw the flower stall. The sudden burst of colour was festive against the dark night, and the crowds gathered around it seemed good-humoured and eager. Stephen felt a sudden impulse of generalized goodwill and togetherness with humanity. He glanced at his watch. He had a window: five minutes.

He craned over the jostling heads, picked a bunch more or less at random (roses, lilies, something feathery, marked £7.99) and waved it at the stall-holder, who seemed to be working out some sort of complex mathematical equation with someone else's change. 'Excuse me!' he called out. 'Can you take for this now, mate? Train to catch!' But the man carried on with his counting, immune to the cone of Cellophane flapping inches from his nose. Stephen glanced at his watch again. He had four minutes now; four minutes to get to the platform and into the carriage. He wondered if a tatty bunch of flowers was worth the trouble. Even as he hesitated, he was aware of a pair of female eyes looking at him from somewhere in the maelstrom of bobbing heads and flailing hands. It was a momentary glance, but there was something about it that made him feel bizarrely unsettled, queasy even – as if he had been caught out in a shameful act. He was so disconcerted he almost put the flowers back, but the stall-holder chose that moment to turn to him, and Stephen, in a reflex action, thrust ten pounds into the man's hand. 'Cheers,' he said. 'Keep the change.'

He started to run towards the main-line platform, hampered by the strangely sail-like quality of the bouquet. As he joined the thickening surge of commuters streaming towards the barrier, he felt a slight tug at his coat. He turned sharply and saw a small, discoloured hand gripping his sleeve. He had a quick impression of a woman with unkempt dark hair, wearing a threadbare black coat. She must be one of the Kosovans or Romanians who hung around the station entrance; someone who'd seen him with his romantic bouquet and thought he was a soft touch. He tried to pull his coat free from her fingers. 'Sorry, love,' he said, pressing on. 'No change!' But the woman hung on, keeping pace with him so that he stopped and turned in exasperation: 'For God's sake, I said, no change!'

That was when their eyes met. When he realized with a start that she was the woman he'd glimpsed at the stall; the one who had caused him that moment of uncertainty and unease. Up close, her face was worn and dirty and her hair was incredibly hacked-about. She was altogether squalid, but he felt again the same confusing, gut-churning sensation that he'd experienced before – and it was much more powerful now she was next to him. She had almost an inviting look, a look that might have been seductive in different circumstances – and even then, on the busy station concourse, gave him a slight frisson. He wanted to smile at her, to engage with her in some way but his rational self took over and he turned away, brusquely. 'Sorry,' he said over his shoulder. 'Try someone else.'

But the woman put her hand on his arm, pulled him back: 'You don't recognize me, do you, Stephen?' He turned, shocked at hearing his name, and even more shocked by the quality of the voice. It was educated and well-produced; totally at odds with the woman's appearance. In fact, it was eerily familiar, like some television voice-over that he couldn't place. He felt the blood come to his cheeks: he must know this woman. His brain rapidly indexed anyone who might fill the bill: mothers of his children's friends, distant neighbours, occasional baby-sitters, school friends of his wife – but no connection would come. Absolutely nobody he knew looked that down and out.

'I'm awfully sorry. You are . . .?' he said, conscious of the crowd rushing past to the train as he stood there in polite suspension, waiting for her to enlighten him. The seats would soon be full, and he'd have to stand the whole way. 'Look, I don't mean to be rude but I'm in danger of missing my train. Are you . . .' He indicated the platform. After all, unlikely though it might seem, she probably lived in Essex, too.

The woman shook her head. And then she smiled. It was a smile of astonishing openness, a smile that transformed her whole face. In the whole of his life, he'd only ever known one smile like that. 'Morella?' he said, peering at her with amazed disbelief, his heart thudding like a die-stamp. '*Morella?*'

Morella Martin had been the love of his life, although he hadn't seen her for fifteen years, not since they were at Cambridge together and she had inexplicably gone off without a word the night after their final exams. He'd been devastated. He'd also been determined to find her again. He didn't think it would be long before he saw her name in lights and he could surprise her at the stage door with flowers. And even if she didn't make the grade as an actress, he was convinced that one day they were bound to jump into the same taxi, or dive out of the rain into the same damp doorway, laughing: *Oh, it's you!* For an entire year he'd haunted every theatre bar in the West End, imagining that at any moment she would creep up behind him, her breath tickling his ear (*Hello, sweetie! Are you actually enjoying this crap?*). And whenever he was at a restaurant alone (and he was usually alone), he would keep half an eye on the door, thinking how envious all the diners would be when she hailed him across the room and came to sit at his table (*Stephen darling, how wonderful to see you – I've just come back from LA!*). But in reality Morella had never appeared in any of his lovingly crafted scenarios. And Stephen had found himself on a personal treadmill of dull work and routine promotion that he seemed powerless to get off. He stopped going to the theatre, stopped going anywhere, in fact. He worked late every night instead, and had no sex-life worth speaking of. Women found him self-pitying and self-absorbed, and didn't stay around. He'd gradually resorted to drowning his sorrows in the proverbial fashion, and had become a late-night bar-propper and a bore. That is, until Sue had come along and rescued him. Sue was patient, kind, and full of good sense, and had made him unexpectedly happy. They'd been married thirteen years now, had two children and he considered himself in every way a reformed and settled man. But he still carried in his head the sacred image of Morella – the entrancing, fawn-like creature of his undergraduate days.

Stephen looked at the stained and grubby woman before him, trying to disguise his feelings of shock. Something awful must have happened to her. Some illness, some terrible accident. The scene was so like a nightmare that he genuinely thought he might be hallucinating. But he could feel the reality of the crowds surging round him as he stood holding a bouquet towards Morella in a parody of a lovers' meeting. He opened his mouth and shut it again. Morella made a wry face: 'Yes I know, Stephen. I've changed.'

'No, no, not at all,' he said automatically. Then, more truthfully, 'Well, that is to say, it's fifteen years. We both have.'

'But some of us more than others. You really didn't recognize me, did you, Stephen?'

He tried desperately to discern the features that had once so enraptured him: the clear eyes with their startling dark-rimmed irises, the high cheek-bones, the delectable, mobile mouth. Everything was essentially there – but everything was washed-out, faded, fallen. She looked a good ten years older than his wife. But she was still Morella. His heart was beating overtime. 'I knew there was some special connection – the minute you caught my eye,' he said, raising his voice over the noise of the station announcer. 'But I was too busy thinking of these damn flowers, and catching the blasted train.' He gestured towards the platforms, the surge of people that was almost pushing them off their feet. He held the bouquet of flowers aloft to avoid the crush. 'And I didn't expect – well, not *you* of all people, not after all this time. It's fantastic, of course,' he added hastily, wishing he had an arm free to embrace her. 'Really fantastic.' But somewhere at the back of his mind he was astonished to find that he was still thinking of his train, his need to get home, to present Sue with the flowers, this tawdry sign of his love and devotion. But even as his mind hovered over the thought, he wondered how he could even contemplate anything so commonplace, when here in front of him, at last, was Morella. And in the manner of a fairy story, the more he looked at her, the less shabby she became. And her face – the way her eyelids slanted curiously at the outward edge, the way her bottom lip quivered gently as she spoke – began to work its old magic.

'I don't want to make you late, of course. Especially on such a *special night*.' She eyed the bouquet. 'But I can't let you go now. Not after all this time. I need to speak to you, Stephen.'

That trick of hers, the way she always used his name repeatedly as if he were special to her, made his heart beat even faster. But he found himself casting a regretful glance towards the platform, and even more unbelievably, to his watch. She picked up the gesture. 'I could come on the train with you, Stephen, if you can't spare the time.'

He almost laughed. The idea was impossible; Morella on the train to Essex, crushed up with all the commuters; Morella walking up the neatly bricked drive to meet Sue in her striped cook's apron; the table laid neatly for two, Bach or Mozart in the background. 'Let's find a pub or something,' he said, squeezing her arm. 'Much more fun.'

She leant into him confidingly, a gesture that had always, quite wrongly, given him hope. 'I hope you have plenty of money, Stephen. I need a serious, *serious* drink.'

'Do you, indeed?' He laughed, relaxed a little. 'Well, I think I can manage a round or two. Unless you're planning on vintage champagne.' Then remembering that champagne was exactly what she'd always liked. Cheap stuff of course, in those days. But in generous quantities, drunk from tumblers: *It makes me happy*.

'That's good, Stephen. That's wonderful.' Her voice was fervent. 'But I have to collect my belongings first. Don't go, will you? I'm so afraid you'll disappear. Like the Fairy Godmother – *poof* – in a cloud of smoke.' She gestured two arcs with her hands, looking more gamine than ever. Her features were more in focus, now. More like his long-ago memory of her. He felt he was salvaging her slowly, bringing her up out of the forgotten deep. The rush of sick pleasure almost choked him.

He wondered what belongings she had, why she had left them behind, unattended in the rush hour. They waded back against the buffeting tide of commuters, Stephen still holding the flowers aloft. Morella made her way to a plastic carrier sagging on the floor near the Tube entrance. It was a cheap yellow bag, crammed so full that the handles wouldn't meet. Not shopping, Stephen sensed. Nothing smart or elegant – Dolce & Gabbana or Harvey Nichols. More the sort of thing bag ladies carried about; intimate belongings indiscriminately thrust together. He watched, shocked, as Morella tucked back something pastel and grubby before hoisting the bag a few inches from the ground, her bony body diagonal with the weight.

'Here – let me take that –' An automatic gesture, but as he took it, the weight surprised him, and the contents clanked a little as he let it graze the ground. 'My God, Morella, what have you *got* in here?'

'My life, Stephen, more or less.' She looked away quickly, then back, eyes bright, shaking a little, he noticed. 'Sorry to ask,' she said with one of her apologetic smiles, 'but I don't suppose you have a ciggie?'

'Sorry –' He mimed helplessness.

'Ah, no, of course. You never did.'

'But let me buy you some.' He put the heavy bag and his briefcase between his knees, the slightly battered bouquet under his arm, and fished out a ten pound note from his wallet. Morella plucked it from his fingers and in a flash she was at the nearby kiosk, pointing out what she wanted, tearing open the Cellophane, lighting up urgently. She put the packet and the change into her pocket with an automatic gesture, and Stephen remembered with a jolt how she'd always done that – pocketed everything as if it were her due.

She turned, looking suddenly chic with the cigarette, like a movie star incognito, her black collar turned up jauntily: 'That's better.' Her hands were brown with nicotine, even the nails. They looked dirty, uncared for – the hands of the beggar he'd supposed her to be. They trembled a little as she held the cigarette. She was even more nervy than he remembered.

'Still addicted, I see.' He'd always hated her chain-smoking. *Nagged her*, she said.

'You wouldn't begrudge me, Stephen, if you knew all that's happened.'

He watched the smoke curl upwards across her face. He thought of Sue, crisp and sweet-smelling in their smoke-free house. And he saw the kitchen clock, ticking away to suppertime; a suppertime he would not make. But this was more important. He had to know what it was that had happened to Morella. 'Have you been ill?' he asked. It seemed the most diplomatic thing to say.

'Ill? Well, yes and no.' She turned to him, that deep intense look that used to shake his bones. 'Stephen, I need help. You will help me, won't you?'

'Of course,' he said, picking up the horrible lolling bag with its seedy contents, and feeling his heart sink. 'Now, for God's sake let's go and have that drink.'

'You're married,' she said, eyeing his wedding ring as he brought the drinks to the table. She'd chosen one in the darkest corner.

'No prizes for that,' replied Stephen. 'What about you?'

'She's expecting you, then.' Morella looked at the flowers lying on the table in their Cellophane wrap, the colours all reduced to shades of salmon pink in the dim red light of the pub. She stroked a wilting petal. 'Will she mind?'

'Mind what?'

Morella shrugged. 'Me. You. This.' She took her vodka and downed it in one.

'Of course not. We trust each other.' But he knew he was never going to tell Sue about Morella. He'd have to think up an excuse. Meeting an old university friend (implication male), going for a quick drink, getting talking, forgetting the time . . .

'What's her name?'

'Sue.' How short it seemed. How plain and ordinary.

'Sue.' She rolled the name around her mouth as if she were tasting it. '*Sweet Sue*. I expect she *is* sweet, isn't she?'

'Yes, as a matter of fact, she is.' He felt himself rise a little in Sue's defence.

'Not like me, then.'

'Rubbish.' He gazed at her. She still had the terrific cheekbones, the kitten face. 'You're very sweet.'

'Do you still think so?' She lit another cigarette. 'Oh, Stephen, I'm really in a mess.'

I'm really in a mess: that had always been a mantra with her, her eyes full of tears, her mane of black hair hanging down over her face as she confided her latest problem. Stephen eyed her threadbare clothes, her hair, her hands, her awful plastic bag. 'So what's the matter?'

She shook her head and twiddled her empty glass. 'I need some money. And somewhere to stay. Just for a short while.'

It had always been short-term with Morella. A loan, a bottle of wine, a packet of cigarettes, the rent. She always promised to repay, but the promise passed with the crisis. And she was frequently in a crisis. That was how he had first met her in the house on Madingley Road when Ian Cresswell had brought her back late one night. 'Just been thrown out of her digs, poor girl. Needs a bed for a couple of nights and Bigsby's round at Sarah's far as I know, so I thought *noblesse oblige* and all that. Could she borrow your sheets, Steve? They're bound to be cleaner than his.' Stephen had dragged his newly washed sheets off his mattress, tucked them into Bigsby's bed at the top of the house, putting his own patchwork coverlet on top. Morella, wide-eyed as a fawn, had smiled at him: 'All this trouble. You're so sweet.' Stephen, lying awake that night on the rough blanket with his dressing gown on top, had not been able to think of anything except Morella's supple body between his sheets, in the room directly above his own.

The next night she was still there, and the following day, too. In fact, she'd just stayed on, and Bigsby, on the nights he was at home, had found himself sharing a mattress in the back bedroom with Paul and his unpleasant rugby boots. Suddenly the bleak, untidy house was full of her sexual presence; the *Carmina Catulli* tapes she played very loud all day and deep into the night; the vases of paper flowers on the landing; the strange green underwear in the bathroom; the poetry she wrote; the paintings she owned. Great abstract canvases hung in prominent positions all over the house. 'That's *Sexual Intercourse*,' she'd explained one day, seeing Stephen scrutinizing a black and purple canvas she'd put on the wall above the kitchen table. He'd tried to make sense of the violent interlocking shapes every morning over his cereals, and wondered whether she had just been teasing him.

Her main passion was acting. Sometimes she'd hide herself upstairs for days, learning lines, creating a sense of seriousness and privacy so strong that Stephen had hesitated to invade it by so much as a knock on the door – although through his ceiling he could hear her moving about, and occasionally detect the tapping of the typewriter above the soaring operatic voices. Sometimes she'd throw herself into days of relentless socializing, turning up with armfuls of groceries to cook spectacular meals for dozens of loud-mouthed people whom Stephen didn't know and who looked at him with barely disguised amusement. She'd paid the rent when she remembered. More often it went out of her mind: 'Oh God, I'm sorry. Next week, I promise.' The five men in the house had put up with it. She seemed exempt from normal censure.

And now, all these years later, she wanted money again. He watched her, wondering what she would ask for. Morella's extravagance had been legendary even in those student days. *Carpe diem*, she always used to say, when she came back laden with wine and oysters and truffles. *Don't be such a killjoy, Stephen my sweet. We could be dead tomorrow.* He looked now at her thin, pale, sexy face and thought with a shock that maybe she really was dying. She looked worryingly frail. 'How much d'you need?'

'What can you manage?' Her hands were trembling again. On her third cigarette in a row, ingesting it almost. He suspected some kind of breakdown. Drugs? Alcohol? On her uppers anyway – that awful bag.

He looked into his flaccid wallet. 'Liquidity's a bit low at the moment.' He laughed wryly. 'But I could get the hotel on my card, and we could stop off at a machine for some cash. Would a hundred do? I think that's all I can get out.'

Morella looked unsure. 'A hotel? I was hoping . . . well, couldn't I stay with you? Just for a day or two? I really won't be any trouble –' She watched his face. 'No, it's impossible. You're saying that, aren't you, Stephen? You're saying your wife won't like it.'

He mumbled, 'Well you know, short notice and all that.' He knew that wasn't the reason. Sue would suppress a sigh at the need to get out clean sheets, move the ironing from the spare room and stretch the supper to accommodate one extra, but she'd be polite and hospitable even while hating the chain-smoking, and the odious appearance of the yellow plastic bag. But he'd have to explain. And the mere idea of Sue and Morella coming together was like a heresy. Sue was part of his sane and rescued life. Sue knew nothing of Morella, of the good old, bad old student days.

'I really wouldn't be a bother, Stephen. I've got a kettle and some pans. I'd cook. I'd fit in.'

'Fit in?' She was straight-faced; he couldn't help a snort of laughter. 'Morella, if there's one thing I remember about you, it's that you always stood out a mile.'

'Is that true? God, how awful . . .' She dropped her head, started to light another cigarette. 'Okay, then. A hotel it is. Thanks.'

Stephen felt guilty. He knew he should take her home, introduce her to Sue and the kids, give her what she wanted, however bizarre. Look after her, not push her away the moment they'd met. But he couldn't face it. He'd never mentioned her name to anyone, or her part in his life. When he talked about his Cambridge days, it was about Ian and Bigsby, Sarah (up to a point), Paul and his rugby boots, even Tom and his crowd. But he had concealed Morella, stowed her away like a sacred icon, rubbed her out of the group photograph. It would sound strange if she started saying how she had shared his life for the best part of three years.

'Would you find somewhere for me? Take me there? Stay a bit? Stephen, please?'

'Of course.' He felt better: a solution. He could stow Morella and her wretched plastic bag safely out of the way, at least for this evening. He realized he was already experiencing those long-forgotten feelings of helplessness, panic and anger, which being with Morella had always induced. He knew the mess she was in would be a big one. He wasn't sure he wanted to hear about it.

'Thanks. You won't dash off straight away, will you, Stephen? Please? I'm a bit wobbly on my own.' The limpid eyes fixed on him. He saw her in a torn dress, holding on to him in her attic bedroom: *Stay with me, stay with me, please!* And curling up with an eiderdown around her, crying into her coffee.

'I'll stay as long as I can, but –' He raised his eyebrows, indicating there were limits. Sue would be waiting, wondering. He thought about ringing her, but decided not to. He wasn't sure he could trust his voice over the phone. Better face to face, with the flowers as a peace-offering. The blooms didn't look so good now, though. They seemed to have been shrivelling by the minute. They were probably half dead when he bought them. A con after all.

Morella looked around the bar. 'Before we go – could I have another vodka, d'you think? Double, if you don't mind.'

He got up, returned with the glass. She took a large gulp. Then she leaned back and asked casually, 'Have you ever thought about me, Stephen?'

He couldn't believe she'd said that. He studied his finished pint, hardly trusting himself to speak. 'Only every day. After all, you almost ruined my life.'

She looked astonished. '*I* did? Stephen, how?' She seemed genuinely shocked, reached for the vodka, finished it.

'Well, tell me if I'm wrong, but as I recall it, you just took your things and went. No goodbye, no address, nothing. I'd seen you every day for the best part of three years and you didn't think I was worth even a telephone call or a bloody postcard.' The pain and fury rushed back as if it had been yesterday and he found himself raising his voice. The couple at the next table turned, glasses half raised to their mouths, and stared at him.

She shook her head. The smoke from her cigarette drifted up between them. 'I did try. But we were never – oh, I don't know . . .' She stared ahead, glazed. 'Why did you have to be so *serious* about me?'

'Because I felt serious.'

'But I wanted a *friend*.' She looked at him with that innocent, injured look, the run-marks of mascara around her cheekbones looking like bruises.

He lowered his voice. 'Well, I *was* your friend. Don't you remember? I ran after you like a puppy-dog, hoping you might throw me the odd bone, the odd old bit of anything. But when you buggered off that night without a word, well, what was I supposed to think? I looked for you, you know. And then I stopped looking. And now, after fifteen years, you appear as if nothing has happened since.'

'Sorry. Sorry, sorry, sorry, sorry. Forget it.' She got up, trying to stub out the cigarette into the thick glass ashtray. Stephen pulled her down again. Her arm felt pathetically thin even through the coat. She was trembling alarmingly now, her face streaked with black. Stephen was overcome with shame. How could he be treating her like this? The woman he'd once adored?

'I'm sorry too. Let's forget the past for a moment. Too complicated. Let's get you to a hotel.'

The room on the seventh floor of the Regency Tower was bland and overheated. Stephen sat on one chintz-covered single bed, she on the other. She had taken off the old black coat, exposing a curious chiffon dress underneath. A layered affair, grey over green, spare and tight over her bones. And she was much bonier, now. She'd lost the wonderful suppleness of her youth. But, pale and pinched as she was, shorn and streaked with tears, her body still had the power to move him. He affected briskness, tried to ignore the arousal he felt. 'I've been expecting to see your name in lights: *Morella Martin triumphs again*. Where the hell have you been hiding all this time?'

She closed her eyes and smiled, a queer, mad smile. 'In a room, Stephen. A really horrid little room. But I escaped, as you see. I packed up my stuff and left. Left it all behind. Because I knew I'd found my future.' She threw herself back on the bed, arms stretched out, cruciform, abandoned. 'You're my rescuer, Stephen. My guardian angel. I knew you'd be there, at the station. Ten minutes past six.'

He laughed uneasily. 'How could you possibly know that?'

She looked up at him from the chintzy pillow, that sultry sideways glance, that sensual fold of skin across the edge of her eye. 'I saw you there yesterday. I could hardly believe it, and –'

'Yesterday?'

'You were dashing past with your briefcase, Mr Commuter. You were too quick for me. But I knew you'd come through again. Same time, same place. You're that sort of person.' She smiled wanly. 'So I packed my things, came back and waited for you.'

His scalp prickled. 'I can't believe you just saw me by accident.'

She flashed the wonderful, engaging smile, just revealing her teeth. 'Me neither. You seemed to appear right out of the blue. I thought what a nice coat you had on.'

'It's the same one I've got on now.' It was making him hot in fact, but he felt safer keeping things formal. Morella's faded little dress was very skimpy, exposing the top part of her breasts. The hemline had ridden high over her thighs revealing a sinuous length of thin black nylon leg, a little white hole near one knee.

She smiled, stretching towards him, touching the cashmere with her fingers: 'It's still nice.'

'Sue chose it.'

She laughed. 'Well, it's still nice.'

'Thanks. But what about all your clothes? Is this really all you've got?' He indicated the yellow bag, spilling open on the textured brown carpet – a knitted jumper, some socks, a tangled bra, a plastic hairbrush, a quilted Air France toilet bag with a broken zip, the glint of something aluminium . . .

'All my worldly goods. Shock you?'

'Well, yes, to be honest.' He'd been embarrassed at the reception desk, Morella so waif-like, him so prosperous. It was as if he were picking up a hooker from the streets.

'You see, I'm in what they call a downward spiral, Stephen. It's ever so easy, but you lose things on the way. Here, there. Your life shrinks. They took my tapes – my *Catulli*, my Verdi, my Puccini. Can you imagine what that did to me? Negative thoughts, they said. It wasn't though, was it? You know that. But I cope without them. You have to, you see.' She eyed the bag. 'I've got more stuff, but I had to leave things behind. Otherwise they would have known. They would have stopped me. I'm not ready, they said. But I tried to be sensible. Practical. A kettle. Some saucepans. I've come to the end of the line, now. I've been in too many places, Stephen, and you're my last chance. I've sort of burned my boats, now. I can't go back –'

Stephen felt confused. Who on earth were these people she was talking about? Possessive husbands? Violent lovers? Relatives of some sort? 'There must have been someone else you could have turned to,' he said. 'Someone closer to you, surely.'

She shook her head. 'Another *man* you mean? Surprise you, does it, Stephen, that there isn't one?' She reached for her coat, got out the almost empty pack of cigarettes, raised herself on her elbow and sat still for a moment. Her throaty voice trembled. 'I've had enough, Stephen. If I have to go back, I'll end it all. Seriously.'

I feel like ending it all! Another mantra. Especially when she'd been mixing it. Dope and booze and God knows what else. He'd held back her beautiful dark hair while she'd vomited into his basin, made her drink plenty of water, and put her to bed on her side. The next morning, *La Traviata* would be blaring out, and Morella would have forgotten everything, chuckling and saying, 'I have a feeling I was a bit skanky last night.'

Morella fumbled a cigarette into her mouth, dropped it in her lap, then started to shake: 'Oh, shit! Shit, shit!' She started to cry. Stephen moved over to sit beside her, put his arm around her. He got a shock as his fingers touched her ribs; she was even thinner than his ten-year-old. He found himself slipping into the soothing croon he'd used with Morella all those years ago: 'It's all right, it's all right.' He never seemed to need such words to comfort Sue. Sue was strong, sensible, sorted: *If you really want to help, Stephen, make me a cup of tea.* She'd probably be making tea now, a quick cup as she prepared vegetables to go with whatever she'd got ready the night before, covered in cling film in the fridge. No special Valentine supper for them: *We're not kids.* He could see her standing at the kitchen worktop, apron neatly tied over her navy blue office suit. He ought to ring her, explain how late he was going to be. But he needed to stay with Morella too. He felt her thin body shivering beneath his arm. He couldn't leave her now, not even to pick up the phone.

'So what is this awful thing that's been happening to you? That's got you into this state?' He took his handkerchief, wiped her cheeks. 'You know, I've never heard *anything* about you all these years. Not a thing. I thought you must have gone somewhere exciting – the States perhaps. Hollywood.'

'Oh, Stephen, I wish that were true.'

'So you've been in London all along?' He felt annoyed. How could she have kept away from him all this time?

'No, I've only been here a couple of months. Moved around twice in that time. They make it difficult, you know. I was in Edinburgh first. Then Leeds. Then somewhere near Birmingham. Always the same, though. Do this, do that. Points for this, points off for that. Oh, Stephen, I was being crushed. When I saw you yesterday it was like a vision, like you really did have angel wings, like you were going to lift me up from all of this –'

'Morella –'

'They didn't trust me, you see. They watched me all the time. No locks. Couldn't even pee in private. Can you believe that?'

'Well, I . . .' He began to wonder if she was actually insane.

She turned and grasped his arms. 'Would you say I'm a risk, Stephen?'

'Of course not.' He wished he could sound more convinced.

'They say it's in the past. But they don't let you get away from it. Ever.'

'Who doesn't? From what? Morella, you're not making sense!'

She paused; a long pause, looking up at the ceiling. 'What would you say if I told you that I'd murdered someone?'

Stephen's heart jumped. He looked sideways at her profile, the way her features were so sweetly, so innocently composed. 'You're not serious?'

'You know I never lie.'

He thought maybe it was an accident. Morella could be overdramatic in her use of words at times. Although he had an awful feeling it was more likely to be a *crime passionnel*. 'What happened?'

'Sharp knife. Opportunity. One, two. Finish.' She mimed a stabbing action. He saw her as Lady Macbeth, the triumph of the year, the rave reviews, the seal set on her bid for fame. She'd been very convincing: *Infirm of purpose! Give me the daggers!* She sighed. She seemed calmer, as if a weight had been lifted from her. She picked up the unlit cigarette from her lap, looked at it carefully as if it were a museum piece. In a reflective tone she said: 'You know, I absolutely lived for these things when I was locked up.'

'You were in prison?' That was one reason he'd never considered to explain her absence from the West End.

'Secure hospital. Same difference. Except the sentence never ends. You have to earn your freedom, and somehow I never had the knack . . .'

'Oh, Morella! Why didn't I know?' It was as if he'd had no right to enjoy himself all these years, to have holidays, to laugh. 'Why didn't anyone tell me?'

She shrugged. 'It was in the Scottish papers: *Cambridge graduate on murder charge* – then months while they tried to work out if I was mad or bad. Do you think I'm mad, Stephen?'

He thought she conceivably might be. She'd always been volatile, extreme. He tried to think of a way to answer her, but couldn't. There was silence. Then he asked, 'Who was it – the man you stabbed? It *was* a man, I suppose?'

'What difference is it to you, Stephen?'

'I'm just trying to understand.'

She sighed. 'You're as bad as they are. Wanting to "understand" all the time. To get inside me. To get under my skin. I've said it over and over – he was just sitting there at the kitchen table. Horrible and thick and blubbery, and so bloody pleased with himself. I just picked up the knife and did it. It was quite easy, really. If he was sitting here now I'd do it again. *Put out the light, and then put out the light!*'

Stephen cogitated. 'A boyfriend, then?'

'No – hardly.' She drew for a long time on the cigarette, brushed away some ash from her skinny lap. 'All right, if you want to know, Stephen, he was my stepfather. My mother's husband.'

'Your stepfather?' It was the first time she had ever mentioned any of her family. She'd always seemed so blithely independent he'd never thought the omission at all odd, as if she'd sprung into adulthood like Athena, fully formed; no bourgeois antecedents, nothing so commonplace as family.

She gave him a sideways look: 'Rory Lennox. You met him, in fact.'

'I did?' Stephen had no recollection of it.

'That first night of *Macbeth*.'

He remembered the fleshy, older man she'd taken up to her room. Someone she had introduced by his first name. Not one of her usual sort: 'I thought he was –' He reddened. 'I mean, I didn't realize he was *related* to you.'

'He wasn't. Not one drop of consanguineous blood. As he was always pointing out.'

Stephen stared stupidly, remembering the man's clammy ownership of Morella, his own impotent jealousy as he'd spirited her away upstairs. The full horror of it struck him with force.

She grimaced. 'Yes, you're right. See what a five-star slut I am. But I had my limits. I told him that night. I said it was all over. He said he knew I'd change my mind when I'd thought about it. When I thought over all that was involved, with my mother's heart being "so very weak".'

Stephen recalled the sinister adult certainty of the man, the frisson of fear he'd aroused with his heavy presence next morning at the breakfast table, Morella in her dressing gown meekly making him toast.

'I called his bluff, Stephen. I said I didn't care; that I was moving to London and that was that. I didn't think he'd tell my mother. It hardly made him look good, after all. But he rang me, the week we finished Finals. You and Ian were out getting pissed and I was on my own. He said my mother was in hospital. Heart failure, he said. *Something must have given her a shock*. So I just got on a train to Edinburgh as quickly as I could. Sorry, Stephen. Sorry I didn't think to leave you a note. Bigsby said he'd tell you . . .' Tears started to roll from Morella's eyes.

Stephen cursed Bigsby. How had he managed to forget such a message? 'And had he told your mother, this Rory?'

'I don't know, Stephen. She was dead before I got there.' Morella was weeping loudly now. 'She was all laid out on the hospital bed. I looked at her, Stephen, and I imagined that she'd died thinking I was the worst daughter in the world . . .'

Stephen gave her a little squeeze. 'You don't know she thought that. He probably didn't tell her anything. After all, why would he? It was his fault. Much more his fault. He was supposed to protect you, not seduce you, for God's sake.'

She shook her head. 'It still felt like my fault. I went a little bit mad, then, taking stuff – uppers and downers; anything I could lay my hands on. It was Rory who looked after me. He was good at that sort of thing; had done it with my mother for years. I thought he was being a proper father to me at last, cooking my meals, keeping the pills away. But it didn't last. One day he put his hand on my tits and said it was payback time. Then I knew it was him or me, and I just picked up the knife.'

'You should have come to me. I would have looked after you.' He stroked her hair – her poor, chopped, shorn hair. Its ugly, rough ends made him want to weep.

'The last thing I wanted was anyone being *kind*, Stephen. I couldn't have borne kindness.' She looked up, wiped her eyes. 'Some days I woke up and thought I was back in Madingley Road, and everything was simple again. You, Ian, Bigsby, Paul, Martin, Gavin.' She smiled, then turned, suddenly: 'Do you still see them?'

'Not really.' She didn't query this, didn't seem surprised he hadn't kept in touch. He added inconsequentially, 'Although I *did* run into Tom about a year back. He's doing very well.'

'Yes, Stephen. He would be.'

Stephen remembered how the subject of Morella had come up; how Tom had laughed his confident barrister's laugh, saying she was *too neurotic by half*. As he'd laughed back, Stephen had pictured Tom and Morella fumbling and thrusting in broad daylight in an alleyway behind the Green Dragon. He'd recalled it with devastating exactitude, like every occasion on which he had seen Morella disappear from a room with someone else's boyfriend, or return home in the smudged and creased garments of the night before. He ventured: 'He's a bit of a prick.'

Morella laughed bitterly. 'Always was.'

There was a silence. Stephen, driven by some envious demon, said, 'But you fucked him all the same.'

She shrugged, eyes wide open. 'I fucked lots of people.'

'Why?'

'Why not?'

'Because you didn't love any of them.'

'Oh, *love*. It's so much balls, Stephen, you know that?' Her eyes flicked over the cone of flowers lying on the bed. 'Or maybe not in your case. Maybe you're one of the lucky ones, with your Sweet Sue. I expect you're faithful to her, as well.'

'I try to be.' He'd never even been tempted to stray. But he felt on a knife-edge now.

'Always the honourable man. You never overstepped the mark, did you, Stephen? Even when I was half-naked on your bed.'

'I was supposed to be your friend, remember? The one you could trust.'

She frowned. 'I know I *said* that, Stephen. But – well, I wasn't conscious half the time.'

He stared at her. 'I wasn't going to rape you, if that's what you mean.'

'Why not?' she said carelessly. 'Other people did.'

His heart started to thump as he remembered her milky skin against the tousled bedclothes, the darker shape of her nipples showing through her pale green bra. 'Well, don't imagine I didn't think about it.' But he had never wanted her that way: limp, wasted, incapable of decision, lacking in any kind of joy. He imagined if it were his daughter in that state – vomiting and shoeless, knickers lost, blouse torn. He shuddered.

'So what stopped you then, Stephen?'

He paused, distracted by his own undeniable arousal. 'Perhaps you were too much of a sex goddess.' He laughed tightly. 'Or I was too much of a gentleman.'

'Well, you can do it now if you like.' She looked at him directly, the dark line around each iris almost hypnotically clear. She leant forward. He could feel her breath as she started to unbutton his coat, loosen his tie, his shirt. He was almost suffocated by the intensity of his desire. He could feel her hands against his bare chest, then around his waist, his belt, his flies. Then she said, matter-of-factly, 'I owe you something, after all.'

He pulled away from her sharply. She looked up, saw his dismay: 'What's the matter?'

'Is this just a payment for services rendered?'

She shrugged, eyes wide and ingenuous. 'It's the least I can do.'

'No.' He slowly rose, started to re-zip and re-button, his fingers shaking. He felt almost ill with the combination of revulsion and desire.

'Well, you don't need to pay me back,' he said roughly. 'I'll help you for free, Morella. For love, if you like. If you know what love means.' He placed the wad of newly drawn notes on the chest of drawers. 'I'm going home now. Thanks for a great evening. Just like old times.' He couldn't control the sarcasm in his voice. He felt a terrible, towering anger towards her. He wondered what he would have done if there'd been a knife handy.

She said nothing. Just sat on the bed, gripping the edge, the small white hole in her tights now the size of a pound coin. He swept up the flowers with a vicious movement. She said in a quiet voice: 'I'm afraid they're dying.'

He said, 'Yes. It's too hot in here. I should have known better.' And he closed the door.

Going down in the lift with its cheap fake wood and pinkish mirrored panels, he felt his anger begin to cool. The hotel was soulless and opaque. As he descended floor by floor, the doors pinging and opening on empty corridors, he kept visualizing Morella sitting alone on the chintzy bed. What would she do with herself tonight, tomorrow? And what would she do for the rest of her life? He'd been her last chance, she said. Her last chance on her flight from the dreadful past, the nightmare of incarceration and halfway houses. He imagined her opening her wash-bag, taking out a razor and cutting herself neatly across her wrist: *Put out the light, and then put out the light.*

A cold horror came over him. He'd been stupid and immature, expecting anything romantic from Morella. She hadn't come to find him because she cherished memories of the old days, but because of what he could offer – Mr Commuter with his expensive cashmere coat. She'd responded simply, as she'd always done; taking what she could, and giving the only thing she had to give. Morella had no scrap of romance in her soul: *It's so much balls.* He felt a gale of compassion for her.

In the foyer he eluded the knowing glance of the receptionist, went straight to the telephone box. Sue answered. Her voice sounded warm and real, and for the first time that evening he felt he could breathe properly. 'I've run into an old friend from Cambridge,' he said. 'She's in a bad way, needs a bed for the night. I've offered. D'you mind?'

'Of course not.'

'And I've got you some flowers.'

'Really?' He could hear her smile.

STAND WELL BACK

I wish I'd never mentioned the damned thing now. I never intended to. Just the usual first Thursday of the month drink: how's the wife, how's the job, that sort of thing. But Tim is the kind of bloke who gets things out of you. He always has, ever since we were schoolboys. His knowing silences always made me feel I had to say the first stupid thing that came into my head. The quieter he was, the more I blathered. The more I blathered, the more he smiled. It's been that way, more or less, for twenty-five years.

I eye him now across the table. His thinning hair, his worn shirt, his cockeyed spectacles, his worthy corduroy trousers – they're everything I loathe. He's gone down in the world since those prep-school days but he still behaves as if I'm the one who has to be patronized, even though I could buy and sell him three times over. It's not as if we have anything in common any more. So why do I go on meeting him – a whole evening once a month just so I can go away feeling terrible? My sister Di says it's survivor's guilt, whatever that means.

Tim's going on about blood being thicker than water. I can't believe it. 'No,' I say. 'Absolutely not.' I don't like to think about blood anyway. It's not what I associate with – well, with the whole Jane thing. So I object to Tim bringing it up. Of course I know why he has. Because although he helped me out, he never approved in the first place. And now he has a chance to say: 'I told you so.'

He puts his fingertips together, leans forward. 'Altruism is all very well, but there's a connection. An inviolable connection. And now it's caught you out.'

'Bollocks.' I start to get up. I've had to fit Tim in between the office and a Kennedy concert. It starts at eight, and I hate being late. 'I should never have told you. I knew you'd be critical.'

'Not critical, Matthew. I just feel you're not being honest with yourself.' He gives me the pitying-but-encouraging look. He's adept at it. He's done a course on it. He's someone with 'counselling skills'. It makes me want to puke. As does the Welsh rarebit congealing on my plate with its forlorn sprig of parsley. Tim seems immune to bad food, having just wolfed down an enormous baked potato filled with bright orange chicken tikka and some kind of bean. A hint of orange clings to his upper lip now. His glass of Speckled Hen sits untouched.

'Honest? For God's sake, Tim! It was a simple transaction. That was the whole beauty of it. I'd no right to barge in after all this time.'

'You may have been a bit, well, rash. But you must see you had a kind of right. An *emotional* right.' (Tim's strong on emotions, the inner child, all that jazz.) 'All you've done is woken up to the implications at last.'

'You would say that, wouldn't you?' I laugh. Tim's the complete New Man, carrying his kids around with him in some sort of papoose, changing nappies on any horizontal surface to hand, reading bedtime stories for hours on end, volunteering for playgroup duty, and so on and so forth. Three little girls, all under five, and a fourth (sex unknown) on the way. *We can't afford it, but we'll manage somehow. Children are the most valuable part of us, aren't they?* (Smile, smile) Ugh. I keep away from his little nest of domesticity as much as I can. It was a nice house once, Victorian, elegantly proportioned. Now it's a kind of kindergarten. The kitchen's impossible, even for a snack – awash with crayons and half-eaten cereal, littered with scribbled drawings which shed bits of glitter and dry macaroni all over the floor. The tiles are a death trap of rolling plastic and spilt drinks. It seems that every time I go, the girls (Tabitha, Freya and Edith) are bouncing about on the sagging sofas with cereal bars in their mouths, dribbling gunge onto my trousers, tugging my jacket out of shape in four different directions at once. In the midst of this, Saint Tim smiles pityingly at me: *Look what you don't have.* I play the game, make jokes, pretend to be a good uncle (and I'm remarkably good at it), but I can't wait to get out. Get back to peace. Privacy. Self. Yes, self, I admit it. I have no problem in admitting it. It may sound smug, but I like my life the way it is.

Tim cocks his head. 'But I'm right, aren't I? Blood *is* thicker than water.'

'You were always one for an original phrase.' I'm sneering again. Tim tends to make me sneer. I could be really hard on him but something always inhibits me from going too far. We have our roles, I suppose. I grit my teeth.

'You know it's not originality that counts, Matthew.' He smiles patiently, as if he has no idea how trite he's being, as if he's saying something incredibly worthwhile. Instead of which he sounds like a woman's magazine, and a downmarket one at that. 'It's not the *phrase*, is it? It's what lies behind it. That's why you're upset.'

'I'm not upset, for God's sake!' But I can hear my voice rising up the scale, and I'm beginning to have that odd feeling again. This thing must really be getting me down. I grope for my wallet. 'Look, I want to get *out* of this thing, not delve in deeper. Anyway, I've no time for your little homilies – I'm meeting Julia in the foyer in half an hour.' I pull out a ten pound note. Eating with Tim is always cheap, but he insists on paying half, counting out his change in the tray of a little leather purse. I've given up trying to argue.

Tim pats my arm, gently depositing some chicken tikka on the elbow of my new suit. 'You're in denial, Matthew. But believe me, it won't go away.'

I'd been mad even to risk it, although of course I never intended to. But when the Chief said we needed to go over to Charlie Gray's home ground if we were ever to get him on board for the Runsgate development, that was fine by me. I don't think I thought twice about it being Finsbury Park. Because, as I kept telling Tim, it honestly didn't bother me. I'd told Jane I'd keep away, and my word is my bond. *You're so beautifully old-fashioned*, she'd said, kissing my forehead. *We're so very, very lucky.* I admit that in the early days there'd been the occasional telephone call, the odd scribbled note. I think Jane and

Barbara had felt obliged – Barbara to a lesser extent, I imagine. But over the months, communication had stopped. And I'd been relieved.

So all Finsbury Park meant to me the day before was a business venue, and a pretty inconvenient one at that. I was mainly concerned that we wouldn't be stuck there all day, given the problems Charlie Gray was throwing up. I wanted to get done quickly and get back early. All my thoughts were on that. It looked like being a warm evening and I fancied sitting out on my balcony with a glass of Rioja, with the Thames in the distance and the early rush hour glittering past beyond the trees. As long as Nick Crisp didn't let me down with the figures and allow Charlie to spin things out till five o'clock. In the event Charlie made no bones. Agreed with all our projections. Thanked us for our hard work. End of story. And there we were out on the front steps at three o'clock in the afternoon. Free.

The weather by then was so glorious it seemed downright criminal to rush straight back into the stale dirt of the Tube. Even more so to share a taxi with Nick, whose main topic of conversation is the Arsenal. I decided to take a walk, a breath of fresh air after that cooped-up office with its smell of charred coffee and overheated copying machines. I left Nick to his own devices, and set off. When I came to the station, I turned left. I swear I might as easily have turned right, but the left looked more inviting. Sunnier, I suppose. I couldn't possibly have recognized anything; it was two years since the other time, and anyway, Tim had done all the navigating, getting lost, and calmly admitting that he didn't know this part of London 'all that well' and had only come to offer me 'moral support'.

So, although it was Finsbury Park, it might just as well have been Timbuktu. My thoughts were on the moment. Entirely on the moment. If I thought ahead in any way, it was to anticipate that early evening drink, or maybe a meal at Giuseppe's with Pippa or Isabel.

I walked on, following my nose, enjoying the freedom of an afternoon off. I crossed a little park and turned down a pleasantish road, thinking where I might go to pick up a taxi, when I saw it – the street name. It was framed neatly against a background of privet: *Primrose Crescent*. The name had always reminded me of Jane, especially the first time I saw her in the basement café at the Courtauld when she looked so small and pale and delicate. She'd been wearing a huge furry coat, and silver earrings. We'd taken to each other straight away.

'Are you sure you're not in love with her?' Tim had kept asking afterwards.

'Are you mad?'

'You talk about her a lot.'

'I always talk about women.'

'Matthew, this is not the same.'

'May I remind you, I am going into this with my eyes open.'

'So you think. But there'll be consequences. You'll see.'

Of course that was the moment to have turned back, poised on the corner of the street. I did think of it. I knew it was the sensible thing to do. But it was such an extraordinary coincidence that it seemed somehow perverse not to take a peep. And I *was* curious, I admit. I told myself it would do no harm just to pass by the door, just satisfy myself with the look of the place. I walked down the road. Then, when I got to the door, my feet seemed to stop of their own accord. And my hand went to open the little gate, and next thing I found myself walking up the path. It was the same time of year as before, and I recognized the creeper growing up the wall by the door – little white star-shaped flowers that I'd stared at so intensely that first time, waiting for the door to open. Not that I'd been nervous; just a little embarrassed. Tim, of course, had fussed around as if it were going to be him, not me, with the clean jam jar in the upstairs bedroom.

I found myself knocking, the same little brass knocker shaped like a leprechaun. They were bound to be out, of course, on such a lovely day. Then I heard a footstep inside, echoing on the tiled floor. I started to panic. Jane could have changed; all sorts of things could have changed. The door opened. It was Barbara.

'Hi, there,' I said, rather too gaily. 'It's Matthew – Matthew Mulholland.'

'Yes. I know who you *are*.'

Her dark brown eyes were blank with hostility. Words deserted me and I blustered something about being unexpectedly in the neighbourhood and feeling it was rude not to drop in. I felt pathetic, the schoolboy with a useless excuse. It was like being back at school, except Tim wasn't there to back me up. I made what I hoped was a wry face. 'Probably not a good idea. On reflection.'

'No.' She didn't help me out.

'No. Yes. Sorry.' But I still stood there; a formal idiot with a briefcase, wilting a little from the heat on the back of my neck.

And, perhaps for politeness, she conceded: 'You'd better come in, I suppose.'

'No, it's okay. Well, just for a minute if that's all right.' I stepped into the tiled hallway. She closed the door.

'They're not here. If that's what you came for –'

I tried to tell her I hadn't come for anything.

'– but they'll be back soon, and I don't want you here then. I don't want to be petty, Matthew, but that was our agreement, wasn't it?'

'Yes, yes, of course. You're right, of course.' I was ridiculously anxious to placate her, remembering how awkward it had always been between us. Jane used to laugh and say Barbara was inclined to be jealous: *Silly old sausage.*

She took me to the back of the house – the kitchen-diner, immaculate and bright with Jane's embroideries and cushions. Coloured building blocks were neatly stacked in a wooden tray. The garden beyond was full of flowers and shrubs. Barbara was a trained gardener, of course, and I'd always imagined her digging away in some market garden while Jane kept house and entertained visitors. In fact, she was wearing an apron and I could smell baking.

'Earl Grey, if I remember rightly?' She took a blue cup down from the dresser.

'That's right.' I was beginning to breathe again. Social niceties are very soothing. 'That's very clever of you. After all this time.'

'We know all your preferences off by heart.'

They'd written everything down, I remembered that now. It was all part of their philosophy. I'd filled in a whole questionnaire. Jane had told me the first time we met, what they were looking for. *It has to be personal,* she'd said. *But you need to keep well away afterwards.* I'd said there'd be no trouble there; I wasn't into complicated relationships. And I was certainly not into children. I told her about Tabitha, Freya and Edith, making such appalled faces that she laughed.

Oh, Matthew, she'd said, tucking into a sandwich. *You're just our type!*

I'd never been sure whether Barbara agreed. I often felt she disapproved of me, although we'd only met three times and I'd always been on my best behaviour. And when I'd looked over the questionnaire – well, without seeming to be too conceited – I felt it gave quite a good account of myself. Good education, good career, healthy, cultured, literate, plenty of interests, a full social life. She had nothing to complain about.

She turned to me suddenly. 'We'll fight you, you know, Matthew.'

I stared at her strong fingers around the cup, imagined for a wild moment she was going to hit me in the face.

'We'll go to court – anything – if you try to get him back.'

So that was the problem. I laughed with relief. 'God, no. Nothing further from my mind –'

'Why have you come, then?' She put her other hand over the first to steady the tremble. She was really worked up. I felt quite surprised.

'I don't know. Honestly. Just because I was here, I suppose. Just seeing that sign: *Primrose Crescent*. It was stupid . . .'

'– Because I won't stand for it. And don't think you can sweet-talk Jane into anything behind my back –'

'Barbara!' I touched her arm. Her brown skin was surprisingly soft. She pulled away sharply. I didn't know if it was me or men in general she disliked, but I felt rebuffed. 'Believe me, the thought never crossed my mind. It's the last thing I'd be interested in. As I said to Jane –'

She wasn't listening. 'David's everything to us. You can't just swan in here and just – impose yourself. Just because you're so well-off and think so much of yourself –'

'Hang on a minute!' My sympathy was ebbing away and I was beginning to feel annoyed. I'd only done the wretched thing in the first place because I was *asked*. Because I felt sorry for them both. Because I liked Jane and thought it would be a simple act of kindness. After all, what were a few million sperm to me, more or less? It was no big deal. However, it was a bit rich, her going on at me. I needed to calm her down. I lowered my voice, spoke slowly, in my best negotiating manner, what Di calls my 'soft soap'. 'Look. Barbara. Believe me,

nothing's changed. Nothing, right? Okay, I've made a mistake, coming here. And now I'm taking myself off. And you are going to forget
I ever came. Is that clear?'

She nodded. I felt magnanimous. I looked at the cup in her hand.
It was a nice piece of Worcester. 'Forget the Earl Grey. A bad idea.
Anyway, I prefer Lapsang these days.'

She smiled for the first time, and stretched to put the cup back on
the dresser. My eyes followed it. And that was when I saw him – the
chubby figure buttoned up against the winter in a blue coat and woolly
hood. He was looking right at me, smiling out of the frame as if he
knew me, as if he were there in the room. David.

I don't know what I said (if I said anything). My whole body was
in shock, as if I'd moved abruptly to another world and back again.
I just remember Barbara's voice, disembodied, as if I were coming
round after anaesthetic, 'Yes, he's really like you, isn't he? I noticed
it at the front door. Gave me a bit of a turn, in fact. Your eyes are
exactly the same.'

I could only manage a grunt. My mouth was dry, my head whirling.
I put out my hand, touched it gently to his cheek through the glass. I
started to stroke his face and found I couldn't stop. My finger went
back and forth, back and forth as if I could rub him into existence
like a genie from a lamp. I wanted the eyes to be looking at me, the
mouth to be making sounds I could hear. I wanted to be able to touch
his skin, speak to him. After a while I sensed Barbara shifting a bit at
my shoulder. 'D'you want to keep it? We'd often wondered, but you'd
never asked, all this time, and so – well, we left it alone.'

I nodded. 'Please.'

She tried to take the frame from me, but my hand wouldn't let it
go. 'Matthew,' she said. 'I'll give it back, you know. I just need to . . .'
She unclasped my fingers one by one, eased out the photo, handed it
back: 'There.'

'Thanks.' I slipped it into my breast pocket, behind my folded
handkerchief. I didn't quite know what to do next. I knew I had to
go, but I hated the idea of leaving the room, the place where he spent
his time with the piled bricks and the wooden toys, the light from the
garden window shining on his hair. I turned to the door, feeling oddly

giddy. Then turned back to Barbara: 'Don't tell Jane. Not just about the photo. This – anything. No need.'

'That's it, then? You don't want to see him?'

I tried to find my old confident voice, and miraculously it came. I grinned at her. 'You know me and kids. Hate the little buggers.'

She took me in her arms and hugged me. She smelt of geraniums and cake.

So – an altogether stupid, unnecessary episode. And now, two nights later, I'm lying here, staring into the dark, unable to sleep. I thought the concert would have put me in a different frame of mind. Kennedy was fantastic, and I came out on a high, the music thrumming through my brain. But the moment I'd put Julia into her taxi, that little face flipped back into my mind. I see him everywhere now. In the Tube. On the stairs to my flat. In the hallway. In every room I go into. I haven't managed a wink in two nights, even with Di's absolute no-fail sleeping pills.

I get up, lie on the sofa, listen to Callas, drink my way through the last of the Reserva Rioja. I've forgotten the concert already. Forgotten what Julia said, her hair, her dress. I just remember *him*, looking like someone I'd like to know. It's insane.

I wash my dirty glass, plump up cushions, tidy my books, listen to the World Service, read yesterday's paper. Tomorrow I'll forget all this nonsense. I have to do it. Tim is wrong; it will go away.

Anna at the office takes one look and says, 'Late night?'

'Couldn't sleep. It must have been that particularly disgusting Welsh rarebit with Tim.'

'Tim with the wonky glasses?' She laughs. Anna is very smart. As in clever and as in looks. She clearly wonders where Tim fits into my life, why I keep up the monthly ritual. She doesn't understand how complex it all is. How much I hate him for his sanctimonious, self-satisfied, wiseacre opinions; how much I love him for them, too. I've always needed Tim to keep me in focus. I need to know he's there; that he still cares enough to turn up rain or shine; that he comes bouncing back even though I abuse him and crow over him, and thrust my rich and wonderful life in his face at every opportunity. I always dread that one day he'll stop coming and that I'll be on my own.

Anna leans over me with a cloud of musky perfume as she brings me up to date with my diary. 'The Chief wants you in his office at ten to congratulate you and Nick on the Westhouse business, and Mr Mohammed Akhtar is coming in at eleven to check on progress with the franchise.' She also tells me over her shoulder that Sarah in Accounts is leaving today and I have to make the farewell speech.

'Remind me again why she's leaving.' I can't remember who Sarah is. Some clerical assistant, off to pastures new, I suppose.

'She's having a baby, Matthew. You signed the card, remember?'

'Baby. Ah, yes.' I pretend to look over the contract from Westhouse. After a minute or two I ask, 'What about the father?'

'*Father?*' Anna looks round, in a puzzled way, from her irrigation of our office fern.

'I suppose there's a man in the picture? Unless, of course, it's an Immaculate Conception.'

'I doubt that, from what I hear of Sarah.' Anna's back with the fern again. 'Anyway, it's not my business.'

And not mine either. After all, I don't remember who she is or what she looks like. And from today she won't even be on the payroll. But I can't help asking, 'Is she going to be all right? For the future, I mean.'

'Bit late now if she isn't.' Anna doesn't seem very concerned, picking off dead fronds. 'Anyway, why shouldn't she be? It's the twentieth century. Who needs a man to bring up a baby?'

'Who indeed?' It's what I've always said: *Light blue touchpaper and stand well back*. I finger the photograph in my breast pocket. It's getting dog-eared. I'll have to find a frame for it soon, or press it between the pages of a book. Soon. But not quite yet. I can't part with it yet. As I think of it, something clots in my chest, something hard and uncomfortable. I clear my throat.

'Are you okay?' Anna looks across at me.

'Just tired.' My face is aching; there's a pain behind my eyes. I need to concentrate on something else. The farewell speech, that's it. I'm good at that sort of thing. I can do it standing on my head. I'll tell Sarah in Accounts how much we have appreciated all the hard work she's done over the (however long) she's been with us. I'll tell her that we'll all miss her, but that we wish her every happiness for the future. Because . . . because, of course, she's got something to look forward to – that's it. And it's sad for us, but it's not sad for her. Because she'll be able to see the child grow up, and, yes, maybe he'll have the same eyes as her. And he'll look at her with that special look that makes your heart want to break . . .

I can feel the wetness on my cheeks. And now here's Anna coming towards me. She's a bit blurred. I can't hear what she's saying. Her face looks uncomprehending. I want to make a joke but I can't seem to make my mouth work. She puts out her hand, but I don't want her near me with her smooth face and smooth clothes and smell of patchouli. I don't want her long elegant fingers and immaculately painted nails. I want the smell of geraniums and baking, and the sight of small hands playing with coloured bricks.

SALAD DAYS

When I get home, she's standing by the cooker. Wearing that pink cotton housecoat that flattens her breasts, gives her a sexless, no-nonsense air. And though she's standing by the cooker, there won't be any food coming out of it. Because it's Friday. And Fridays are salad days. Winter and summer, year in, year out.

She raises her eyes, gives me the look she's been perfecting all day: depressed and aggressive at the same time. It makes her face bleak, but I pretend I haven't noticed. Last thing I want to do is start an argument.

I come towards her with a smile. I haven't brought flowers – too obvious under the circumstances. I open my arms instead, move towards her lips: 'Hello, sweetheart.'

She moves her head aside so I catch the edge of her ear and a strand of the wispy hair that has escaped from her dragged-back ponytail. All she says is, 'You're late. And that peppermint trick doesn't fool me.'

I brazen it out. I tell her Janet Sims passed a packet round to show her appreciation for us all staying late on a Friday. And it's not exactly a lie; Janet *did* get out the Extra Strongs at one stage. Okay, some of us went for a jar after that, but there's no point in telling Denise the truth because she gets it all out of proportion. It's not as if she doesn't know what it's like after work. After all, she used to come with us when she was part of the Section. Sitting in the corner twiddling her Babycham, watching me all the time out of the corner of her eye. Smiling then. Laughing at my jokes. Looking sweet and lovely. But she's forgotten all that.

'It's the same every flaming Friday.' She picks up a tea towel and wipes a perfectly clean worktop. 'Other people get back *early* at the weekend. Other people *care* about their wives.'

'Well, *other people* aren't in the Emergency Payments Section, are they? And you know what it's like there on Friday afternoons – queues practically round the block. You'd think, wouldn't you, that they'd spread their domestic crises through the week a bit, to give us poor sloggers a chance to get the giros out. But there you go – no consideration. They don't seem to realize that we've got wives and families too.'

She looks at me, weighing me up. She doesn't understand irony. And she doesn't understand the system. It actually makes no odds how late we work on Fridays, the payments won't get there before Monday – and I couldn't care less. But Denise looks a bit ashamed. She used to be a real bleeding heart in the old days, coming up from the interviews practically crying, saying how could this man leave his wife and kids with nothing to live on, *just nothing at all*? She went a bit over the top, to be honest, and Janet had to take her off the desk and move her upstairs. Opposite me, in fact. Which was where it all began.

I gesture to the pristine oven: 'Can I give you a hand?'

'It's only salad.' She's waiting for me to say something, but I'm not going to put myself in the wrong.

'Fine,' I say, brightly.

'Cheese salad.' She waits again. She knows I hate cheese. At least, I hate the cheap vacuum-packed stuff she sticks on the plate. Dry and sour-tasting, like concentrated earwax.

'Fine,' I say. 'Haven't had a *decent* piece of cheese for ages.'

'Well, I can't be expected to do everything. Not on a Friday.'

'Cheese is fine.'

'I know you're not keen on it, but it's all I could manage.'

'Cheese is wonderful.'

'Why do I have to rush around all the time? On Fridays too?'

'You don't have to, sweetheart.' (Not that she does. She's home all day, mooning around.) 'I've told you, I'll go down the pub. Have a pie and a pint.'

'A pie and five pints. Or not even the pie, just the pints. I know you, Philip Bessant.'

Yes siree, she knows me all right. She makes a career out of knowing me, all my weaknesses. If only she'd just lay off, we could manage. Instead, she keeps at it, the broken record: 'Yes, I know *you* all right.'

'I think we've had that line.' I sit myself at the kitchen table. It's laid for two, her idea of high style. Stainless steel knives and forks, stainless steel condiment set, beige paper napkins folded into triangles, tumblers with coloured patterns, a glass jug with some kind of murky squash.

'Oh, very funny.' She goes over to the fridge and takes out two plates of salad. Not only unappetizing, but ice-cold, too. She casts them onto the Formica – like pearls before swine – and sits down.

I stare at the leathery green leaves, the mound of little cheesy shavings, the aniline colour of beetroot bleeding into a hard-boiled egg.

'Pretty,' I say.

She glares. We eat in silence.

I chase a baby beetroot round the plate with my fork. The salad is fibrous as well as icy. It sticks in my teeth, gives me toothache. I really hate Fridays.

Denise puts her plate to one side, looks at the clock. 'Well, I'd better go and get ready. She's coming at seven.'

'Right.'

'Well, I don't want to keep her waiting, do I?'

'Of course not.'

'There you go again.'

'I haven't said a word.'

'That's just it. Silent sarcasm.'

'*Silent* sarcasm!' I raise my eyebrows, impressed.

She gets up, pushing her chair back noisily against the floor tiles. 'There you are! That's exactly what I mean!'

I pick a bit of lettuce stalk from my teeth. 'I don't know why you make yourself rushed like this. Why don't you get yourself something earlier? No need to wait for me.'

'I'm not starting that. We eat together.' She whacks the plates on top of each other, crushing my leftover beetroot till it trickles its juice down her hand.

'One night a week wouldn't hurt. Just stick the meal in the oven.' I smile. 'Unless, of course, it's salad.'

'There you go again!' She slams the dishes in the sink, runs a conversation-drowning gush of hot water on them.

'For God's sake, Denise! Just a –'

'And I'm not putting your dinner in the oven. Ever! Do you hear?'

Difficult not to. But I know what the trouble is. Her bloody dad; all those burnt remains thrown at the wall week after week.

'Okay,' I say. 'If that's what you want. I was only trying to help.'

But I can't help. Not any more. Once, I could make her laugh. I could comfort her, and she was grateful. Now, everything I say is wrong.

The baby business started it off, I suppose. I didn't think she'd be keen, after what she'd been through. I thought that was the point of getting married – to get her away from all that family stuff; liberate her, give her new experiences. God knows I tried. But every month she was there with the calendar, doing the calculations, then crying in the lavatory when she came on. Of course it was my mistake, not taking it seriously. I used to tell her it was 'early days'. I used to say, 'let's enjoy ourselves a bit first'. But she'd look at me as if I'd hit her.

I got to dreading it every month when she'd come to me red-eyed, holding a hot water bottle to her belly, saying she wasn't going in to work: 'It hurts too much.' I don't know what was worse, those awful days when I felt so useless, or the ones that came after – when she'd put on her night clothes as soon as we finished supper and turn off the telly with a meaningful look. She'd pull me off the sofa and rush me upstairs like we had a quota to meet. I didn't always feel like it, to tell you the truth. I wanted to have a drink or two, watch the sport. Not get all hot and bothered at eight o'clock at night. And she was so bloody intense that it was difficult to get in the mood, in spite of the heavy doses of Obsession and the lacy underwear. And as time went on, she got so anxious and tight, she would hardly let me inside her. And then she'd wince and dig in her nails, and I'd shrivel up completely.

After a while she gave up work and took to lying on the bed for hours, staring up at the ceiling, not saying a word. Every evening I'd sit downstairs on my own, propped up on the settee with her brick-hard scatter cushions sticking in my back, just waiting for a movement, some kind of sound from above. I'd watch everything on the box, any kind of rubbish, and read the paper till it nearly fell apart. But she never called to me, never came down. Eventually I started to nip down to the pub for a breather, to speak to somebody who'd bother to reply. She started to say I didn't care. I started to wonder if I did.

Now we only snipe at each other. For some reason, the whole thing's my fault. I don't know – perhaps it is. Perhaps I shouldn't have married her. Feeling sorry for her wasn't enough. But in the early days when she used to lean over my desk with that pile of unnecessary filing and that terrible need in her eyes, I thought I was the one who could make her happy.

I sit at the kitchen table contemplating an Apple Pie For One. I can hear her getting ready upstairs. I can hear the floorboards creak in the lavatory just above me. Now the flush. Now the stomp across the landing. Now the wardrobe door and the jangle of wire hangers. Now silence, while she gets into her dress, wriggling and grasping for the zip.

I open the packet and take out the pie. It smells stale. The apple filling is smooth and boiled-down, like jam. Cheap jam, too: all sugar, no fruit. But I'm hungry, so I'll eat it all the same.

Now I hear the sound of the dressing-table drawer, the one that sticks and then comes free with a jerk, sending all her little bottles rolling around inside. She'll be sitting in front of the mirror, now, staring at her face, thinking she's too pale. Then on it'll all go – basecoat, topcoat, gloss varnish, the lot. She'll be stretching her face in all directions, opening her mouth to do her eyelashes, munching at a tissue to wipe off her lipstick, brushing and drawing and painting until she's satisfied.

I eat my pie in silence.

Now she's up again. More stomping, harder this time with her heels on. Bang of the wardrobe door. Twice. Now the bedroom door opening: 'Has she come yet?'

'No.' I finish my tart, throw away the foil dish. Open the fridge.

She's in the lav again. Another flush, hiss of aerosol, thunk of bolt. 'Isn't she here yet?'

'No.' I close the fridge.

I don't know why she gets so worked up. It's only a lot of women.

*   *   *

'You don't like me going out, do you?' She's come down, looking at herself in the hall mirror, combing her hair. Parting it first one side then the other.

'Rubbish.'

'I know you don't.'

'Then you know wrong.'

'But you like to go out. Why shouldn't I go out too?'

'No reason.'

'It's only for a couple of hours.'

It's usually much longer than that, but Denise has an elastic notion of 'a couple'. I say: 'I don't mind. Enjoy yourself.'

'I suppose you'll be off to the Buccaneer the moment my back is turned.'

'Maybe. Just for a couple of drinks.' My notion of a couple can be just as elastic.

'You know, you never ask.'

'Never ask what?'

'What we're going to do. On Fridays.'

'None of my business.'

'Aren't you curious?'

'I can cope with the burden of ignorance.'

She throws down the comb. 'There you go again!'

I suppose it's silent sarcasm, but I don't have to defend myself because the doorbell rings. It's Gill. She steps just inside the door. Reluctantly, as if the house might contaminate her. She's very tall and has a very loud voice, which she uses all the time. It always makes me feel exhausted just to listen. Not that I do. But Denise is obsessed by Gill's ideas. She's always into some new therapy or other. One week it was a completely raw diet – sunflower and pumpkin seeds. We couldn't even eat bread. Luckily Denise didn't like it any more than I did, and we were back to cold meat salads in a trice. I don't think Gill could have stuck with it either because they all went for a carvery two weeks later. Roast beef or turkey with a choice of six veg. Traditional veg, that is.

Gill ignores me. 'Okay?' she says to Denise, jingling her car keys.

'Hello, Gill. How are you keeping?' I wave to her from the sitting-room door with a can of beer I've just opened.

'Fine, thanks.' She can be terse when she wants to. But after the door is closed I can hear them both laughing. Gill's telling some anecdote. I can't hear the words, but I can imagine the sort of thing she's saying. I hear the car door slam.

I hate being alone in the house. My day crowds in on me. I don't know why I go on doing this job; it's the same thing over and over again. You'd think they'd come up with something original, but I could tell you what's on the bloody forms before I look at them. The boyfriend who smashes the place up. The husband who spends all the giro. The ex-lover who breaks back in and nicks the furniture. Slashed mattresses, water pipes pulled out of the wall, injunctions, robbery, violence, money for crime. I don't know how they get themselves in this state. It depresses the hell out of me. So I think I'm entitled to the odd drink. It's not a lot to ask.

I generally go to the Buccaneer. There's usually someone I know. Mostly it's Nick. He's an estate agent – or rather an estate agent's lackey. Shows people around houses, that sort of thing. Nothing major league. He's talking about his wife, as usual. He hates her, and makes the mistake of thinking the rest of us are interested. 'She wants me to be there while she paints her flaming nails. Or chats to her bloody friends on the phone for hours. I'm not having that, Phil. Understand me? Understand what I mean?' Nick's a bore. And a drunk. I don't know why I put up with him. I order a couple of whiskies and settle down for the night.

I'm a bit drunk myself when I come home. I admit it. And it's a bit later than I intended, too. Denise is back. The light's blazing from the bedroom.

She's lying fully dressed on top of the duvet, shoes halfway across the room. She's staring up at the ceiling. She looks particularly small and thin.

I drape myself casually in the doorway: 'Had a good time?'

'Thank you. You have too, I see.'

Not-so-silent sarcasm from the little lady. But I let it pass. 'Only so-so, as matterafact. Got stuck with Nick. Impossible to get away.'

She stares at the ceiling. 'It's his wife I feel sorry for.'

'Naturally.'

She turns her head to look at me. 'What do you mean – *naturally*?'

'Because – bless her – she's painting her fingernails to the bone to keep a decent home for him, and he's a soak, a lush, an alky. Nuff said.'

She sits up, gives me one of her stares, the sort where she tries to work out if I'm being funny. She can't decide. She lies back. 'Some people feel sorry for *me*.'

I suppose she's been on about the baby thing again, drumming up some sympathy from the Sisterhood. You'd think she'd let it rest. 'Never mind, petal. Take no notice.'

She seems to be expecting something more. I smile, try: 'Just forget about 'em. Don't know what they're talking about. You're okay, Denise, you're okay.'

'I know I'm okay. It's not me that's the problem.'

'Oh?' I'm not really following her now. I can see she's upset, though. I need to take it carefully. It's easy to make a mistake in situations like these. Delicate situations. Delicate – things. My head feels blurry.

'You know what I mean. Please don't pretend.' There's a childish wobble in her voice that reminds me of how she used to be. When she used to tell me about her dad and all the quarrels and how she couldn't bear being at home. And I would listen to her. And put my arm around her. And protect her. I want to protect her now, to love her. She's rolled away from me, now. I can see her dress is undone. The long zip is open all the way down her back. I can see the whiteness of her bra, the top of her pants.

'Denise. Sweetheart –' I try to move forward, but the room has become suddenly treacherous. I have to hold on to the dressing table. The bottles and jars rattle. My fingers are sweaty on the kidney-shaped glass that covers the surface.

Her back's still turned. Her voice comes out flat. 'Gill's right. Every bit of my life's been ruined by drink.'

'Oh, bloody brilliant. As if you needed telling. Didn't you say she's a bit slow off the mark with her amazing insight?'

But I don't understand this *every bit* of my life' angle. After all, it's in the past. Denise is over all that now. Well over. Last time she even saw her father was at our wedding – when he'd grabbed at every passing sleeve to say how 'bloody, bloody beautiful' she was, before falling under the bar stool for the duration. She hasn't spoken to him since, thank God. And Denise, bless her, *never* drinks, except for silly little things like shandy. Or Babycham. So Gill's just making trouble.

I start towards the bed. I want to make her laugh. 'Never mind, Denise. You'll be all right, petal. Babycham doesn't count.'

But she doesn't laugh. In fact, I think she might be crying. The sound's muffled by the pillow but the bed's shaking. Her shoulders are shaking too. She's looking tiny and childlike.

I want to hug her, make it better. The bed looks a long way off but I think I can make it. Once I've got her in my arms it'll be all right. 'Never mind,' I say. 'You don't need to worry.'

'You don't understand.' Her voice is thick; she's definitely crying. All this talk has brought it all back. I'll have to speak to Gill, tell her to lay off. Explain that Denise is very vulnerable where drink's concerned. And she gets things all mixed up. Like now. She's murmuring, 'It's not *me* I'm worried about.'

'Well, who else then, sweetheart? It's not as if we had any –' I hear the quick hiss of indrawn breath. Bit of a mistake to bring that up, specially this time of night. But it's too late. I see her shoulders tense.

She turns on me. 'Between you and my dad, it's a good thing we *haven't* got any kids.'

I stare at her. She has got it so wrong. 'Look, I may overdo it sometimes – but I'm not an alcoholic, for God's sake!'

'Nobody ever is.' Her mascara is smudged, streaked down her cheeks. Her panda eyes look ridiculous with her blond hair. 'How many have you had tonight, for example?'

I can see where she is going wrong. Tonight wasn't typical. Not typical at all. That's where she's making her mistake. She just can't compare me with her father. There's a world of difference; she needs to get that straight. I tell her: 'Not all that many.'

She continues looking at me, so I give in a bit. 'Well, perhaps a few more than usual. You know what Nick's like. Won't take no for an answer.'

'Shorts, I suppose?'

'A coupla whiskies. So what? Nick was paying. You know what he's like.'

'I know what *you're* like.' The same old record. She turns away again, wipes her eyes on the duvet cover, leaving black smudges on the pink candy stripes. 'They all know.'

This is a new one, a new development. 'All who?'

She doesn't answer.

'All *who*?' I'm beginning to get annoyed. This is typical of Denise. She starts things, then goes all silent on me.

'They all feel sorry for me. The way you carry on. Arguing and drinking.'

I get it. The bloody Sisterhood. They've got their knives out, as per usual. Nick, me, any poor bloke in their sight'll cop it. Oh yes. I don't know why I let her go out with them. Poisonous bitches, the lot of them.

'What do *they* know about it then? Unless a certain little birdie has been flitting around saying a whole lot of things she shouldn't?'

She laughs. Her lipstick is all smeared, like jam against the pale pastry of her face. 'Lies! That's a good one. The girls don't need me to tell them anything about you. They can see it for themselves. You're a drunk. *A self-righteous, self-pitying, and depressive drunk* – that's what Gill said.'

I see Gill saying it. They're just her kind of words. And I see the rest of them, heads together, mouths opening and shutting like some bloody chorus. I'm enraged. I'm incandescent: 'That's nice. That's bloody nice. So they think they know me, do they? Think they know what makes me tick? I'd like to have them here. I'd wipe the smile off their bloody faces. Who do they think they are, bloody Gill and Co., some kind of bloody psychol-ologists?' I have difficulty getting the word out.

Denise laughs again. 'There you are! Can't even talk properly!'

She lies there on my bed. In the house I pay for. In the dress I bought her. Laughing. She has no right to laugh. A skinny, panda-eyed woman who can't cook, can't have babies, won't have sex. What kind of woman is that? She's making a fool of me, I can see that now. It's gone on too long. Far too long.

I lurch towards her, tripping over her shoes, her stupid high heels catching on the shagpile. I kick them out of the way. She sees me coming and starts to scramble off the bed on the other side, dragging the duvet with her. But I'm there already. I grab her by the wrist and pull her back on the bed. She's light, like a doll, like a dummy. Her dress is coming off. She's starting to scream.

Afterwards, I'm sorry. I tell her that. I put her back on the pillow, wipe her eyes, stroke her hair. I love her really. I tell her that too, and she seems to be listening. Her eyes are swollen, but she seems to be looking at me. I keep telling her I just had one too many. I keep telling her it won't happen again.

She doesn't move but I think she understands. I think she's smiling.

ROOM FOR MANOEUVRE

It was a single room – a servant's room – up on the eighth floor in an unfashionable quarter. It was a very small room and very plain. I hated it. But Paris was expensive and it was all I could afford.

When I'd moved in I'd had plans for redecorating. Nobody, I thought, could live in so hideous a room for long. High cold light came in from a high cold window. A large ornate wardrobe gave a semblance of style, but it had doors that refused to stay shut. The rest of the furniture was cheap and ugly – a narrow bed, a trestle table, a wooden chair, a cramped miniature cooker. Opposite the wardrobe, over the mantelpiece, was a small mirror. It was badly cracked, as if a former tenant, driven to despair, had savagely attacked it. The world it now reflected was jagged and prismatic and the face that looked back at me was disjointed and crazy. That object at least I felt belonged to me.

The facilities of the room were as limited as the furnishings. There was no basin, no tap. All water had to be collected in a tall enamel jug from the communal sink on the landing. The management had, however, provided me with a portable bidet so difficult to conceal that I gave up any pretence of doing so, using it as a prop to keep the wardrobe doors closed. But it was rather too light for the purpose, and at regular intervals it would crash to the floor as the doors returned to their preferred position obstructing the middle of the room.

When I'd got on the boat train at Waterloo two months before, I'd still been in the artificial high spirits which had buoyed me up since walking out of Gerald's life. I was exuberant. I'd freed myself of two whole years of subjugation, of moulding all my thoughts and actions around one man's desires and preferences. London was Gerald's city: but Paris was mine. It was where I'd been happiest and where I'd first led an independent life. It was the obvious place to go. And there had been one of those moments of serendipity when it feels that Fate is on your side. A bursary had become available from the Photographic Society, and I'd got it with hardly any effort. I'd never done such a brilliant interview; never been so assertive, so confident. I'd convinced them that, given a chance to spend six months wandering the lesser-known streets of Paris, I would bring home a portfolio of pictures to rival Cartier-Bresson.

But all that manic energy had broken down once I'd arrived. I realized too late that it was one thing to be wretched; it was quite another to be wretched in a foreign city without friends. I lost my briefly acquired nerve and drifted into isolation – or what passed for isolation, because Gerald was always in my thoughts. I kept wondering if I could have acted differently if there had been another way out. I even asked myself if I'd been fair to him; if I had behaved unreasonably – high-handedly even – in walking out the way I did and not giving him another chance. I was in the right, I told myself. But every night I lay awake until the small hours, re-enacting that final disruptive scene, trying to give it a more satisfactory ending.

I'd been in the flat when Gerald had come back from work. It was only three-thirty, and although he finished early from time to time, the moment I saw him I sensed that something serious was wrong. His skin was puffy and his eyes were too bright. I knew the signs of heavy drinking in Gerald by then, though they were not easy to detect. To anyone else he would have simply seemed a self-possessed man with more than his fair share of energy and vigour. He threw down his keys and stood for a moment in the middle of the room, giving me a long look. Long looks in the afternoon usually meant sex, but not this time. This time he seemed almost stunned. 'Oh, Jenny,' he said, shaking his head sadly, tears starting to his eyes. 'Something's happened. I can't really believe I've made such a fool of myself. But I want you to know – and believe – that I still love you.'

'Well, that's good.' I said, trying to sound light-hearted. I'd never known him to be maudlin before. He always held his drink remarkably well.

He came forward and almost fell on me. I could smell his sweet winey breath, the aftermath of a rich meal. 'You have to forgive me,' he muttered.

'For what?' I laughed, trying to fend him off. I felt embarrassed. But underneath my embarrassment was a cold, lurching fear. Gerald never admitted guilt for anything, and certainly never asked for forgiveness. Things didn't trouble him the way they troubled other people. He only acknowledged problems in so far as they offered an opportunity for solutions, and he never voiced regrets. (*What's the point?* he'd say.) So for him to be even the slightest bit emotional was unusual. And it couldn't all be down to drink.

Eventually he let me go and fell back on the sofa, sinking his face in his hands in a gesture that seemed too theatrical to be sincere. He gave a long sigh and paused, as if expecting me to say something. Something soothing, no doubt, something that would make him feel better. But I was at a loss, my mind spooling out wildly like a broken film. I could only think that he'd been found out in some kind of fraud; something the gutter press would latch on to, something that would mean the end of his career. I discounted as a matter of course that it might be a love affair. After all, I knew Gerald wasn't faithful, and he knew I knew. Although we never spoke of it, on certain days I could tell that he'd taken another woman to bed because of his heightened animation and effulgent vivacity. I never made even an oblique comment. As long as he came back to me I decided I wouldn't stir up trouble. Gerald hated women who nagged and fussed.

'Forgive you for what?' I said again. He rubbed his hair with his hands and in bits and pieces began to bluster his way through the explanation. I stood like stone as the story came out. It seemed he had 'somehow or other' got engaged to be married. That very lunchtime, in fact, in a restaurant in Soho. To a woman called Sarah Latimer whom he had been meeting on and off at 'various events' for the last six months. She'd taken quite a shine to him, he didn't know why. In fact, she had called the shots and more or less made the proposal herself. She was a nice girl. A very nice girl, so that Gerald had been taken aback. Caught off-balance. Made to feel sorry for her. Agreed to it in a kind of whirl without thinking of the consequences.

I stood in front of him, astounded. 'Jenny darling –' He raised his big puppy eyes to me. 'I didn't mean it to happen this way – well, *any* way, in fact. But she's very sweet, and I can't get out of this without a hell of a lot of bother. Damaging bother. And it needn't be that way. If you stick with me, I'll make it up to you. Because you're the only one who matters to me. Sarah will help me get on, of course. She's been brought up to this sort of life and can only do me good, but that will help you too.' He paused. 'Look, I know it's not ideal, but we could make this thing work. It could be great for both of us . . .'

I could see it all – Gerald weekending in the country with Sarah, weekdaying in Whitehall with other up-and-coming men, and popping back to see me about bedtime. I was enraged. How dare he propose such a shabby second-rate relationship for both us women? I told him he was contemptible. He winced: 'You're right. I don't deserve you – either of you.' And then he threw himself back on his plump silk cushions in a gesture so tragic that it almost made me laugh. He had nerve, Gerald. He really thought he'd get away with it.

But he didn't. I packed and left him the same day. All my friends said I was doing the right thing, cheered me on, patted me on the back, gave me tea and sympathy and lots of vodka: *The cheek of him,* they said. *You're far better off on your own. He was just holding you back. You can follow your own career now.* But I was used to Gerald, to his expansive nature, to his ability to make decisions, to take me places, and to make me laugh. I was miserable without him. And Paris and that wretched room was making everything worse. I had hardly spoken to anyone since I'd arrived. Some days I'd go and sift through the archives in the library, or shut myself up in one of the Academy darkrooms, passing only the time of day with the curators or caretakers, asking brief questions as to where I might find fixing solutions or developing trays. Most days, however, I walked about on my own, trying to collect material for my projected exhibition back in London. In spite of my big talk about following in the footsteps of Cartier-Bresson, I felt inhibited by the Master as I wandered the very streets he had wandered. I'd hoped to see French working life from an outsider's point of view, but I found myself photographing the same old clichés of Parisian life as I sat on park benches in the Tuileries watching children at play in sandpits, or sailing boats in the *grand basin* across the river, supervised by foreign au pairs. And everywhere I looked there were promenading lovers. I photographed waiters in pavement cafés in the Latin Quarter, street cleaners in Porte de la Villette, and streetwalkers in Pigalle. But everything seemed hackneyed. My eye and hand felt dull. I was wandering about like a ghost, covering a great deal of ground but not making much headway. Each night I would return, jaded, to the dreadful room.

I hated it every time I opened the door. It was so awful it was not even worth decorating. I took to flicking through the pages of *Le Figaro* to see what other rooms might be to let, but all the ads were for two-room apartments and always too expensive. There was a crisis among the *immobiliers* I was told. Rents in Paris were sky-high, especially if you wanted to live in the central arrondissements. So I resigned myself to sticking it out. It was only for another four months after all, and I was away most of the day. I'd taken to eating at a little café on the corner – almost as cheap as cooking my own, and a good deal better. And I'd found somewhere to wash – a hall of residence for Catholic students. They didn't seem to mind that I was not, strictly speaking, a student or indeed a Catholic. They were happy to take my one franc fifty for the use of their showers and laundry room. I could thus avoid using the unspeakable encrusted lavatory on the eighth floor, which could only be opened by the insertion of a portable doorknob into the spindle-hole, and which, once entered, gave off a smell that made the gorge rise. I had only used it once and couldn't help wondering how the other tenants managed to cope with it every day. Mademoiselle Regnier, for example. She had the room opposite mine, a single servant's box room (as they all were on the eighth floor), and she was old and frail. I'd sometimes see her in the dim corridor, painfully dragging the enamel jug to and from the tap. I'd never spoken to her. She avoided my glance. I only knew her name by the faded white card pinned to the frame of her door by a rusty drawing pin. *Mademoiselle Regnier,* it said in full. *Sonnez fort S.V.P.*

The sad but assertive singularity of her title made me curious about her, as did the odd hours she kept. Sometimes if I was awake at night, I heard her emerging from her room, breathing heavily, walking slowly down the creaking stairs. Once, coming home in the early hours, I'd seen her emerge from the shadows of the entrance arch and set off into the dark street. Sometimes her solitude reinforced mine, and I saw myself foreshadowed in her existence. I wanted to know more about her.

This curiosity was quickened when I had a conversation with Cherbal. He was the unofficial caretaker of the flats. There was no concierge – the apartments were too lowly for that – but Cherbal, who was a fruit porter, undertook the general maintenance of the building. Every morning he hosed down the courtyard and once a week he saw to the collection of the bins. He was a big, muscular man with flashing white teeth and the air of a circus performer. He lashed the water from his hose around the walls and windows of the courtyard like a lion tamer. Whenever he saw me coming, he would pretend to direct the hose at me, then turn instead to flush out some rotten cabbage leaf from a corner. *Passez! Passez, Mademoiselle*! he would shout urgently, as if his ringmaster skills would soon fail and the wild water hose get the better of him.

However, one day he'd stopped me in the courtyard for more protracted conversation. He wanted to know if I had the key to the top-floor lavatory. It was important to keep it locked, he said, so it would not be rendered unfit by unauthorized users. A propos of this I expressed sympathy with poor little Mademoiselle Regnier, so old, and with so many stairs to climb. Cherbal shook his head and lifted an admonitory finger. 'Keep away from that woman,' he warned me, his eyes fierce. I expressed surprise. She seemed such a sweet little lady, I said. But Cherbal repeated the head-shaking and the finger-wagging. '*Méfiez-vous, Mademoiselle,*' he reiterated. '*Méfiez-vous de cette femme.*'

I decided there was something unstable about Cherbal's flashing eyes and flashing teeth and general air of performance, and that I would make my own mind up about Mademoiselle Regnier. But moments later she became of marginal interest to me when I unlocked my letterbox and found a letter from Gerald. I'd taken great care to pass on my address to all the friends whom I'd thought Gerald might approach for information. I'd been quite depressed when I'd heard nothing. Two years of being a mere appendage to Gerald had made me angry. But not angry enough to do without him entirely.

His letter was humorous, decisive and sure of itself. A wave of physical desire came over me as I stood reading the confident, well-formed handwriting. I leant up against the wall, my hands shaking. Gerald made no mention of Sarah or the engagement. He simply said he had an appointment in Paris the following Saturday and would like to come and see me in the afternoon – '*chez toi* unless you tell me otherwise'.

I decided I would not reply. I wanted Gerald to think that the strong and self-confident woman who had rejected his shoddy compromises and walked out of his flat to make a life for herself was still strong and self-confident; that she was too absorbed in her work, too busy (or too disdainful) to reply. I knew he'd come all the same. And I would be ready for him.

Ironically, the prospect of seeing Gerald again revitalized all the energy I'd once thought I'd regained as a result of leaving him. I looked at the room with a new eye. I photographed my chair in all its plainness, as if it were van Gogh's chair at Arles. I photographed the wardrobe with its doors open, a combination of strange angles and absurd gaping mysteries. I photographed my bed, with the cold little window above it almost aching with loneliness. I photographed myself in the mirror – shattered, divided. I felt enthusiastic about my street project for the first time since my arrival. I decided I would go down to the wholesale markets that night and see if I could catch Cherbal at his work. I hung around in the Place de l'Opéra taking long shots across the square, till the cafés closed and the streets emptied. Then I took the Métro to Les Halles. There was a lot to see and I got some good compositions. I looked out for Cherbal, but he was not to be seen. Some flower porters gave me a bunch of carnations and I was carrying them back home, stepping over the crates and debris strewn over the road, when I saw the little figure in black, hobbling along ahead of me, a bulging string bag in each hand. It was four a.m. and the streets were still dark, and I couldn't be sure at first, but I hurried alongside her and fell into step.

'*Bonjour, Madame*,' I began, bending to look into her face. She looked up at me, slightly suspicious, slightly cross. Then she recognized me.

'Ah,' she said, 'my young neighbour. Good day to you, Mademoiselle.' She put down her shopping and shook my hand. A porter, doing a passable imitation of Cherbal with a lively hosepipe, sluiced our legs as he passed. Mademoiselle Regnier cursed him with an expression which was unknown to me, but elicited a ripe reply from the porter. Then she turned to me with a lovely smile, and I could see she had once been a beauty: 'Take no notice. He is an ignoramus.'

I went to pick up her shopping bags, now lying in a puddle at our feet. 'Let me help you with these. You're out very late.'

'No,' she replied, 'very early. They sell off the damaged fruit for next to nothing, and practically throw away the vegetables. Look at this –' She ferreted in one of her bags and produced a creamy white cauliflower. 'I picked this up from the pavement. Perfectly good. You see, Mademoiselle, I am not rich. I must take advantage of opportunities.'

We walked back together, slowly. We climbed the eight floors even more slowly.

'This is a long way up for you,' I remarked.

She shrugged her shoulders. 'One lives how one can.'

My old desire to know more about Mademoiselle Regnier took hold of me. 'Will you have coffee with me, Madame?' I paused by my door.

'*Non, merci, Mademoiselle*, I will not intrude.'

'Oh, please. It would be *my* pleasure.'

She inclined her scarfed head with the graciousness of a princess and followed me into my room. Its bleakness struck me anew, as I saw it through the old woman's eyes.

'You must forgive the mess,' I said, hastily clearing negatives and prints from the hard chair. 'I'm not here for long. And I'm not at home very much.'

Mademoiselle Regnier sat down and put her bags on the floor at her feet. She glanced around the room with an expression that was almost rueful. The enamel jug was empty and so I went out to the landing to fill the cafetière. When I returned, Mademoiselle Regnier was studying the photograph of Gerald which I had left lying on the table.

'Very handsome,' she remarked. '*Très, très beau.* He is your lover?'

I was disconcerted by her directness, and answered in rather a flustered fashion. 'He was once. A while back. I'm afraid he's marrying someone else now.'

'I see.' Mademoiselle Regnier looked at me and then the photo. 'Then you would be better to put this man out of your life, Mademoiselle. Let him go – *Bye-bye*!' (She said that in English, waving her hand like a child.) 'There is no future for you there. Believe me, Mademoiselle, I speak from experience.'

'That's why I'm here – in Paris,' I said. 'I've come to forget.' I avoided her eye, concentrated on making the coffee. There was a silence. The cafetière spluttered and splashed coffee over the cramped cooker. I lifted it and hastily poured two cups. Mademoiselle Regnier took one in her bony, misshapen hand.

'I've had a lot of trouble with men,' she said finally, as she swallowed. 'It is not too much to say that men have ruined me. Especially handsome men. Especially those. You see, Mademoiselle, I am not exactly the sort of woman it does you good to have coffee with. I have a bad reputation.'

I half laughed. 'Surely not,' I said.

'Assuredly so. People don't care so much now – now that I'm old. They put up with me now. But I've had a lot of hard words. No doubt Cherbal has given you his usual warning . . .' Her eyes twinkled attractively in the wrinkled mask of her face, a face still powdered, still a little rouged.

I didn't reply, but she obviously knew he had talked about her. 'Well, Cherbal has not got much finesse.' She smiled. 'A porter after all, only a porter. At least the men in my life had some charm, some culture . . .' She got up painfully slowly and went to the mantelpiece where I'd roughly arranged some contact prints. She picked out the pictures I'd taken of the women in Pigalle. It had been difficult to get those; the women had been annoyed when they saw my camera, turning their backs and making rude gestures. Two of them had threatened me in the end, saying I was embarrassing their clients and spoiling their livelihood, and I'd had to stop. Mademoiselle Regnier looked at them and said, 'These are yours? You are a professional photographer, Mademoiselle?'

'Of a kind.' I felt embarrassed. I took the prints from her and put them face downwards. 'These are not very good. Just experimenting.'

She shrugged. 'Don't be embarrassed on my account. It's a way of life after all. And you don't have to depend on one man, always waiting at his beck and call. But there you are, I was ignorant and stupid. But that's all in the past. Girls these days don't make that kind of mistake, do they? They're much more independent.' She picked up Gerald's picture again and then propped it up on the mantelpiece. '*Très beau,*' she said with a sigh. '*Très, très beau.*' And then she said it was late and she needed to lie down for an hour or two: 'I'm always tired, but I never sleep. It must be my bad conscience.' She laughed, shook my hand and wished me good night.

On the Saturday I went down to the shops and got fruit, cheese, wine, eggs. I'd decided I could just about manage an omelette on the little cooker. I chose some pictures to pin around the room to show off my prowess. I'd developed my shots of Les Halles and I was pleased with them. I loved the sensual heaps of vegetables and fruit, the early morning light filtering through the darkness and the casual grace of the porters as they carried the crates about. I thought Gerald might be impressed.

He arrived about three. I heard his voice in the courtyard, loud and confident as always, interrogating Cherbal. 'Eighth floor,' said Cherbal, pointing. 'Right up to the top.' I sat on the narrow bed and waited for him. I felt panic-stricken, as if I were standing on a bridge, deciding whether to jump, and finding my feet suddenly leaving the rail. Simultaneously, Gerald knocked at the door.

He'd brought champagne and flowers. What a cliché, I thought. But I felt alive for the first time since I'd set foot in France. Gerald looked around at the room and frowned with disbelief. I knew what he was thinking. How could I have exchanged his soft sofas and silk lampshades for this condemned cell? He said nothing about it, however. He popped the cork and poured the wine into coffee cups: 'To us! *Vive l'amour!*' And then he kissed me.

We drank the champagne and made love for what seemed like hours. The bed was too narrow and the wardrobe doors kept opening at inopportune moments and we were light-headed with wine, but I felt happy. I cooked him an omelette – a *pièce de résistance*, he said. But he couldn't wait for my elaborately arranged platter of cheeses; he had to rush because he was meeting a man at the Quai d'Orsay at eight. I started to panic: we hadn't discussed Sarah, we hadn't mentioned the engagement or what was to happen to us from now on. Gerald saw the look in my eyes. 'Don't spoil things,' he said before I could speak. He gave me the sort of kiss that was unfair in the circumstances, grabbed his document case, and left. As I stood in the doorway, watching his elegant back disappear down the stairs, I heard the click of Mademoiselle Regnier's door, and saw her old brown eyes looking at Gerald, then looking at me.

I turned and went quickly back into the room. I looked at my divided face in the shattered mirror. Then I sat down on the bed, which was still knotted and wrinkled from love-making, and stared at the monstrous wardrobe, the hideous bidet, the ghastly table, the uncompromising chair. For Gerald's next visit it was obvious I would have to redecorate the room.

FRENCH COFFEE

It was the beginning of the conference, and Jim knew already that he was out of step with the Europeans. For one thing, he was too big. They seemed such tiny guys, these French and Spaniards, these Italians and Belgians. They nipped round him like tugs round a liner. And they nipped about intellectually too. While he was trying to work out the language, they were on to something else. He felt out of things; his high-school French stilted and plangent, his accent risible with its slow childish drawl. He listened to the Europeans slipping smoothly between one another's languages – and felt a fool.

He'd managed to deal with breakfast only because there'd been a woman at his table. Babette had seen his hesitation with the waiter, had guessed his problem. 'He asks if you want coffee with milk. And if you want bread or croissants.' She smiled encouragingly. She wore a yellow scarf wound round her head and was smoking a cigarette.

He'd seen her the night before, at the opening seminar. She'd asked a question in French. He didn't know what she'd said – someone had forgotten to translate it. There'd been a bit of a linguistic free-for-all after that, and he'd felt like he was the only one who didn't know what was going on. Some of the delegates got very excited. A woman with long blond hair had walked out, shouting. The chairman, French, had given a shrug of theatrical proportions.

Jim smiled, first at Babette, then the waiter. 'Oh, *oui*. Milk – *lait*. And some croissants, please. *Merci*.'

The waiter rushed off impatiently. Jim turned to his rescuer. 'Gee, thanks. I haven't got the hang of this yet. I'm glad at least someone speaks English.'

'Not very well, I regret.'

'Well, better than my French.'

'Perhaps you can speak German? A lot of people –'

'No.'

'Spanish?'

'Not really. Hello and goodbye. Things like that.'

'Italian?'

He shook his head. 'I guess I only speak American.'

He felt ashamed. He'd spent hours with the phrase book on the flight over. He'd begun to feel confident as his school exercises returned to his memory. He'd counted to twenty, he'd asked himself the time, he'd enquired after his health, he'd reminded himself of colours, he'd asked directions to the Town Hall. But the moment he landed, it all went out of his head. In Customs, in the Arrivals Hall, in the queue for taxis, he'd been assaulted by a barrage of vowels and consonants crushed unrecognizably together. Everything he tried to say was met by a series of blank, cross faces. He felt like a deaf man, asking everyone to repeat everything. *'Je ne comprends pas!'* became the one phrase he could state with conviction.

Babette had noticed him the previous night, too. How he'd stood out. Not just because he was so tall and broad in the chest – and tanned in the comprehensive way only Californians could make look natural – but because he'd looked lost and disarmingly puzzled. He'd carried a note-book, rather obviously new, but had written nothing in it. He'd chewed his pencil instead, watching people's faces and gestures; clearly oblivious to most of what was being said. The translation service hadn't found its feet yet. Philippe had skimped on that, asking delegates to volunteer on a rota basis, but they'd got caught up in the arguments themselves and had forgotten their duties. Philippe would have to sort that out, she thought. But she wasn't convinced he would; he was already edgy trying to cope with last minute cancellations, rearranging the schedules of the key speakers, making sure all the lodging arrangements were satisfactory.

'Is your room okay?' Babette knew Americans expected high material standards; student residences didn't always fill the bill. One professor had refused to share sanitary arrangements with some other participants and had had to be moved out to a three-star hotel.

'I guess. I was so jet-lagged I'd have slept in a barrel.' But as she'd brought the subject up, he thought he'd probe a little. 'Although I am a little confused as to bathroom etiquette round here.'

'*Bathroom* etiquette?' Babette frowned.

'It's just kinda public.' He winced. 'This morning, for example, the women –'

The waiter slid himself between them, deposited a bowl of *café au lait* in front of Jim and laid a basket of croissants on the checked cloth, muttering something.

'What? What did he say?' He watched the waiter. His efficiency with the tray and the cloth and the dishes exuded contempt for the non-francophone.

'Just *bon appetit*.'

'Oh, right. So let's tuck in.' Jim looked round for a plate. There was only a small square of flimsy paper napkin in front of him. He reached for a croissant, and bit into it self-consciously. The flakes of pastry fell all over the table: 'Excuse me.'

'But you were saying – about the women?' Babette's eyes were round and prominent and golden brown. Bedroom eyes, he would have said. She was a good deal younger than he was, but those eyes were well-travelled.

'Well, I didn't like to ask. I mean, I thought I'd made a mistake. They were all – well – hardly dressed. I mean they were wearing T-shirts but just covering . . . you know . . .' He gestured, hand cutting across his lap.

Babette finished her cigarette, ground it into the ashtray, smiling. 'How terrible for you.'

Jim watched her small fingers prodding the cork tip. As the acrid smell drifted upwards he couldn't help commenting, 'Say, don't you have a no-smoking rule in restaurants round here? Back home you can't smoke anywhere now. Except the john. And even that's getting problematical.'

Babette shrugged, watched his eyes. 'You Americans think too much about health.'

'Well, I guess it's important. That's why we're all here after all.'

'Of course.' She was gathering her stuff together – a stylish handbag, a serious-looking cardboard folder heavy with manuscript. 'Excuse me, I have to talk to someone. Perhaps we can meet later. You can tell me what else you have observed about – bathroom etiquette.'

She got up and went over to another table. It was dominated by the loud voice of Philippe Leconte, expounding in three languages. Every so often there was a burst of laughter. It all sounded mature and witty. As he saw her bend elegantly over Leconte's shoulder, Jim felt envious, embarrassed. He was an unsophisticated middle-aged man with unsophisticated anxieties. How could he have said all those things about 'bathroom etiquette'? Okay, it'd been on his mind all morning, but why did he have to blurt it all out like that, like he was totally naïve?

But he felt naïve. He'd been feeling that way since touchdown on French soil. His customary props – language, status, know-how – had been knocked from under him. He no longer felt secure as an adult, let alone a tenured professor of fifteen years' standing. He was still recovering from the shock of finding himself taking a leak in mixed company. He'd opened the door marked *douches/sanitaires,* seen the urinal in the corner, and assumed in spite of the absence of the word *hommes* that this was the safe haven of the men's room. He'd had a hell of a shock moments later to find half-clad women walking past him to the showers, as he stood there dick in hand.

After breakfast, he walked to the conference hall. He looked round for Babette. She was sitting next to Leconte, looking chic in her light brown suit. Its colour seemed to merge with her skin. She looked up, caught Jim's glance and waved almost imperceptibly with her fingertips. He waved back more clumsily, feeling conspicuous as he towered head and shoulders above everyone around him, a Gulliver in the midst of the Lilliputians.

The translators were operational this morning, and Jim could just about follow the introductions and opening speeches. He wasn't sure how he was going to cope for a whole week; the concentration needed for flipping between two languages was something else. He studied the schedule for the day. As usual, interesting speakers were always on at the same time. But he decided to stay put for Hans Muller's talk on aspects of memory loss. It sounded relevant to his own research. And more to the point, Germans usually spoke English.

But before Dr Muller could begin, Leconte was on his feet again, explaining, in rapid conversational French, something about lunch. It was very important, he seemed to be saying. There would be two sittings – delegates would possess either red or yellow tickets and should make sure to do . . . something or other. This something or other was vital – *imperatif*. At the end Leconte asked in English if everybody had understood: 'Okay?' he said, grinning around at everyone. There was a general murmur of assent. Jim gazed quietly at his blue ticket, but guessed that if he followed the others he'd manage. Everybody round him seemed very much at home, busy in conversation with one another. A Babel of voices rose around him like walls. But he had no one to chat with. Babette was miles away.

He wondered if he'd made a mistake coming here. He was a bit old to start this kind of thing. Not that he was new to the conference circuit – over the years he'd regularly gone north to Toronto and Vancouver, south to Mexico City, and west to Japan. And at some time he'd visited most everywhere in the States that had a department of neurophysiology worth its salt. But he'd missed out on Europe; as a student, as a tourist, and as an academic. That's what had made him come now. France, in particular, with its reputation for gaiety and romance, had attracted him. He'd suddenly realized that his life had gotten a whole lot duller since Betty had divorced him, and the worst thing was he hadn't noticed. His daughter had said it would be great for him. She was a Europe veteran, a much-travelled member of the Spring County Episcopalian choir. 'You'll love it, Dad,' she said, her warm voice hugging him down the phone.

His son had gone for the underbelly: 'You can't speak French, can you? D'you reckon you'll be okay?'

'Who says I don't speak French?'

'Well, you never helped me any.' Charlie always whined. Even at twenty-four he was remembering high-school grudges.

'I don't remember you ever asking for help.'

'I didn't. I thought you only knew science and math.'

'So I can still surprise you. Anyway, I'm going. It'll be an opportunity to get a response to my research paper.'

'Hey, don't say too much before publication. You don't know these guys.'

'I think I'm old enough to look after myself.'

He wondered now if that were true.

Babette was only half listening to Hans Muller. She'd heard him before in Vienna. And Amsterdam. It was the same sort of stuff; not really her area of interest. So it was easy to concentrate on Philippe, his profile judiciously grave in the next seat, his body thin under his designer shirt. Stress never stopped him looking immaculate. He was inordinately vain, something she had initially rather liked about him. It had amused her. 'You're pleased with yourself, aren't you?' she'd said, that first time in Bavaria.

'Of course,' he'd said, showing a larger-than-life set of perfect white teeth. 'That's why I'm so good to be with.'

It had been true. For three years, those snatched meetings in European cities had been the highlights of her life. International fornication; no time to get into boring habits. But he'd been tense recently, preoccupied; not so much fun. She had seriously wondered if there'd be any point coming here this summer. She had to finish her current project by October or her increasingly paranoid Head of Department would freak out. She'd almost not filled out the application form, but the prospect of the Loire valley had been an inducement. Philippe had said they'd go to Blois and Anjou, take a picnic, find a *dégustation*, get drunk. 'But not too drunk, you know,' he'd said, laughing seductively down the line. It sounded for a moment as though things would be on their old footing.

But now she was here, he wasn't finding time even for breakfast together, let alone anything as romantic as *déjeuner sur l'herbe*. He'd booked them both into a hotel (two kilometres from the university in discreet consideration for his wife and daughters in Toulouse), but he'd been so busy he'd not set foot there yet. He'd whispered to her in a corner the first night: 'Babette, my sweet, I'm so sorry – but you know Gregoire has left me with everything to do – and none of the speakers are coming at the right time – either a day early or two days late. I'll be up all night working it out. It's crazy.'

Babette didn't want to make demands. She left that to the wife in Toulouse. But she knew that the hunger had gone from their relationship. As she watched him, saw his mind so wholly concentrated elsewhere, she began planning to end the affair. Vanity had had its day. A little humility might now be piquant. And she had a fancy for the big, blundering American.

'How ya doin'?' A welcome voice whispered at the back of Jim's head as Hans Muller's applause rippled away and the audience stared to disperse. He turned. A pale man with horn-rims was extending his hand. Jim recognized him vaguely.

'Roger Greenberg, Columbia, remember? Guess you've just arrived.'

Jim pumped his arm gratefully. 'Hi there, Roger. Jim Benchley, California Institute. Great to see you again. It's a real relief, finding a fellow American. I was feeling all at sea.'

'Not been to Europe before?'

'That obvious, is it?'

'Hey, don't worry, you'll get used to it – get your eye in, so to speak. Or should I say ear?' He laughed, wheezily. 'And this is my wife, Sophie. We come every year.'

'What, here?'

'Wherever something interesting's going on. Madrid last year. And I hear talk of Milan or Frankfurt next spring. The important thing is to book early, get your own en suite.'

'Is that the trick?' Jim laughed. 'But I don't think I'll be making the trip again . . .'

'Oh, gee, why not?' Sophie wrinkled her little blue eyes. She put her hand confidentially on Jim's arm, as far as her five foot nothing would allow. 'You get to know people real well.'

Jim's gaze rested on Babette, standing near the door of the hall, smoking. 'Is that so? I have to say I've been feeling kind of detached.'

'Oh, we'll introduce you to everyone.' Sophie whisked him off to meet Hans Muller, Daniel Frink, David Donovan and Alicia Rodermeyer.

They all spoke English. They all smiled kindly at him. 'We'll take you to lunch. Tickets? Oh don't bother with that nonsense. Sit where you like.'

They all sat together. Jim sat by Sophie. She gave him a potted biography of everyone in sight, munching and waving her fork. She eventually got round to Babette. 'Oh, now there's a dark horse. She's been having some sort of thing with Philippe. But they're real discreet – he's married, of course.'

'Why of course?'

'Jim, honey! A man like that! Of course he's been snapped up.'

As if on cue, Philippe caught Sophie's eye and gave her his dog-smile, all flashing white teeth.

The Americans are all on the same table, thought Babette. Seeking cultural reassurance. Eating in that funny way. She saw both Sophie Greenberg and the big American look at her simultaneously, then look away. They were talking about her. She wondered what they were saying. And then she knew, as their glances switched from her to Philippe. She was aware that he was touching her knee under the table in an abstracted fashion; a substitute for his attention, a casual gesture of apology. She withdrew her leg. Philippe appeared not to notice.

'It's kind of small.' Jim looked at the tiny cup of coffee he'd been given after asking proudly for *un café*.

'Well, it's *un express*. That's what you get after a meal. Unless you ask for *un grand* – that's a big cup –' Roger's Brooklyn vowels were insistent. He was in instructional mode. Jim could imagine him in the classroom.

'– But it'll always be black,' Sophie added. 'Unless you ask for it *au lait*.' (She pronounced it *olé* – as in Spanish.)

'Same with tea,' said David, who was English and wearing a summery T-shirt with a terrible design. 'They never bring you milk unless you ask. And then it's hot and frothy.'

'I see I've got a lot to learn.'

But he felt happier, more relaxed.

'You look happy. More relaxed, perhaps.' Babette was walking in step with him as they crossed the courtyard. 'Is that because of Mrs Greenberg? She is very easy, I think.'

'Easy-going. "Easy" means something else – not very polite. But I guess you're right. It's a relief to speak your own language.' He was evading her eyes, watching her feet on the gravel. She had nice feet, neat and brown, in neat sandals. He wondered if the rest of her was the same, compact and understated. He couldn't think what to say. He blurted out, 'What's your field, then?'

'Field?'

'Specialism.' He paused. *'Sujet spécial.'*

'Ah. Sex.'

He blushed. 'Pardon me?'

'Impotency – is that right? And too-sudden ejaculation. What about you?'

'Me?' He stared at her in horror. 'Oh, no problems like that.'

'I mean your – *sujet spécial.'*

'Sorry.' He blushed again, wincing inwardly at his idiocy, trying to remember what it was that he did for a living. 'Brain damage.' He touched his head. 'Post-CVA patterns of learning.' He caught her blank look, tried again. 'CVA – that's "stroke" – you know that word?'

'Ah, yes.'

'Not as interesting as sex, I guess.'

'Oh.' She shrugged. 'Many statistics, like for everyone. It is an occupation only.'

Jim couldn't remember exactly how it happened. Except that it was perfectly natural and easy.

'I have a hotel room,' she said. 'It's just two kilometres away.'

'What's that in miles?' he asked stupidly.

'Not far,' she said. 'Even an American could walk there.'

'I'm fit,' he said. 'Let's go.'

She was so matter-of-fact as they strolled along that he wondered whether he might have misunderstood her offer and was about to make a faux pas of a horrendous kind. Maybe all that talk of sex had given him the wrong idea. Maybe his sense of cultural alienation was affecting his judgement, and her invitation was just a friendly gesture, colleague to colleague – a chance to chill out, away from Philippe and the gang. If he made a move, she might be embarrassed by his crassness. Then he'd have to spend the next two weeks avoiding her eye. He couldn't face that: he really liked her, and she seemed to be his one chance of fitting in. He told himself to take it slowly; keep his eyes open for every nuance of meaning, be ready to back off. But when they got to her room, she locked the door, kicked off her sandals and slipped her hand under his shirt in a way that left no room for doubt. All his confidence came back, then. This was a language he knew by heart.

She had a body just like he'd imagined. And a few ideas he hadn't imagined. He was a bit afraid that he might suffer the too-sudden ejaculation, but he focused his mind on Roger Greenberg's coffee lecture, and managed to keep control. '*Olé!*' he cried out when the moment came.

IN THE STREET OF THE ROSE-GATHERERS

I t's November and very cold. It's our last night in Paris, and we seem to have been walking around for hours. I am silent; he is full of words. Finally I say I am hungry. He smiles as if he has been waiting for that. 'We could go to that place. You know, the one Anders so kindly suggested – the Dangerous Place.' He takes out a piece of paper: '*La rue des rosiers* . . . That's not far.'

We cross the river on the footbridge, the lamps fuzzy in the drizzle, the water lapping underneath. On the other side, the streets are dark and narrow. There's a Turkish bath-house, a Jewish bakery with Hebrew above the door. The place we're looking for is on the corner, blue neon light flashing: a six-point star. In front, there's a delicatessen: sides of spiced beef, jars of pickles, rows of smoked eels on a white marble slab, everything bathed in fluorescent light.

We plunge in, grateful for the warmth, discarding damp coats. *It's the river,* they say. *It's always cold by the river.* The restaurant is up a flight of stairs, a dim refuge of tobacco smoke and music, opera-red décor suggesting a lost Bohemia. Out-of-date playbills cover the walls. Amateur portraits, relics of long-ago customers, stare down at us. The room is long and narrow. Couples face one another down each side, as if reflected into infinity. There's a duo of gypsy fiddlers working the tables. They smile and stamp, spilling out the fierce rhythms of Middle Europe. 'How corny,' says my husband, sliding into the plush banquette against the wall.

I take the outer seat, a bentwood chair. I have my back to the room, to the other row of diners, to the gypsies and the waiters. I prefer the banquette, but I say nothing. I brush the sleeve of the woman next to me as I unfold my napkin. I mumble apologies. She glances back, disturbed from her conversation, nodding briefly. She is young, and has a sad, Ingres face, brown hair wound over her head in braids: a pure, old-fashioned look. Across from her is a young man, bearded, Orthodox, intense – wielding an authoritative knife. They murmur. *It's always the same with Lalage . . . She's always the same . . .*

My husband looks at the menu, raises his eyebrows. 'I hope you like sauerkraut, my darling. It seems to be Cabbage With Everything.' Across the table, his smile is thin, composed. We choose, heads down. There are blinis, goulash, dumplings, salami, fish. I don't know what to pick. I am exhausted, and my hunger has gone. Suddenly the violins swing past; a hint of cummerbund, a ripple of applause. Somewhere behind me, a group of people starts to sing 'Happy Birthday'. They sing in English (badly). A cake is brought, hot with candles and the smell of melting wax. A wrinkled man rises, suit immaculate, eyes old as sin. He smiles with duplicitous courtesy: *Merci, mes amis – merci, merci!* He raises his hands, palms down. He deprecates their congratulations. After all, he says with a laugh, it is not a great achievement to grow old. They are delighted with his *jeu d'esprit* and applaud some more. Next to him, his woman, thin and shiny as a racehorse, shows her teeth in a royal acknowledgement. She sits, expensive, in her strapless dress and her tight pearl collar. The old man kisses her, hieratically and for show. She glances in the mirror and meets my eye as his lips nibble her necklace. (Anders and I saw one like it today at the *Musée des Arts. Collar for a Decorative Dog,* it said. The best thing there.)

The gypsies strike up again. They play animatedly in the aisle between the tables: *See how we evoke the Magyars and the wild romance of the plains!* They move towards us, eyes gleaming in anticipation of a tip. They pause at my back. I cannot see them, only hear the music at my neck, feel the movement of the air, sense their satin ruffles quivering away. I wonder if I should look them in the eye. And how much should I pay for this embarrassment? But my husband is prepared. He has a coin or two already in his hand. He drops them casually, gives me a sideways glance as the violinists bow and move away. 'More Topol than Chagall, don't you think? More *Fiddler on the Roof* than *Hungarian Rhapsody?*'

He doesn't wait for an answer. He's not waiting for answers at all tonight. He slides his index finger down the menu, eyebrows raised, lips puckered, hovering over dumplings: an important choice, he says. And of course we should have pickles, however crude. As part of the real 'experience' of the place. I am, he has become suddenly aware, very susceptible to novelty these days. 'The strangest things seem to suit your taste.' He shakes his head. 'A pity Anders isn't here to guide us through, give us, as you might say, the Orthodox view. Still, it was good of him to look after you this week. I hope he was a satisfactory guide. You know how I hate you to be bored.'

I don't reply. I think about Anders, the flower market, the red rose I put in my coat as we walked about and then threw in the Seine when we parted. I can't decide about pickles. My husband has chosen, but I still demur. Soup perhaps, or . . .

He won't wait, calls the waiter with a finger-click. *Enfin*, he will order for us both, 'As Madame's mind is elsewhere at the moment. Madame has – how should we say – overstretched herself. The demands of a new culture, *oh là là!*' The waiter smiles and nods: He is, alas, only too aware that people in Paris do this kind of thing. Paris can weave a spell; she takes you by surprise. He tweaks the menu from my listless grasp, tucks it firmly under his arm and sashays back along the aisle. Behind me, middle-aged waitresses flick open beer and wine, plump breasts straining against sateen and lace. Heavy platters sway above our heads: *Excusez, Monsieur'dame. Take care! Take care!*

'How are your pickled herrings? Ethnic enough?' I look at my fish fillets, grey and soggy on the plate. He has ordered borscht and dumplings, and tucks in with a crazy grin. He pauses, looks up; waits for me to start. I cut a piece. It's sour and furry in my mouth. I nearly retch, but smile and give some kind of nod. He beams at me: 'Good choice on my part, then?'

More music. More customers. The restaurant is very full, the shop downstairs is fuller. I can see the heads and hats of people as they come to buy meat and fish and bread. A queue forms near the stairs, waiting for spare tables; but no one leaves. The birthday party is in full swing, the Godfather and his woman are embracing again. She laughs and feeds him like a child.

My husband looks at the complimentary matchbox again. 'I see they don't close till two. And open seven days a week. That's the way to make money. And Anders – he must have money too. He has plenty of time for walking around, pursuing pleasure, wouldn't you say?'

I affect not to hear. I have no appetite, but he is wolfish; he eats for two. He is trying smoked fish, now, pooling pickles on his plate. 'Yes, and on the subject of our *Swedish* friend . . . his father was a tailor, did he tell you that? Doesn't exactly fit with the Aryan good looks. But I imagine he has a certain *dreamy* charm.'

I watch his chewing mouth, his busy jaw. I try the goulash, burn my tongue.

It's late, now. The tables have been cleared and the water jugs are dry. The queue has dissipated, the party people are long gone. The violinists wilt in a corner, cummerbunds companionably awry, *vodka maison* in little glasses. A huge dog pads past the tables, unremarked. Two waitresses are singing, arm in arm. My husband's downing schnapps: one glass, then two. He reads the playbills, coffee cup in hand, holding humorously forth about a string quartet, and symphonies by Mahler (naturally). Now he is saying something about Mendelssohn and Brahms.

I hear, but do not listen. Behind his head I see a mirror shattered by bullet-holes. Painted blood runs down from six-point stars. There is murder in the mirror, but his solid head talks on imperviously.

We're outside now, out coats hunched tight. It's midnight, and the street is freezing. Frost coats the vegetables left outside in crates and our breath steams white against the dark. My husband knows his way, he says. We're not far from the rue de Rivoli, best place for a taxi, and we can walk there easily. A little walk will be good for me, a last chance to enjoy the special flavour of the *quartier*; after all, we won't be here again. He marches me along the pavement. He squeezes me between parked cars, over runnels of dark liquid, decaying vegetables. A sudden rectangle of light displays some haute couture, a dress of dizzying green – three thousand francs (a snip). He jerks my elbow, makes me stop and look. 'Now, *if I were a rich man . . .*' He laughs softly as he hums the tune, chinks his coins deep in his pockets.

There are, after all, no taxis free on the rue de Rivoli. We cross under trees, descend to the Metro instead, strap-hanging through *St Paul, Hotel de Ville, Louvre*, a mixture of burnt soot and screeching brakes. There are more gypsies in the carriage. These are real, and have hard looks and an accordion. My husband proffers a handful of small change, which they take without a smile. He whispers: 'You see, I pander to your ethnic tastes.' At *Palais Royale* we ascend to wide streets and café-lights. We come to our hotel, the shadowy lobby, the desiccated plants. At the desk, the night porter watches a silent football match onscreen, hands us the keys without a glance: *Bon nuit, Monsieur'dame, bon nuit!*

I am undressing. My husband lies on the hotel bed, socks still on, orange lamplight across his hair, guide book in hand. It's one a.m. and he's reading it aloud, plangent lullaby, drowning the tinkling of the tooth mug as I brush my teeth. He wiggles his toes, unbuttons his shirt. The ancient plumbing gurgles and gushes. Strange feet creak the floorboards outside the door, faint keys open distant rooms. He puts the book down with a sigh. 'Well, well,' he says. 'What was Anders thinking sending us there? Dangerous is hardly the word. Twenty-two injured, six killed – gunfire in the street and a grenade through the window. But *we*'ve survived, my darling, have we not?'

I wake up at dawn, and breakfast alone: one croissant, one pat of butter, one sachet of jam; coffee with everything. Now I sit in the lobby, suitcase at my feet. My husband is still in the bathroom, a razor at his jaw, his face tilting in the basin mirror.

I sit on a small bench, *Paris Match* in my hand. On the cover a film star goes off with someone's husband. In the lobby mirror I see people arriving, departing, handing over keys, shifting luggage, waiting for the lift. Then I see Anders come in. He is tall and stands out from the seething crowd like a mast at sea. His blond reflection smiles at me.

Then I see a hole in his chest. I see him behind trickles of red blood. I see the Ingres girl, the young rabbi, the old man and his thin woman all jerking in the air, eyes and mouths *Guernica*-wide. The white shirts of the waiters are splattered with crimson, the violins are crushed, the pictures hang askew. Borscht and goulash stain the tablecloths. I turn from the mirror. Anders comes towards me with a smile. He is holding a red rose against the whiteness of his shirt. He bows and kisses my hand. He says, 'Are you ready, Natalie?'

I nod. Then he lifts up my suitcase and we walk out into the street.

SIX WEEKS WITH KIMBERLEY

Our Linda used to laugh at me when she was expecting and I used to carry her shopping for her and help lift her up out of the easy chair. 'Gerraway, Mick!' she'd say. 'I kin manage. You'll gerron me nerves in a minute.' She thought I was just fussing, but I just wanted to be part of it all. I loved looking after her and watching her grow bigger. And when Kimberley was born – well, I can't say how I felt, then. I couldn't get over it. Such a little wrinkled thing she was, kind of strange and familiar at the same time. And all ours. When they put her in me arms I just wanted to burst out crying, like a big kid. 'You're a reel softie, Mick,' said Linda. 'Honest you are.'

She was always saying things like that, teasing me. But she was right in a way. She was the strong one out of the two of us. From the first time we started going out she said she could see she'd have to take me in hand else I'd get walked over by some designing woman. But I knew from the first that the only designing woman I wanted was her. When we got married, she looked so lovely coming down the aisle that I was the one in tears.

And then, when we took Kimberley home and laid her down in her cot all wrapped up and sleeping, I felt as if the whole world had blossomed like a flower, and we three was tucked right deep down in the middle of it. I hated getting up and going to work, leaving Kimberley snuggled up next to Linda in the double bed. They seemed so happy and warm together, and everything else seemed so cold.

It *was* cold, mind. It was February. And although I was on a job inside that month, the place I was working on was as bleak as hell. It was an old house in Small Heath – nothing special, just a corner terrace. I reckon it hadn't been touched for years – no proper kitchen, no bathroom, just all this brown wallpaper and green paint. And that smell. They always stink, these old places. Rot, I suppose. And rats. Hardly worth the effort of messing about with, I thought, but renovation was getting to be all the rage.

To be honest, I'd had me fill of old houses when Doody's was first doing the demolition. I'd just left school and they'd taken me on no problem (that was when you could walk into any job easy). Of course I loved all that knocking down and smashing up; it was a great job for a young lad. But it gave me a shock, too, seeing how some people lived. I thought I'd been brought up pretty rough meself; seven of us in a little terraced house, Mom with a widow's pension and a cleaning job to make up the difference – but we lived like kings compared to some of what I saw when we was demolishing the slums. I could hardly believe the state of some of the houses: all the filthy yards, filthy entries, filthy piles of rubbish. Every day I went to work I'd tear into them old places like a tiger, ripping them apart with sheer joy. And when we'd knocked everything down, and all the bricks and timber had been taken away, I used to look at the flattened streets and think what a great job we'd done.

The paper was full of it. Sometimes I used to sit at our kitchen table having me tea and looking at the plans in the *Evening Mail*. 'Artist's Impression,' it would say, and I used to think that if Birmingham got built like that, it was going to be a real space-age city: motorways up on stilts, underpasses with tunnels, roads going up and over other roads in great big curves like a fairground ride. And everywhere there was tower blocks and new houses set in green spaces, like a big park. I reckoned Paradise was going to come for all us Brummies. We'd have new flats, central heating, fitted kitchens – everything we'd never had before. So, as soon as Linda and me got engaged, I put our names down for a council flat. I didn't want us starting married life with my mom – not sharing a kitchen and bathroom and having to keep all our wedding presents under the bed.

As it happened, we had to wait a bit, but six months after we got married, we were given the keys to a maisonette in Nechells. All clean and new; fitted cupboards and Formica tops in the kitchen, and an inside toilet. We were dead chuffed. I even pretended to carry Linda over the doorstep, but she said we'd look like fools in front of the neighbours, so I put her down and just give her a kiss instead, saying I didn't care what the neighbours thought of that. I didn't mind moving to a new area with people I'd never seen before. After all, they'd been on the waiting list for years, just like us. I reckon if you treat people fair you'll get on with them. All the people in our Close was grateful to have a decent house to bring up their kids in.

Not everybody felt the same, mind. Some people from the slums had been moved right out to Chelmsley Wood and they was all moaning for the Housing to let them come back to the old terraces. But there was nowhere for them to come back to. We'd knocked nearly everything down, and what'd been left standing had been taken over. Whole families of Asians had been moving in. They were running all the old corner shops, selling everything under the sun including curry and rice, and nattering away in their own lingo.

The house I was working on when Kimberley was born belonged to one of these Asians. Ali – something or another. Never saw him, though. Mr Doody just told me what to do and left me to get on with it. He'd promise me a lad to give me a hand, but ten to one I was on me own most of the day. Mr Doody knew he could rely on me. Turn me hand to anything I could – and still can. I'm just the sort of bloke for a small job with a lot of different things to be done.

Well, this particular day I was refitting the upstairs window. I'd pulled out the rotten old sash and was putting in a nice new louvre. I'd been having a sly look at the Indian women across the street with their bright veils and bits of gold and silver. Nice, they looked. I'd have liked to have give them a wave, be friendly; but I didn't want no trouble from their husbands. So I just went along with what I was doing, transistor on the mantelpiece, listening to Dave Lee Travis, whistling to meself.

Then I saw this blond woman getting out of her car. Really struggling, she was, her belly out like a balloon. She must have been a good eight months gone. In fact, she looked as if she might start off in labour any minute. I stopped with a handful of panel pins in me mouth, watching her. She was a little thing, much shorter than our Linda, and she was just wearing this loose cotton dress, no coat, in spite of the bitter cold. I couldn't help wondering what she was up to. I'd never seen her in the street before. No one ever parked outside, except us builders – and Mr Doody when he came by in the Rover – so this woman's car stood out a mile: bright canary yellow. Looked foreign, too; a French thing. Anyway, she made a beeline for the skip we'd got outside, and started to poke about in it.

Now if she'd a been a bloke, I'd have tapped the window and yelled at her: 'What the bloody hell d'yer think yer up to? Clear off!' But being as she was a woman, and pregnant, I was more worried about her than anything else. That skip was too bloody full (I'd been telling Mr Doody about it all week, but he'd let things drift as usual), and some of the stuff was ready to take a flyer. I could just see her trapped under a purling or one of them heavy bits of cast we'd just ripped out. I thought about shouting out to warn her, but I was afraid I'd make her jump, and then God knows what might have happened. I knew I'd have to do things more gently.

It took me a few minutes to get to ground level because we'd pulled out the stairs the week before, and I had to use a ladder. When I got down, the woman was already in the house, bold as brass, standing in the middle of the passageway between two split bags of browning. 'Hey, watch yerself, bab,' I said. 'This is no place for a woman in your condition. One slip and I'll be running you up to Marston Green.' That was where Kimberley had been born.

She laughed at that. 'Oh, it's all right,' she said. 'I'm quite used to it. My house is a building site too. Probably worse.'

I was a bit shocked by that. I couldn't imagine our Linda living on a building site when Kimberley was practically ready to be born. She'd had everything decorated and ready months before – new bedroom, new cot, new quilted eiderdown, soft fluffy carpet – everything perfect. She was a really great organizer. And she used to budget down to the last halfpenny. In them days we didn't have much left over, once we'd paid the rent and the bills. But I knew that with Linda in charge, Kimberley wouldn't want for anything.

Anyway, this woman started peering in at all the rooms. 'I'm looking for a fireplace,' she said. 'You know, a grate. I saw some bits of cast iron in the skip, and I wondered if you were throwing out any old ones. I'm desperate to get one in before the baby's due.'

I must admit I felt sorry for her. A well-spoken woman she was – quite posh in fact – but she had no winter coat and she was having to scavenge around in skips to find a fireplace for herself. 'Look, love,' I said, 'you don't want to be messing about with all this dirty old stuff. I can tell you where you can get a really nice modern grate for next to cost price: Coventry Road, friend of mine. He supplies all the stuff for Doody's. Tell him Mick Hanlon sent you. He'll sort you out.'

She kind of smiled at that. 'No,' she said, 'I don't want a modern grate. It's a Victorian one I want. Could I just see if there is anything else here?' She started to poke round before I could stop her. 'Oh look, here's one!' she said. She was looking at the one Terry and me had tried to get out the day before. Bloody great thing. 'Oh, it's broken!' she said, pointing at the front bars where Terry'd put his crowbar. 'What a shame!' She looked up at me. 'Are there any others?'

'There might be one in the back room,' I said. 'It's covered up, so I'm not sure what it's like.' We went into the back room, me holding on to her by the arm, afraid she'd slip. The electrician had had half the floorboards up, and hadn't come back – typical. There was this old mantelpiece with a big sheet of rusted metal over the grate, and a broken gas fire sitting in front. I picked up me claw hammer. 'Let's see what's behind here,' I said.

I got the stuff off easy enough; there wasn't much holding it together. Underneath was this filthy old fireplace, the grate still with the ashes in it, and cobwebs full of thick brown dust. But the woman sort of knelt down in front of it. 'Oh, it's lovely!' she said. 'Just look at those beautiful tiles!'

I couldn't see anything in them meself. Real Olde Worlde stuff. Gave me the creeps. Get rid of it – that was my motto. But this woman was really thrilled. 'Do you think the owners will want it?'

'Bloody hell, no!' I said. 'We're renovating. All this old stuff's going out on the skip. This place is gonna be all nice and clean and new.' (Poor kid, I thought. That's what you could do with – something all comfortable and clean.)

'Would you pull it out for me?' she said. 'I'd pay you.' She took out her purse. 'How much?'

I could see then that she wasn't wearing a wedding ring. That explained a lot. 'I'll do it for you free, bab,' I said, 'but how'll you take it with yer?'

'Oh, it'll go in the car,' she said. 'The back comes right down. I can get loads of things in there. But I must pay you. Is this enough?' She held out a pound note.

'Yer on,' I said, thinking it was an easy bit of work. But in the end, it took me best part of an hour to get the flaming thing out. The woman kept getting in me way every time I picked up the chisel, saying, 'Please be careful,' and, 'Mind the tiles, won't you?' After a bit I said, 'I'll get it out for you, love, as long as you stay well away. Otherwise I won't be responsible for that babby of yours.' So she sat down on a bucket as best she could, and stayed quiet. I went round and round the frame, easing the whole thing out. She kept smiling at me as if she was really pleased the way I was doing it. She looked really pretty when she smiled, and I couldn't help thinking about how she'd look tucked up in bed with her baby all nice and cosy, and the fire burning away in the grate.

Getting the thing into the boot of her little car was what really buggered me up. She couldn't help, of course, and it was really a two-man job.

'You're daft, you are, Mick,' said Linda when I went home that night. 'Fancy doing all that work for a quid!' She was even more annoyed the next day when I couldn't get out of bed and she had to ring Doody's to say I'd done me back in.

In the finish I was off work for six weeks, just getting me sick pay and no overtime – just when we needed the extra because of Linda giving up her job at the hairdresser's. But I couldn't say I minded, because suddenly I had all day with Kimberley. I didn't have to go out in the cold and leave her behind; I could nurse her as much as I liked. I looked after her every time Linda went out to the shops, and I gave her all her feeds because I was stuck in bed and Linda said I might as well make myself useful. I couldn't have been happier. We built up a real relationship, Kimberley and me. I'd chat to her and she'd look at me, intelligent-like, and grab tight at me little finger. I hardly remembered about me back, and Linda started to joke that I'd put the whole thing on, just so I could skive off with me daughter. 'I bet she'll grow up to be a real daddy's girl,' she said. 'I kin see it already.'

Kimberley's eight now. And I have to admit she's a bit spoiled, being the only one. We'd have liked more, but somehow it didn't happen. Linda pretends to be strict with her, but she isn't really; buys her a whole load of Barbies and My Little Ponies and fancy things to put in her hair. And me – well I can't say no to her, not when she looks up at me in that way, her eyes all clear and beautiful, just like when she was a babby them first six weeks. And I can't help remembering what first brought us together: that little woman and her bloody two-ton grate.

I've often thought about that woman over the years, and wondered how things turned out for her in the end. Her own kid would be just Kimberley's age, of course. A little girl, I liked to think, blonde like her mother. Every time I see a yellow car I think it might be her, but it never is. Our meeting in that house was a bit of a one-off. We only came together because she saw that skip, and I was looking out of the window.

But she came into my head again last week. I was driving down the Moseley Road and it caught my eye: a shop practically bursting with fireplaces. There was loads of them, stacked up in the window and half over the pavement. Of course I'd realized that all these Victoriana type things was coming back into fashion since Mr Doody started asking us to take them out in one piece, and put them aside for the reclamation yards. But I didn't think many people would go back to laying coals and lighting fires with sticks and paper, when they could have central heating at the flick of a switch. But from the look of this shop, it seemed that I was wrong. I decided to park the van and take a look, just to see what all the fuss was about, and maybe thinking, somewhere in my heart of hearts, that I might run into the woman and her kid.

When I went inside, I was really knocked back. There was all sorts of fireplaces, some with mantels and mirrors and fenders, and a fair number with coloured tiles. They was all really bright and polished, quite attractive really. And in the middle of the shop there was the spitting image of the one I'd shifted.

A lad with a plait and filthy jeans came out of a back room. 'Can I help?' he says, posher than I expected.

'How much yer rushing us fer this one?' I asked, pointing it out.

'One-fifty,' he said. 'The tiles are especially nice.'

'One-fifty? Is that all?' I laughed. 'I did well, then, flogging one off for a quid a few years back.'

The bloke stared at me like I was daft. Then he said, 'A *hundred* and fifty pounds. A good working grate like this costs a *hundred* and fifty.'

I nearly had a fit, thinking of what I could do with that sort of money – but I nodded, pretending I'd known all along. Of course, looking at it again, I realized it'd cost more than a couple of quid, all that cast iron with patterns and scrolls, all those tiles with flowers on them, all that gleaming black polish.

'Yes,' I said to the bloke. 'That's what I meant. The way the value's gone up, like. That's the thing, isn't it? You never know how much things are really worth at the time.'

But I do know, of course. And if I met that little woman, I'd shake her by the hand and tell her that taking out that grate was the best couple of hours' work I ever did.

TAKING PEOPLE IN

I sense it from the minute I wake up: I'm reaching the perfect pressure. I lie on the bed unclothed, feeling the warmth of my body evaporate into the air, and the warmth of the air seep back through the pores of my skin. There's a complete osmosis, an exact equilibrium of heat. Days like this are rare, even in high summer, and the year has been disappointing until now. Grey, rainy, heavy. Lows on the chart and in the heart. I've stayed indoors.

But now I will get up. I will wash and breakfast. And I will go to the park and walk among the flowerbeds, inhale the moistness of the glasshouses, and lie on the grass by the lake. Someone will come past. And stop. Things will repeat themselves.

I prepare eggs, toast, marmalade. In the morning room, on the mahogany table, I set a cup and saucer, two kinds of plates, a toast rack, butter in a dish. I like the ritual of breakfast, the habit since childhood of starting the day properly. In this I am different from Rob. And from the others; the friends he brought to stay. They would get up at midday and stand at my windows half-dressed, squinting at the light, gulping at coffee and cigarettes. A little later they might bite at a biscuit, or crunch at an apple they would leave to brown on the sill.

Don't fuss, Rob would say if I cleaned up the crumbs or rinsed out a cup. *Just relax, princess. Relax and be beautiful.*

I tried so hard. It seemed such a good thing not to care about the material things in life, to be free from the slavery of habit. I watched the others, trying to copy what they did. But I don't smoke. And coffee makes me ill. And I am used to a tablecloth and cutlery. I am used to sitting down at eight o'clock sharp, clean and brushed and smelling of soap.

I sit down now. I pour myself tea from the big silver pot, milk from the silver jug. It is satisfying and civilized. I enjoy watching the clear liquid arc into my cup, the milk mingling it to opaque. *It's really no more trouble*, I would tell Rob, *than a tea bag in a mug. And a lot less wasteful.* But more ostentatious he thought. And infinitely more bourgeois. 'Bourgeois' was his favourite word of condemnation as he lay on the Persian carpet, propped up with tasselled cushions, watching my colour TV.

He's gone now, of course. They've all gone. The whole thing was an aberration, a kind of hiatus in the pattern. They moved in, and then moved on. It's now quite a while since they were here. But I dare say they remember me fondly enough, look back with a smile at my old-fashioned and solitary life. Quaint Octavia – that's how they saw me. A girl with a big house and a lot of money. A girl who was good to look at. A girl who always said yes.

'You're like a little kitten.' Rob would stroke my long blond hair while he read a book or talked to the others. They all did it, stroking, patting, as if they couldn't keep their hands off me. But they didn't seem to hear me when I spoke. They'd smile in my face, saying, 'You don't mind, do you? If we have the meeting here? If we have the party here? If we move in for a while? If we invite our friends?' It was understood without question that they could all come to Octavia's house. That they could all eat Octavia's food. Drink Octavia's drink. Sleep in Octavia's bed. They thought I didn't mind; that I took sex like I took tea – calmly and with good manners. They didn't notice how stiff I was, how quietly I cried.

It was not what I'd been brought up to. It was not what Mummy and Daddy would have expected, at all. But they were gone years ago and the big house had become so very lonely. The neighbours had carefully minded their business and I had carefully minded mine. But one blazing midsummer day by the lake, Rob had smiled and said I was beautiful. And I had taken him home.

He'd been kind at first. He said he respected my quaint way of life. 'Don't ever change, princess.' But then he brought the others, with their easy laughter and their easy ways – and I felt out of step.

I watched them carefully – how they moved, how they talked, what they said. I believed that if I tried hard enough it would happen; that I would mirror them unthinkingly until eventually there would be no difference between us. I was twenty-one – just like they were. It couldn't be too hard. I rode with them on buses and the backs of motorbikes. I ate with them in greasy cafeterias. I sat with them on draughty walls outside corner pubs and drank beer in thick glass mugs. But it didn't work.

'Just keep quiet,' Rob would whisper whenever I tried to give an opinion. 'I think your lot have had enough to say for the last few hundred years. Give the proletariat a chance.'

Jeni would put her heavy arms around me and tell him not to be so cruel: 'It's not her fault. Octavia's not like the rest of them, are you? Anyway, it's her house, isn't it? And I think it's fantastic. Millions of times better than the last place we were in.'

Jeni liked my kitchen especially. She'd sit there, devouring handfuls of cornflakes straight from the packet, and concocting tumblers of thick pink slimming drinks: 'Oh God, Octavia, something's got to work!'

The rest of them scattered through the house, the bedrooms, the library, Daddy's study – but mainly they occupied the drawing-room floor. They liked the Indian rugs, the cushions and embroideries, and the long curtains they could draw against the light. It had atmosphere, they said. Karen would sit cross-legged for hours, singing quietly to the Bob Dylan records Carl had told me I must buy, while Rob and Steve lay with their tangled hair against the sofa, smoking something strong and scenty and writing angry things on pieces of crumpled paper. They'd brood and chuckle together for hours. Often, Beverley would pull my head onto her flower-patterned lap and plait my hair the way she did hers – lots of little strands woven with coloured beads. Then we'd go into my room to look at ourselves in the tall cheval glass, my pale arm linked in her olive-skinned one.

'You have such lovely things,' she'd whisper, plunging her whole body into my wardrobe, caressing silk caftans, cashmere jumpers, chiffon cocktail frocks I'd never worn. She'd look at the labels and say, 'Zandra Rhodes! Oh, fabulous!' And I'd let her have things, although she was a size bigger than me and split the zips in places where she couldn't see. And she'd kiss me and say, 'Don't let Rob know.' And she'd wear them when he wasn't around, twirling on the polished floors, catching her reflection in the window glass. 'You're really kind, Octavia.'

Rob, of course, said kindness was meaningless, that it clouded the issues, the real class struggle, that there were no exemptions. 'Property is theft,' he'd say with a grin, taking a five pound note from my purse. I used to think about it a lot. And one day I told him that he was right. I'd give it all up. I'd sell the house, the furniture, the clothes, give all my money to charity, get a job in a shop, be ordinary. They were all silent. Then they shrieked with laughter. 'Oh, Octavia, you are funny!'

Rob laughed too. But later on he came to my room, kissed my forehead and looked in my eyes: 'Now listen, Octavia – about what you said. I think, my angel, I need to protect you from yourself. You don't seem to realize what a sheltered life you've led – nannies and governesses and all that crap. And money whenever you want it. I don't think you realize what the real world's like. It's dog-eat-dog out there you know. Basically, princess, you wouldn't survive.' He put his finger under my chin and lifted my face, smiling in that way he had. 'Now, I'm not getting at you. It's not your fault. You can't help your weirdo parents and their weirdo ideas. But promise me like a good girl you won't do anything rash.'

I kissed him and promised, and he smiled and lit a cigarette.

Rob was always rude about my parents. About anyone's parents. About families in general. They were bourgeois of course. And a drag, to be cast off as soon as possible. He said I was well rid of mine: 'You're a free spirit, you see. God, I wish I had your luck!' He always assumed I felt the same way. Only once did he mention his two sisters: older, married, and living in 'ticky-tacky houses' in suburbs too bourgeois for words. He'd been lying propped on the bed with an arm round me, drawing on a joint and rambling a little. But when I wanted to know more, he turned away on the pillow: 'They're not important.' His mother telephoned once, late at night: someone was ill, he needed to come back. He refused to speak to her, wouldn't take the phone from my hand: 'I don't know where she got this number, but if she rings again, hang up.'

But he was forever staring at the silver-framed photos on the piano and the mounted snapshots in the stiff, brown pages of the old albums. He loved the pictures of my grandparents, formal on studio furniture with potted palms; my bachelor uncles – overcoats and dogs in the Highlands, light suits and gins in front of Raffles Hotel. And most recently, the end of our life in Delhi – my father against the white façade of government offices, our bungalow with its garden, the servants lined up, me a blond child in Manjit's arms just months before we came back to England. Rob would pore over them for hours, jeering at my father's moustache and droopy linen jacket, my mother's Dior afternoon dresses, wide-brimmed hats and long white gloves. 'Look at them! The remnants of our glorious colonial history. Thank God you were too young to remember it all!'

But I did remember it. The pressure of the air. And the brilliance of the flowers – the huge red dahlias blazing just in front of the house. And the distant clatter of china cups in the afternoon shade as I lay on my mattress inside the veranda. We'd been happy, all three of us. Perfectly happy. But I didn't tell Rob all this. Rob always misunderstood about Mummy and Daddy. He'd turn the pages and snigger: 'What parasites!'

I'd tried to tell him that it wasn't like that. Daddy had worked himself to death, staying up late into the night with his boxes of papers. Everyone in the Service had respected him. And they'd loved my mother; she was so hospitable – always tea parties and guests for supper. Rob would look at photograph after photograph, faded smiles in bright light: 'She certainly knew a lot of handsome young men.'

So I stopped telling him anything, let him go on drawing his conclusions. It pleased him to make fun. *'Righting the balance,'* he said as he tried on Daddy's silk scarves and Panama hats, striding up and down, snapping his fingers: 'I say, you there, boy! A cup of char for myself and the memsahib!'

Rob made them all laugh, and I tried not to mind. I tried not to mind when he started wearing my father's suits every day, staining them with food and cigarette ash; and when Jeni went out to a disco in my mother's pearls and came back without them. And when Karen and Steve broke the Royal Worcester plates by sitting on them. And when Mandy burnt a hole in the pale blue Wilton when she fell asleep, stoned. They are my friends, I said to myself. And they must share what I have.

They stayed a long time, sharing. I can't remember how long. But gradually they drifted away, got jobs, sent me postcards: *Can you believe we've got our own mortgage and Bev is having a baby? And Steve's been offered this fantastic job in Hong Kong? And Carl and Jeni have a book shop in Bath?*

'Wankers,' said Rob. He'd been the last to go. In the final months he lay about the floor, unshaven, gnawing at leftover food, slinking along the landings, turning knobs, opening boxes, pulling and picking at my life.

I couldn't stand it in the end.

And now, today, this warm summer's day, I will have to go the long way round to the park. When we first came to this house, Mummy and I could run straight there, out of our back garden gate, down to the lake. We'd lie in the sunshine under the dahlias, pretending we were back at the bungalow and someone would soon bring us tea. But the back gate is padlocked now, jammed tight with damp, and I will have to go along the Crescent, past the mansion flats, through the railinged gate. But it won't matter. No one will be watching. Everything will be quiet.

It's almost noon as I leave the house, and the light is falling in solid blocks, cutting shapes on the masonry, dividing the road with hard edges of shadow, the geometry of pointed gables in triangles along the middle of the tarmac. A few parked cars reflect the sun along the bright side of the road, but there is no one on the pavements. The residents of the Crescent are very private. They sometimes smile at me as I walk along, but they never speak. Most of them are old, and stay indoors.

I have put on my big straw hat and my dark glasses. I have to protect myself from the sun. My skin is just as ivory-pale as it's always been. My eyes are just as large and blue. On a day like this I have to hide them from view. I wear gloves. A lady always wears gloves. I have many pairs. Today they are pale lilac, to match my frock. It's my favourite, a Jean Muir original. It makes all the difference.

I visit the glasshouses first. As a child, walking with Mummy into the sudden wall of heat, I was reminded of India. And I am again, now. I see splashes of shimmering red, a jungle of deep green. Everything moist, warm, scented. I drift along the rows of terracotta pots. My high heels skid a little on the red tiled floor. Hoses snake across my path. Sprinklers start up suddenly, tingling on my skin. My dress is damp. It clings a little to my back, my thighs. The heat is building up. I remove my hat, my glasses. It is time.

I choose the spot. I am superstitious; I keep to the same routine. Here in view of the lake, on a quiet piece of lawn, near the bed of dahlias. Spiky red dahlias. They are very tall; they reach my shoulder as I stand beside them. They have no smell; they attract by show. I hold out my hand, touch their tubular petals, their splayed open centres. I lie down. The heat of the day will soon start to wane.

I know him at once. I smell him, the acid of his aftershave, the faint odour of tobacco and sweat. The sun is behind his head as he stands over me. He is a dark shadow. Thinner than Rob. Taller. He pauses, deciding. I know what he will decide. The dahlias vibrate in the background.

'You make a beautiful picture.'

The usual words. I smile my usual smile.

He eases himself down beside me. He has long legs, grey trousers – grey flannel trousers. His face, as he turns, is pale and avid. He will be no trouble.

We talk a little. Very little. Then we walk, slowly, in the heat. 'We can go indoors,' I say. 'My house is very near.' I point out the back wall, the glistening windows of the Crescent rising above the trees.

As a lover, he is indifferent. I expect no more. He is too eager, too flattered to consider much beyond himself. He is a man who wears grey flannel trousers on a summer's day and is at the mercy of strangers.

He exerts himself, sweats a little, groans. Afterwards he strokes my hair. He looks around – the cornices, the mirrors, the mahogany furniture: 'It's a massive place. Do you live here all alone?'

'Not quite.' I like to tease on these occasions. He looks nervous, eyes the door. 'You needn't worry. We won't be disturbed.'

He senses something. He wants to be away, but my body is across his chest, my fan of hair, still blond, scarfing his pitted complexion. He subsides. Strokes my hair again. 'I can't make you out. You're very – different – do you know that?'

Of course I know that. I accept that now. I smile. 'You're not the first to say that.' No, not the first.

He asks to get his cigarettes. They are in his shirt pocket, on the rosewood chair. I say I don't allow smoking. He laughs and says that isn't fair. I tell him this is my house and I make the rules.

But I bring him some tea. Indian tea. Strong and pungent. I bring it to him on a tray. White cloth, china cup. And a red dahlia head floating in a shallow glass vase.

He lifts the cup, reluctant: 'I don't drink tea, normally.'

But today isn't normal. Surely he can see that? Today is very particular. I tell him, 'It's a special blend.'

The temperature has dropped now. The pressure is falling. The windows rattle a little with the evening wind.

I make myself supper. A slice of melon, cold consommé, anchovies on toast, a water ice. I cover the little folding table in my father's study with an embroidered cloth. I put out a silver knife, fork and spoon. I pin the dahlia in my hair. I pour myself a glass of wine.

No one will disturb me tonight.

LYING TOGETHER

We'd chosen the countryside because it seemed the right thing. Honest, in a sort of way (more than we'd been, anyway). We'd savoured the thought in those last days cooped up together: two weeks in the open air, regular meals, exercise. And no drinking.

'What about country pubs?' I'd asked.

He shook his head: 'No drinking.'

'Maybe a shandy?'

'No drinking.'

We'd allowed ourselves cigarettes instead. A hundred each to start off with. Sister Jenkins had looked at us. '*They*'ll kill you just the same.'

'Have a heart,' we said.

We'd chosen Wales. Or at least I had. Going home in a way, although the Marches were a bit off my track. I come from Newport; one of those towns people can't get the hang of; neutral, faceless, confused – neither English nor Welsh. Just like me with my disappeared Welsh mother and my dear drunk English dad. But we'd always gone on day-trips up the Usk and the Wye. 'Best scenery in the world,' I said, remembering school outings, picnics by the river, ruined castles, endless sun. So Bill took me up on it, because I was always boasting and lying. 'We'll see if you're right, you little toad. Little pissed Welsh newt.'

We'd hired a car. Gary, my ex (ex-what, I'd like to know, he'd never committed himself), let us have one of his write-offs as long as Bill was doing the driving. He doesn't know about Bill; thinks I'm the unsafe one. I didn't tell him. Gary does quite a business now, but doesn't spend more than he has to. I imagine life above the garage is just as it used to be. Sex and engine oil. And invoices. Gary's got a new girl, now. Blond, naturally, and bonded-on stilettos. But I could see engine oil at her roots. Gary insured the car (third party), did all the paperwork in his own name – some scam or other – and got a hundred quid from Bill. 'For a rotten beat-up Mini?' I said, but Bill said beggars can't be choosers.

When the time came, I was nervous. Fourteen days. Fourteen days of being alone. And being alone together. I'd got too used to living in the public eye. There's a kind of protection there; safety in numbers. Dr Barker said I'd been in too long. He was always saying that. It was his theme tune: *What are you afraid of, Glenys?* I'd been afraid of all the usual things before, but now it was Bill. I was afraid of Bill's private reality, but I wasn't telling Dr Barker that. I'd spent a year sitting in a room full of nutters, trading insults, smoking, watching the jagging picture on the telly and (in the last few months) watching Bill from the corner of my eye as Fat Margaret tried to park herself on his lap, with Dempster going on and on about the wicked ways of women before Sister Jenkins came to break it up. Our smiles across the room weren't private. Always someone to comment, and someone else to bring it up on Mondays: *Have Bill and Glenys got something to tell us?* 'Mind your own fucking business,' I'd say. But even fucking wasn't private when the only place to do it was behind a big prickly bush with some nosy bastard always coming past. It was our drinking place, though, that bush. When we had our famous lapses and sneaked off like kids with a bottle of Johnnie Walker, throwing up in the corner near the wheelie bins before the heavy brigade came to get us. Not a normal life, exactly. Not Mr and Mrs. But something we were used to.

Suddenly, sitting next to him in the Mini, having to make conversation, I was scared stiff. An hour after we'd got on the road, my ashtray was spilling over. And my nails bitten down worse than ever, starting to bleed. I used to have nice nails once. And nice hair – real blond, not bottle. I don't know when it went mousy. When I went into that place, I think. Before that, I was a proper Marilyn Monroe.

'She was peroxide,' said Bill.

'Well, Princess Di, then. My dad always said I looked like Princess Di.'

'You're such a liar,' said Bill. 'Such a terrible little liar.'

The pubs along the valley were bright and beautiful, with fairy lights and striped umbrellas and baskets of flowers. Best pubs I'd ever seen. But we'd agreed no stopping, not even for a lemonade, not even to have a pee. Ground rules, Bill had said. Only common sense. Sister Jenkins had been unconvinced: 'How long do you honestly think you'll last?'

'We'll show you,' we'd said, deciding on B&B for the nights. Farm-houses, we'd said. Off the beaten track, well out of danger. 'Don't people drink in the country, little newt?' said Bill, but he knew what I was after.

The first farmhouse was up a lane. It was so far up I thought we'd missed it. Then a muddy farmyard and mangy old dogs barking like crazy, running out under the wheels of the car, Bill braking hard enough to send us nearly through the windscreen. We had a picture of a plump farmer's wife: a smooth white apron, a welcoming smile, but everything looked dead and ramshackle. The dogs went on barking and we could hear the fog-horning of some cows in the distance, but no sign of human beings, not a flicker of welcome. We couldn't get out, not with those dogs ready to take a leg off us, so we just sat there: helpless and surrounded. After a bit, Bill slammed the window down and leant on the horn, shouting at the top of his voice. The dogs went manic, jumping and showing their teeth, but nobody came.

'Deaf buggers! Ignorant bloody peasants!' Bill shoved the car into reverse, dogs scattering and yelping. 'Stupid bloody animals! They should be kept under control!' He gripped the steering wheel hard, nearly scraping the gatepost as we shot out of the yard. He wouldn't look at me as we went back down the hill.

After that, we thought we'd keep it simple. Something on the main road. No lanes, no dogs, just a straightforward guest house. And there it was, a swinging sign – *Ty Gwyn*. A neat white house with geraniums and a polished brass doorstep. And two single ladies reluctant to let us in. 'Don't want their rooms dirtied,' said Bill as he pulled our bags from the boot. 'Don't really want anyone actually staying at all.'

I thought it was the car that put them off. Gary hadn't bothered to fix the dent in the side.

'One night only,' they said. 'And single beds.'

We nodded.

'Oh, and cash in advance.' They thought they had our number, but Bill drew out his wad, what was left of his lump sum, and they let us in.

'And breakfast at eight, no later mind, as we have to tidy up by nine. And out of the room by half past, please, so we can change the sheets.'

They watched us, hoping we'd change our minds, go away, give them a reprieve. I expect we looked the sort to want to lie in all day, but hospital gets you out of that, breakfast at seven most days. Eight was a treat. So we nodded and ran up the stairs and fell on their pristine sheets in our shoes.

A tap on the door: 'And no smoking.'

'Perish the thought,' said Bill, sitting up and unwinding the Cellophane from our second pack.

We opened the window and leant out, letting the ash float secretly onto the neat chips of gravel. 'Almost yellow,' I said, looking down on them.

'*Muffin*,' murmured Bill, who'd spent hours decorating the marital semi before Cheryl upped and left. He had the colour cards off by heart: Driftwood, Oatmeal, Cornsilk, Honeycomb, Harvest Moon, Buttermilk. He laughed. 'Or maybe, *Crumpet*?'

We pushed the single beds together, rucking up the thin square of carpet, scraping the polished floor. We stopped, holding our breath, expecting the women to come. But they didn't. We laughed: *Too busy polishing the fridge!*

Then undressing. Both of us nervous with buttons and zips. He had old-fashioned Y-fronts and dark socks that came up to his knees. And part of me was laughing and part of me was gritting my teeth, not wanting him to go any further, not to take off any more. It's stupid, with all the blokes I've been with, but I'd never seen a man naked, not close up, not all over. They'd all kept their kit on, as far as I remember; which of course isn't much. Even Gary couldn't be bothered to take his jeans off most of the time and always fell on me with some sort of greasy T-shirt flapping around his tackle. And I'd close my eyes anyway, knowing he'd be quick. Now I felt shy in my new white undies. Like a bride. Like a virgin. We both laughed and Bill started to sing that song by Madonna, and I was still laughing when I knew I couldn't do it, when he caught hold of me and the blackness opened up in my head, and I couldn't stop shaking. He thought I was shaking with wanting him so much, and nearly didn't stop.

I had to bite hard, pinch and tear at him with my stupid blunt nail-less fingers. I heard myself shouting, saying I hated him (Dr Barker's face: *Who is it you hate? Him? Or yourself?*). I started to cry, and Bill slammed his hand against the wall: 'This is bloody great, this is!' Then he calmed down and said he was sorry, knowing all he knew and everything. And we both said how much we needed a drink.

In the morning, the women watched us while we ate off little square flowered plates with scalloped corners. One pale sausage, one rasher, and a poached egg each; two pieces of toast in a polished silver rack, and an egg-cupful of marmalade; china pot with one teabag, little label over the edge. Bill laughed. 'Well, I'm not sure I'll be able to move after all this hearty country fare!' I watched everything he did, grateful for its ordinariness. Discovering the way he stirred his tea, spread his butter, wanting to do it for him. I'd never noticed what he ate before, when he'd been squashed up in the day room on the other side of a vinyl table, sticky tray crowded with dishes. Didn't always notice what I ate myself, fretting about pills and ciggies, and who was getting what and going where. Meals were a blur. My whole life was a blur. After Dad, after Gary. Before Bill, after Bill. All a blur.

That's why they say I'm a liar. I just can't remember. And what I can't remember, I make up. Why not? It's more interesting. You can't keep saying, 'I can't remember.' It's pathetic. And for all I know everything I say might be true. I've told it so often, it's not surprising the story changes a bit, that it's mixed up with all the other stories, with what Dad said, with what Stevie said (could he remember himself?). And then Gary. I don't know what's real any more. It's not clear.

I kept telling them I was usually drunk; stupid drunk. So I could have been wrong. I could have remembered it wrong. *Could have?* Dr Barker looking clever made me more confused. *Why are you making excuses for him?* 'I'm just trying to explain,' I'd say. 'Trying to get my thoughts straight through the mist.'

I can picture Dad passing me a can when we watched telly together. On the sofa together, side by side. To keep him company, he'd say. Won't hurt you. Anyway, who's to know? He'd smile, all relaxed and nice. I remember that bit. Then getting warm and comfortable. I remember that too. Next thing, not wanting to go anywhere, meet anybody. Missing school, teachers wanting me to talk about my 'problem', me not wanting to. People looking at me – that Edwards girl. Wanting not to be that girl, to forget everything, not to have to think or make decisions. 'I was a bad girl,' I told Dr Barker. 'I liked being drunk.' *Liked it? Or needed it?* He looked me in the eye. I said, 'How do I bloody know?'

Dr Barker says it wasn't my fault, I was only a child. He says I must believe that. I don't know. I don't know if I believe that. I was fifteen at the end, not exactly a kid. But I was lonely too, Mam gone, and Stevie with Auntie Mags, and no friends I could talk to. I used to shut the door, pretend I couldn't hear Dad whispering. But I can't really remember. And everyone says I'm a terrible liar.

Gary wanted to save me. For himself. He was my first real boyfriend. Steady, I mean, after all the one-night stands. He said that a lovely kid like me didn't want to be hanging around pubs. There were better things to do. Like helping him with his business. He fancied himself, did Gary. He was twenty-four and a bit of a self-made man. He wanted to have me better myself. And he wanted to have me in the process – he wasn't that charitable. We had sex all the time and Gary thought it was what I needed to keep me on the rails. But he never took me anywhere or gave me anything, except sheaves of invoices to check through. 'Earn your keep, Blondie,' he'd say, throwing them down on the bed and smiling as if that made it all right. And the flat was filthy – oily and smelly and full of spare parts – and he never gave me any money for cleaning things in case I spent it on drink. 'Cruel to be kind,' he'd say. And then he said I threw his kindness back in his face. He told me I'd broken his heart. He's a liar too. He just didn't like to think his mates had seen me in the pub car park with the punters. 'Reverting to type,' he'd said. 'Trying to blame your poor old dad, too. You don't want anyone halfway decent. You're a lying little slag, and you always will be.'

I watched Bill over the breakfast table. He had that same fresh, just-ironed look that had struck me so much when he'd first come onto the ward. He'd seemed out of place, as if he'd just strolled through the patio window of his tidy little garden and stepped suddenly into Weirdo World. Too bloody healthy-looking for a drunk, I'd thought. Too neat, too clean, too calm. 'My, we are one for the stereotypes,' said Jenkins when I brought it up at the meeting. 'Not everyone feels obliged to dress the part.' She was getting at the way I looked after myself – or didn't. I knew the weekly reports by heart: Self-care poor, self-esteem low, self-mutilation an ongoing problem. Dr Barker doing the firmness bit: *If you don't care about yourself, how do you expect anyone else to?* I didn't expect anyone else to. Couldn't he see that was just the point? Some shrinks are really thick. It was easier to let things slide, to have no expectations. *Then you can't get hurt?* Too right. I wanted to be a shadow. Invisible, irresponsible. And not thinking. Never having to think. Saying whatever came into my head. Yes, no, three bags full, whatever you say. Believe what you like. Just don't bother me.

But Bill bothered me. He made me take notice. It was those clean jeans, that open-necked shirt, those blue eyes that didn't at first glance look bloodshot. He seemed to smell of the open air – gardens with lawns, trips out with the kids. As if he'd never been in a saloon bar in his life.

He used to joke that he was with us by accident. Although he had a history (we soon got the tale of his marriage to Cheryl), the night in question he was under the limit. And the kid had come from nowhere. A six-year-old, out at nearly midnight; it was hardly Bill's fault. And he made a good showing in the witness box, could never forgive himself and all that crap. Got off with a six-month ban, walking out of court thinking it was all over. But then there was all the stuff in the papers, and the letters from the kid's family, and then the nightmares. He'd gone on week-long binges, lost his nice comfy job. Then the lovely Cheryl had ditched him, and since then he'd done everything – detox, the lot – and landed up with us. Dempster did his bit, warned him off me the first day: 'She's bad news, that one. A sex-fiend. And a liar. She'll get you into trouble.'

Well, I had to, hadn't I? He was asking for it, coming in looking so smug, joking with Jenkins, giving the impression he wasn't staying long. I had to prove he was just like the rest of us. And I did it. Pulled him down with me and my bottle behind that old prickly bush, made him slurred and swollen, helpless as a baby, jeans stained with grass and vomit, shirt creased and sweaty. I could have killed him for making it so easy.

I nearly did kill him, that last time when he'd gone on Antibuse and I didn't know. 'Happy now?' said Jenkins when he'd been taken off to Intensive Care, babbling rubbish. 'Now you've brought him down to your level? Now he's half-psychotic?'

Dempster started on about how Bill should have taken his advice, but some men could never resist a bit of skirt, the cheaper the better. I went for him with Jenkins's pencil, stabbing his cheek: 'It's not my fault! I didn't mean to hurt him.' Of course, I wanted to say, 'I love him.' But I can't use that word.

'Liar,' said Fat Margaret, turning the tap on like she always does. 'Dirty little liar! You'll go to Hell!'

'Glenys isn't going anywhere.' Jenkins gave me one of her more meaningful looks. 'Glenys is set fair to be one of our permanent residents.'

I don't know why it came as such a shock. Up till then I'd have welcomed the idea of staying around on a permanent basis. I'd always panicked when they started the crap about Halfway Houses and Taking a Step into the Community. I always made sure I did something really spectacular to disgrace myself, persuade Dr Barker I just wasn't ready for the outside world. *Just when you were doing so well, too. Is this significant, Glenys?*

But Permanent Resident was scary. I looked into the metal mirror in the bathroom and saw myself old and grey. Other people coming and going, whispering, 'Take no notice; she's the Permanent Resident.' I'd be a ghost, a sort of non-person. It would be better to finish it, stop everything right there, dead before my time, a tragic loss. If they left me long enough, I could do it. The window glass in the toilets was thick and grey, but it could be broken.

I used both hands and all my strength, bringing my wrists down together. So when the window suddenly opened – swung out as though it had been oiled – I nearly fell out. I'd geared myself up for the thud of pain, the spurt of blood and the sound of my own screaming, so the sight of trees and the fresh smell of earth came as a shock. It was an ordinary afternoon, but it was so bright and real it was like a kind of vision. I could see the red tops of the buses sweeping along the main road behind the brick wall. And there were people walking past the gates and taking a short cut through the grounds – women, men, children, dogs. I supposed they'd always been there, but I'd never really seen them. It made everything in the hospital behind me seem tawdry – the horrible shiny walls, the squeaky high-backed chairs, the drab notice-boards, the ripped baize of the pool table in the corridor, the stink of food and medication. And the everlasting noise of the television, somebody always talking through it, irritating someone else. Suddenly it wasn't a cosy place any more. And I wanted to escape. Properly. Like a normal person. Walking out of the front door. Walking out of the gates. Getting on a bus and going somewhere ordinary.

I haunted the windows every day after that, re-learning the ordinary things, trying to hold them in my head. I watched the gardener plant a flowerbed. It took him all morning – digging each hole, setting in each plant, putting back the earth, firming it down. Then the next one, same routine. I sat in my dressing gown until he had finished. I felt as satisfied as if I had done the whole thing myself.

Then I asked to go shopping. I bought underwear, pure white, respectable. I bought a blue suit and a pink dress, and a soft woollen jumper. I had my hair done (not too blond). I was going to be a normal person. I was going where normal people go. On holiday perhaps. One thing was definite, I was not coming back. They all laughed. *You're not going anywhere. You like it here.*

But Bill didn't laugh. He said we'd do a deal. If I stayed off the bottle and didn't try to do him in again, he wouldn't mind giving it a go. We'd have a trial run, four weeks under Jenkins's eye. Then off to the wide blue yonder.

I couldn't believe he'd said it. Since he'd come back from Intensive Care, I'd lain in bed imagining the two of us together, walking in the country, holding hands, laughing. But he'd sat on the other side of the circle every Monday, and never looked me in the eye once. Perhaps it was the new hair that decided him. Or the blue suit. I'd paraded them in front of him, trying to show him I'd changed. But I didn't really believe it myself, so when he said that, the old feelings closed in. And when he started getting out maps and talking about dates I had a go sniffing the aerosols in the cupboard.

'You are disgusting!' said Jenkins when she found me. But I couldn't face it. Bill was a stranger. I knew every bit about his agonies, his wife, the accident, his guilt – but I'd never walked down the street with him or knew what he liked to do in the evenings. Except drink. All we had in common was drink. And that was out. So I was scared rigid. And, as usual, covering it up with all sorts of stupid remarks, lying my head off. Yes, Gary and I had often gone touring. Yes, I'd been abroad; Spain I think, couldn't quite remember the place. I thought my mother might be living abroad, too. She had some foreign blood.

The driving was Bill's idea. To lay the ghost. And getting the car from Gary was mine. I hadn't spoken to him since we broke up, but he was willing enough: *I always had a soft spot for you, Blondie.* Kidding himself he looked big in Bill's eyes as he passed me on with his blessing like some kind of godfather.

The real terror came when we were on the road. The empty space between us, how the conversation drifted into silence, into stilted questions and short answers. O, Land of My Fathers, I was so scared it was all going to spoil; that it was going to be me as usual who'd spoil it.

The night in Ty Gwyn was so near the edge, I couldn't believe the next day that we'd slept so well, that breakfast was so nice and ordinary; that perhaps, after all, the women thought we were no different from hundreds of other tourist couples. They got quite chatty and told us about some Celtic cross we should look at, and waved goodbye from the front door, smiling.

'Let me empty the ashtrays,' I said. 'They really stink.' I got a paper bag and felt pleased with myself. I thought that in my new life I might like to be tidy.

'Filthy habit, smoking.' Bill screwed up his second-to-last pack and threw it on the grass. 'Come on, Newt, stop being the perfect housewife. I need you to navigate.'

'What about the Celtic cross?'

'If you like. We'll pass it anyway.'

It wasn't far, a little triangle of grass and a grey carved column. We got out and looked at it. Then got in again. In the wing mirror I saw another couple come after us and do the same.

We came to a crossroads. 'Come on. You're supposed to know the route. Abergavenny or Raglan?'

I looked at the map, all wiggly lines and black print. I had no idea where we were, where we were going. But I wanted to make the right choice. 'There's a castle at Raglan.'

'Worth seeing?'

'Oh, yes.' Please God.

'Bet you can't remember, Newt.'

'Yes I can. It's ruins.' Always a good guess.

'I like ruins.' He smiled.

We turned off, passing the Red Dragon on our left, pointing the Mini uphill. I had the bag of fag-ends on my lap, and Bill's hands were almost firm on the steering wheel.

About the Author

Photo: Richard Battye

Gaynor Arnold was born and brought up in Cardiff, and read English at St Hilda's College, Oxford. She now lives in Birmingham, where she was until recently a social worker with the city's Adoption and Fostering Service. She is married with two grown-up children and is now a full-time writer.

Acknowledgements

With thanks to my fellow writers in Tindal Street Fiction Group for their advice and encouragement over the period when most of these stories were written. Thanks also to all at Tindal Street Press, especially my indefatigable editor, Alan Mahar.

GIRL IN A BLUE DRESS

GAYNOR ARNOLD

'Fabulously indulgent Victoriana' – *Observer*

Longlisted for the Man Booker and Orange Prizes –
a novel based on the lives of Catherine and Charles Dickens.

Beloved writer Alfred Gibson's funeral is taking place at Westminster Abbey, and Dorothea, his wife of twenty years, has not been invited. Dorothea hasn't left her apartment for years, but when she receives a surprise invitation to a private audience with Queen Victoria, she is shocked to find she has much in common with Her Majesty. With her renewed confidence Dorothea is spurred to examine her past and confront not only her family but also the pretty young actress Miss Ricketts.

This beautiful new edition of the re-imagining of Catherine and Charles Dickens's marriage looks forward to Gaynor Arnold's next Victorian novel in 2012.

'Arnold's knowledge of Dickens is impeccable . . .
Beautifully written, entirely satisfying' – *The Times*

'A fine work of imagination and compassion' – *Daily Telegraph*

£7.99 from all good bookshops and from: www.tindalstreet.co.uk
Ebook also available.